THE HOUSE ON DOWNSHIRE HILL

THE HOUSE ON DOWNSHIRE HILL

Book 5 in the Hampstead Murders

GUY FRASER-SAMPSON

Urbane
PUBLICATIONS

urbanepublications.com

First published in Great Britain in 2018 by Urbane Publications Ltd
Suite 3, Brown Europe House, 33/34 Gleaming Wood Drive, Chatham,
Kent ME5 8RZ
Copyright © Guy Fraser-Sampson, 2018

A CIP catalogue record for this book is available from the British Library.

ISBN 978-1-912666-11-9
MOBI 978-1-912666-13-3
EPUB 978-1-912666-12-6

Design and Typeset by Julie Martin
Cover by Author Design Studio

Printed and bound by 4edge UK

Urbane
PUBLICATIONS

urbanepublications.com

The House on Downshire Hill is the fifth volume of the Hampstead Murders. Readers are invited to sample the series in the correct order for maximum enjoyment.

CHAPTER 1

Detective Inspector Bob Metcalfe had various reasons to be cheerful as he made his way from Frognal towards Hampstead police station. First, as he took the small footpath beside the former residence of Gracie Fields which led past the graveyard and up into Church Row the sun, which had been attempting to break through some rather hazy clouds, finally did so. After the grey, damp weather of the previous few days this marked a welcome change.

Second, he and the rest of the team had recently received favourable comments from the powers that be at Scotland Yard for successfully concluding an investigation into a suspicious death at an exclusive club for female university graduates. This meant a few days of quiet as they waited for assignment to a new enquiry, and having a respite from the long hours and intense efforts which normally attended a homicide investigation was always agreeable. Last, and by no means least, he had recently become engaged to be married, a development which even a few months ago would have seemed extremely unlikely given the highs and lows (mostly lows, to be honest) of his personal life.

He crossed Fitzjohns Avenue, one of the two main roads which meet at the top of the hill by Hampstead tube station, and cut down Perrin's Court which brought him swiftly to the second, Rosslyn Hill. From here it was a right turn and a walk down the hill to the police station, passing the King William IV pub, commonly known as 'the Willy', where he and his colleagues had been known to take a modest drink or two after work. He stayed on this side of the road as he progressed down the hill, since it kept him away from the window shoppers and aggressive pram wielders who tended to clog the other pavement. He crossed the road at the zebra crossing and completed his brief but agreeable walk to work.

The desk Sergeant said "good morning, sir."

Since he would normally have used the informal 'guv' Metcalfe looked at him sharply, for they had been uniformed constables together, and it was always difficult to know whether someone was 'extracting the Michael' as DCI Tom Allen would have said. He wondered if this newfound formality was for the benefit of a trainee constable who had started work a few days previously, but a subtle jerk of the sergeant's head indicated the presence of Detective Superintendent Collison, who was leafing through some papers away in the corner of the room in a rather desultory fashion. As he dropped them back into the tray he caught sight of Metcalfe.

"Morning, Bob."

"Good morning, guv. Anything happening?"

"No, not really."

"Excuse me, sir," the desk Sergeant said diffidently, "but there is that missing person's report."

"Yes, I was just looking at that. Is there anything to it, do you think? It all seems a bit tenuous."

"I saw the lady when she came in, sir. I'd say she was genuinely upset. Shall I ask someone from uniform to call on her? It's only just round the corner after all."

"No," Collison said after deliberating for a moment. "On reflection I think you're right. Let's do the job properly and send somebody from CID. Who's free, Bob?"

"Just about everybody at the moment, guv. What about Priya?"

"Okay then. Have that sent up to DC Desai, will you please, Sergeant?"

"So how are the wedding plans coming along then?" Collison asked as they walked up the stairs together.

"Oh, quietly you know. We haven't even set a date yet. It's all been a bit sudden to be honest. I'm still trying to get used to the idea."

"No second thoughts I hope?"

"Absolutely not, no."

"Good. Lisa seems like a really nice girl."

They walked past the door to the operations room, currently eerily empty since the conclusion of their most recent case.

"Now, let's see, where is Priya? I think she's sharing an office with Timothy isn't she?"

He knocked briefly at the next door they came to and poked his head into the room. Timothy Evans was eating a large pastry, much of which he seemed to have spread across his desk. Priya Desai was watching him and trying to look disapproving. Priya never had to try very hard to look disapproving.

"Priya, do you have much on at the moment?"

"No, sir, just getting rid of the last of the filing actually."

"Good. I was just taking a look at some papers downstairs and I came across a missing person's report which was filed yesterday. Because it doesn't deal with a child it wasn't treated as a matter of urgency. There's also some doubt about whether it actually discloses anything sinister. Apparently some lady hasn't been able to contact one of her neighbours for a while. Do you think you might be able to pop round and have a word with her? It's only just round the corner in Downshire Hill."

"Yes of course, guv. It'll be nice to get out of the station."

As she said this she cast a pointed glance at the snowfield of sugar and crumbs on her colleague's desk.

"Good. I've asked the desk Sergeant to send up the report. Ah, here it is I believe. That was quick. Thank you, Constable."

He stood aside to let the trainee constable hand an internal brown envelope to Desai.

"Report back to DI Metcalfe, will you? Depending on how you see things, we'll decide whether to take things further or not."

Where a missing person's report concerned neither a child nor a vulnerable adult the police had a wide measure of discretion as to how seriously or urgently to press their enquiries. Where the concern expressed amounted to little more than an elderly neighbour not answering the door, usually a visit from uniform was enough. There was hardly a serving officer in the Metropolitan police who had not, as a young constable, forced entry to a house to discover the natural death of its occupant. DCI Tom Allen, who delighted in regaling younger officers with the gory details of his early career, had a fund of such stories, including his pièce de résistance which concerned an elderly man who had died over a year previously and whose body had been largely mummified by the cool breeze from an open window.

Metcalfe ducked into his own office while Collison continued along the corridor. He was feeling at least as much at a loose end as the rest of the team, but was trying very hard not to show it. An old university friend who now worked at an investment bank had described to him over dinner the unnatural calm which descended on a corporate finance department once a deal completed. He had explained how everyone took the opportunity to schedule anything from a weekend away to a dental appointment as quickly as possible, since they all knew it was only a matter of time before the next merger or equity issue arrived on their desks from one of the rainmakers on the directors' floor upstairs. He had reflected at the time that this sounded pretty similar to what CID went through when a homicide investigation closed down. He couldn't quite decide whether it felt like the beginning of term, or the end.

One of the doors he passed was open, and he saw Detective Sergeant Karen Willis putting a file into her out tray. Presumably she, like Desai, was just tying up the few loose ends which remained in documenting the Athena Club case. She looked up at him and smiled, tossing her dark hair back as she did so.

"Good morning, guv."

"Good morning, Karen. How are you? And how's Peter?"

"We're both fine, thank you."

Karen's boyfriend was Dr Peter Collins, who had for some time been an official psychological adviser to the Met, and whose skills Collison had used extensively since he had first come to Hampstead as a Detective Superintendent.

"That's good," he replied and then wondered what to say next.

"It feels strange, doesn't it?" she asked. "I suppose it always does, but I went on leave the last couple of times so it didn't really hit me the way it has now. I don't think I'll ever get used to being completely committed to a big case one day, and it suddenly all being declared over the next. It's a sort of flat feeling, isn't it? I suppose it might have something to do with stress, and adrenaline, and all that sort of thing."

"Yes, I suppose so. Still, if history's anything to go by we won't have long to wait for something else to crop up, so I should make the most of it if I were you."

"Good, then I shall."

"Actually, while I'm here, there's something I wanted to talk to you about."

He came in and closed the door behind him.

"This is all very speculative, but every time I see the ACC he seems to have some new idea about my future. As you know, all I really want to do is to stay here and get on with solving crimes, but he seems to see things rather differently."

"That's hardly surprising is it, guv? You've been marked out as a high-flyer, everyone knows that. They're grooming you for a top job, perhaps *the* top job. They'll want you to be sitting on committees, briefing civil servants, that sort of thing."

"You're right of course, but I wish you weren't. It's all very flattering being apparently held in high regard by the ACC but I'd much rather just take my chances like everyone else."

"How do you mean?"

"Well, other officers are going to see me being promoted ahead of them and they're likely to resent it, aren't they? It's only human nature."

"I would have thought you'd be used to that by now, guv. Wasn't that an issue when you first came here to Hampstead?"

"You know it was. And it put me under a lot of extra pressure, I don't mind admitting. If we hadn't been able to crack that first case it would have been extremely embarrassing – not just for me, but for the ACC as well."

"Well, you did crack it. So what's the problem?"

Collison gave a wry smile.

"Why is it you sound like my wife so often?"

"How is Caroline? And the baby?"

"They're both very well thank you, but listen: this is what I wanted to talk about."

He sat down, glanced out of the window to marshal his thoughts, and then went on.

"I said that the ACC seems to have lots of different ideas about my future career. Well, that's true, but there's one that he keeps coming back to and it involves quite a senior post with Special Branch."

"Well, that wouldn't be as bad as sitting on a committee now, would it? And the branch is a traditional route to the very top, as I understand it. Didn't the present Commissioner used to be Commander there?"

"Yes he did, as everyone keeps reminding me. But here's the thing. As a sweetener, he's suggested once or twice that I might be able to take either you or Bob with me. How would you feel about that? It would mean a promotion, I assume."

"I'm very flattered, guv, but why are you asking me? Bob is a much more experienced officer."

Collison shifted awkwardly on the chair.

"Bob's got a natural leg up coming here as a DCI on homicide. He's overdue for it in my view, as I've told the ACC repeatedly. That's not true of you. If you wanted it, I think this could be a great opportunity for you. Like I say, I think if I press them they might make you a DI immediately."

"Have you had this conversation with Bob?" she asked quietly.

"No, I haven't. To be perfectly honest I think you would be my number one choice. That's why I wanted to hear your reaction first. Bob's a great copper and he knows his way around a homicide enquiry with his eyes shut, but the branch is different. It needs a flexible, imaginative approach, and I don't think that would be playing to his strengths. Also, he's a really nice bloke and that might not be a good fit with what goes on at the branch."

"What does go on?"

"Well I can't be sure, but don't forget I got quite involved with them over that business at Burgh House. So I know some of the things that went on, and I can guess at others. Let's just say that once you move into the security world you need a rather different perspective on things. You need to be able to do things because you're comfortable that they're in the national interest without worrying too much about the ethics of it all."

"And you think that I could do that? I'm not sure whether to be flattered or not."

"I'm sorry, I don't think I'm putting this very well am I?"

"No, I see exactly where you're coming from, guv, and I think you're right to be concerned. I'm not sure how I'd handle that, to be honest. If this ever becomes a serious enquiry then I'd need some time to think about it."

Collison gave a little laugh.

"That's exactly what I've been telling the ACC for the last six months or so."

CHAPTER 2

If Hampstead has every claim to being the most beautiful area of London, then Downshire Hill has an equal claim to being its most beautiful Street. The police station actually nestles on the corner of Downshire Hill, and the entrance to its attached Magistrate's court gives onto the street itself. It was from this doorway that Priya Desai emerged, shutting it securely behind her, as she went in search of Wentworth House, the inhabitants of Downshire Hill being naturally far too refined to make use of anything so vulgar as a house number.

She passed a number of breathtakingly elegant houses on each side of the road, some large and some small, but all set back from the street behind gardens which could for the most part have held their heads up proudly in any leading horticultural show. 'For the most part' since there was one garden which, as she approached it, stood out from all the others. Though she was no gardener she could see very plainly that it was horribly neglected, little more than an overgrown tangle of grass and weeds in fact. Once she could make out the name on the gate, badly faded and in need of repainting as it was, she realised with a shock that she had in fact arrived at her destination.

As she stood there for a moment and surveyed the scene

it became apparent that the house seemed every bit as neglected as the garden. Tiles were missing from the roof, the woodwork appeared not to have been painted for some decades, and an old television aerial had become partially detached from the chimney and hung dejectedly down at one side of the building. She shook her head, opened the gate, and walked up the pathway.

Three steps lead up to a small porch area, where she stood as she rang the bell. Actually, 'rang' may not have been quite the right word for, listen hard as she might, she was unable to hear any bells sounding within the house. Noticing that there was an old knocker in the middle of the door, she gave it two or three peremptory raps.

She waited a minute or two and, this having elicited no response, repeated the process. After a while, she did so once again. Just as she was turning to leave, the front door of the neighbouring house opened and a middle-aged woman came hesitantly outside. Desai reached into her shoulder bag for her warrant card, and showed it to the new arrival.

"Police. Can you tell me anything about the man who lives here, please?"

"His name is Taylor, but I haven't seen anything of him for some weeks. Are you from the police station at the top of the road? It was me who came in and saw the Sergeant at the desk there. I'm Helen Barnes."

"Ah yes, of course. I recognise the name. Your report was passed to me to follow up, which is what I'm trying to do, but I can't get any answer. Is there anyone in there do you think?"

"Beats me, dear. I haven't been able to get any answer

either. Come inside if you like. I was just going to put the kettle on."

Had it been a man who had just called her 'dear' Priya would have been seriously upset, perhaps even to the extent of suggesting an impromptu demonstration of unarmed combat. The fact that it was a woman made it a little easier to accept, but only just.

"Thank you," she said stiffly. "As long as it's no trouble."

"No trouble at all."

She stood aside as Desai came in and nodded for her to go through into the kitchen at the end. As she looked around the gleaming work surfaces and appliances she speculated that the kitchen and its installation may well have cost as much as somebody else's one-bedroom apartment.

"Do sit down," Helen Barnes urged her. "Tea or coffee?"

"I'll have coffee if it's going, thank you very much."

She perched on a stool which would not have been out of place in a Mayfair cocktail bar and watched with interest while the woman took coffee beans from a sealed container in a fridge whose doors seemed to run uninterrupted from floor-to-ceiling. These were introduced into a grinder, which ran briefly but noisily, and finally to a silver coffee machine festooned with knobs, tubes, and gauges.

"Would you like milk with it?"

"No, I'm fine with black, thank you."

It seemed that the machine was largely automatic in its functioning, for Mrs Barnes now simply selected a position on a dial, pressed a button, and stood waiting while a small quantity of fragrant black coffee collected in the small coffee cup which she had placed under the outlet, forming a perfect crema. She passed it to Desai, who raised it to her nose and sniffed appreciatively.

"What an amazing machine."

"Yes, isn't it? It's one of my husband's toys, actually. One of the toys of my husband, I should say. I only have the one, naturally – husband, I mean."

She smiled, and Desai began to warm to her.

"So what can you tell me about next door?"

"Well, we've only lived here for about two years. When we moved in I went and knocked on the door, you know – the way you do with new neighbours. He seemed a little suspicious when he answered the door, and even after I explained what I was doing there he seemed reluctant to let me in. I found out later, from people at the church across the road, that he is a real recluse. Hates visitors, and all that."

"But he let you in?"

"Yes, just into a little front room off the hallway. It was quite an experience, I can tell you."

"Why was that?"

"Well, everywhere, all over the floor, there were papers."

"You mean newspapers?"

"Partly, yes, and I couldn't help noticing that some of them must have been very old. They'd gone yellow, you know – the way old newspapers do. But there were other things as well, things that looked like journals or professional magazines, and even just loose sheets of paper with typewriting on them. And when I say they were all over the floor, I mean they were deep. It wasn't just a few things scattered around, it was like wading through water halfway up to your knees. They told me later at the church that he's highly eccentric. It certainly seemed that way to me, I can tell you."

"How long were you there?"

"It seemed like a long time, but it was probably only 10 minutes or so. Certainly nobody seemed to want to make me feel welcome."

"Nobody? You mean he wasn't on his own?"

"No, there was this really strange man. Indian, I think he may have been. They seemed to be living there together, although on what sort of ... you know, basis, I'm really not sure."

"How was he strange?"

"Well, he just sat there and stared at me. He didn't greet me, didn't introduce himself, just came into the room, sat, and stared. I tried asking him a few questions but he just sat there quite impassively."

"Do you think he understood you? Did he speak English?"

"No idea, but he must at least have understood it, don't you think? I found out later that he'd been living there for at least the last year or so."

"Hm, yes that does sound very strange, doesn't it? What about Mr Taylor? What did he have to say for himself?"

"Not very much, really. He was just answering my questions, not asking me anything himself. He did say that he had lived there for a long time."

"Can you remember anything specific at all?"

"Yes, now you come to mention it, I can. I asked him if any of his family were living with him, and he reacted really strangely. It seemed an innocent enough question, but his reaction was almost as if I'd asked something shocking, something rude. Do you know what I mean?"

"Yes, I think so. You struck a nerve, as it were."

"Yes, exactly."

"Do you know anything about his family and what might have happened to them?"

"Nothing directly. But you might speak to Jack. Oh, he's the neighbour on the other side by the way. He's retired and I think that he travels quite a lot so he's not always there. He's lived there a long time like Mr Taylor, so they go way back together, although they're not very close. They hardly speak at all."

"Why's that? Have they fallen out over something?"

"No, I don't think so. I think it's just Mr Taylor. He won't let anyone get close to him. Jack's fine with me. He told me that Conrad – that's what he calls Mr Taylor – has been living at the house for as long as he can remember, but he very rarely goes out and almost never lets anybody in."

"Maybe I should see if I can have a word with him. What's his full name?"

"Jack Rowbotham. He used to be in property, I believe. I'm sure he said something about that."

Desai jotted some notes in her book and then looked up.

"And what was it that worried you enough to approach the police? Did you notice anything out of the ordinary?"

"No, not really. It was just that I suddenly realised I hadn't seen anybody – nobody at all – going in or out of the house for some weeks. Normally I would see at least the Indian chap every day or two. I think he used to walk down to the supermarket of Belsize Park to do their shopping. But I haven't seen sight nor sound of anyone. I've even tried banging on the door a few times, like you just did, but there's no sign of life at all. It's just that sometimes you get a feeling, you know? A feeling that something's not right."

"Did you speak to Mr Rowbotham about this at all?"

"Yes, he came round with me the last time I tried knocking at the door. We tried peering through the letterbox, but all we could see was lots of papers. That's when I said we should go to the police."

"And what did he think of that idea?"

"Not a lot, actually. I think in his own quiet way he's a bit of a recluse as well. Said he didn't want to get involved. I tried to persuade him, of course. I said 'imagine if that poor old man is lying sick or injured somewhere', that sort of thing."

"But he wasn't concerned?"

"Not really, no. Oh, you know what men are like. They don't like making a fuss about anything, do they? So then I decided to go to the police anyway myself – and here you are."

"And here I am, as you say. Well now, I'm not really sure where we go from here. I think I need to go back to the police station and have a chat with my guvnor."

"That's what you call your boss, isn't it?"

"Yes, I'm sorry, it's police slang. It was he who suggested I call, actually."

"Isn't there some procedure as to what happens next?"

"Not really, no. If it was a child or a vulnerable adult who'd been reported missing then we'd have a major manhunt mounted within an hour or two, but with adults it's different. So many go missing all the time, you see, and most of them show up again sooner or later. If we investigated every report we wouldn't have any officers left to do anything else."

"But surely it's usually something like a wife running away from a husband, or vice versa, or a teenager running away from home, something like that?"

"Usually, yes. And like I say, they either show up again or they are deliberately concealing their whereabouts for reasons which are usually nothing to do with the police."

"But this isn't like that is it?" Helen Barnes persisted. "I've really been wracking my brains as to why that poor old man might have just gone missing, but I really can't think of anything. I'm sure something is wrong. Just a feeling, I know, but a very strong one."

"Well," Desai said as she put her notebook back in her shoulder bag, "I'll have a chat with Mr Collison straightaway. It's his decision at the end of the day."

CHAPTER 3

"That does sound rather strange, I must admit," Collison said later as Desai sat in front of his desk in what felt like a very large office for just one person; Hampstead police station was still officially slated for closure and the room had originally accommodated four detectives.

He stood up and gazed out of the window while he marshalled his thoughts. As seemed to be the case pretty much whenever he looked out of the window, an ambulance went past with its lights and siren noisily active – what the police called 'blues and twos'– on its way down the road to the Royal Free Hospital.

"Have you checked public records: you know, the electoral register, that sort of thing?" he asked as he turned around.

"Yes, guv. There's a record of Conrad Taylor living at the house right enough, but nobody else, so this Indian guy, whoever he may be, is a bit of a puzzle."

"What about family?"

"I had to go and rummage around in the archives for that. Would you believe it's still on microfiche? But anyway, there's been no record of anyone except Taylor for about the last 20 years. Before that a family lived there, name of Schneider. Two adults and two children, a girl and a boy. I cross checked with the land registry, and their records match. There's a change of owner logged around the same time."

Collison thought deeply for a moment. Whatever decision he made might have serious implications. On the one hand, launching an investigation might just lead to the discovery of a crime, perhaps even homicide. On the other hand, this could tie up significant police resources on what might ultimately turn out to have been a wild goose chase.

"What's your recommendation, Priya? You must have come to some views."

"I don't like it, guv. Mrs Barnes seemed very genuine and very concerned. There's something not right about this."

"Copper's nose?"

"If you like, yes. But it would be awful, wouldn't it, if he was lying in there dead and nobody did anything about it?"

"Yes, you're right of course, but I have to look at the wider picture. We could get a new major homicide coming through the door any day, and I need to make sure that we have people available to handle it when it does."

There was a pause. Priya looked obstinate and a little angry, but then she often looked obstinate and a little angry. Collison sighed.

"Tell you what, Priya. Before we make a final decision one way or the other what if you can see that other neighbour, let me see... Jack Rowbotham it says here in your note. It's just possible he might know more than he's let on to Helen Barnes."

"And if he doesn't?"

"Let's cross that bridge when we come to it, shall we? Thank you anyway, Priya. Good work."

●

A few doors away along the corridor Metcalfe was in conversation with Willis.

"You getting bored yet?" he asked, glancing aimlessly at the various administrative emails which were all that filled his inbox.

"Yes, I don't mind admitting that I am. Curious, isn't it? When you're on an investigation you sometimes think it will never come to an end and then suddenly it does, and you're left with nothing to do. So you end up wishing the next investigation would land on your desk right away. Awful really, I suppose. After all, somebody has to wind up dead in order for us to have something new to do, so I suppose in a sense I'm wishing somebody dead."

"I guess so," he replied as he repeatedly hit 'delete'.

"How the plans for the wedding coming along? I haven't heard you and Lisa discussing it very much. Where is she by the way? I thought she was supposed to have moved in – officially, I mean."

He and Willis shared a large house in Frognal with her partner, Peter Collins. Metcalfe and his girlfriend, Lisa Atkins, had recently become engaged and she had become something of a fixture at the house.

"Oh she's away staying with her mother while she has some more tests done. Just routine, I think."

"Let's hope so," Willis said fervently.

Lisa had been attacked in the course of a previous

investigation, which was how she and Metcalfe had met. She had been left in a coma for a considerable time with a fractured skull which also seemed to have resulted in the onset of epilepsy. The doctors were still trying to discover exactly what might be the consequences of her injuries.

"No second thoughts then?"

"Strange, Collison just asked me the same thing. No, no second thoughts at all. Lisa and I are very happy together. To tell you the truth, I still can't quite believe that I could get so lucky twice. Well, you know what I mean ..."

"I know."

She nodded awkwardly. The two of them had for a while been a publicly acknowledged couple and there were many of their colleagues who remained curious about precisely how that relationship had come to an end. Not acrimoniously, obviously, since there remained an easy intimacy between them.

"Peter was wondering if there was anything he might do to help."

"Financially, do you mean?"

"Yes, I think so. He's too embarrassed to ask you himself. He wasn't sure what Lisa's mother's circumstances might be."

"To be honest, neither am I. But it's fine, really. We're not planning a big wedding at all. The four of us, the guvnor and his wife, Lisa's mum. That's about it. Maybe just sign the book at the registry office and then have lunch somewhere."

"Sounds good. Sensible actually. After all, Lisa gets tired quite quickly at the moment, doesn't she? So a big wedding might be a bit of a strain for her."

"Yes, I thought that too."

He closed down his email and looked at his watch.

"This is bad," he said. "Very bored, but too early to go home."

"I know. I was thinking of going out to do some shopping but I can't really summon up any enthusiasm even for that."

"Hm. By the way, have you seen the guvnor today?"

"Yes why?"

"Oh, is just something I heard in the canteen earlier. It seems that rumour has resurfaced about him being posted to the Branch. Did he mention anything about it to you?"

"Not really, no."

It felt wrong to be lying to him, even in a good cause, and she felt herself flush slightly.

"Bob, there's something I've been meaning to talk to you about. Something I was chatting about with Peter, actually, and he felt the same."

"That sounds serious. What is it?"

"Well, we were both wondering if you'd ever thought about writing a paper? You know, like the guvnor did for the ACC about reorganising the homicide teams."

"Good God, no. Why should I want to do something like that? Apart from anything else, do you have any idea how much time it took him? He was moaning about it to me for months."

"Yes, yes, I know all about that, but I do wish you'd think about it anyway. They say the Commissioner really likes the intellectual approach, so it might do wonders for your career."

"What's wrong with my career? Have you heard something?"

She hesitated. This was more difficult than she had imagined. Metcalfe had recently only narrowly avoided a disciplinary enquiry, and had been passed over for promotion as a result. It was only natural that he should feel touchy on the subject, she reflected.

"No, nothing like that, don't worry. But have you thought about what you're going to do when you do get promoted to DCI? The next one after that is a big one, and it might really improve your prospects as a potential Superintendent if you had something like a paper under your belt. You know, something you could go around giving talks about. Peter said he'd be very happy to help you with it."

"What on earth would I write about? I'm no academic, you know that. I didn't go to university like you."

She was starting to get cramp in one of her legs, so she stood up and performed a few little pirouettes on the old parquet floor.

"Of course, you had dancing lessons, didn't you?" Metcalfe observed. "It shows."

She did a little ballerina curtsy and then sat down again.

"You remember that day we had lunch together? When we were just getting to know each other?"

"You mean *the* lunch. Of course I remember. It was the guvnor's idea, wasn't it? We just finished all the papers on that murder case, the first one where he was SIO, and he sent us away to go to lunch somewhere."

They both fell silent and looked at each other. The

relationship which had caused them both so much pain and ended unfortunately had begun over that lunch table. Come to think of it, the court case to which he was referring had not had a happy outcome either.

"Yes, well, I didn't mean to rake up any bad memories," she said hesitantly, reading his mind. "What I was thinking of was that conversation we had about serial killers. It was your theory, wasn't it? Do you remember? You were talking about the number of people who just go missing every year, adults who just go out one day to work, or a party, or a football match or something, and are never seen again."

"Yes, of course I remember, and we've discussed it again since haven't we? But what about it? My point was simply that if you look at the numbers it seems very difficult to explain it in any other way. Particularly now in the information age, when it's almost impossible to do anything at all without leaving some sort of electronic signature behind you. How would you get around in London without an Oyster card, for example? Or draw money out of an ATM without a cash card?"

"But that's it exactly, Bob, don't you see? It would make a marvellous paper. And it wouldn't take that long, either. The guvnor's was different. That was on human resources and organisational behaviour and there's a huge amount of stuff – articles, 'literature' they call it – that you need to read and review before you can even get started on your own work."

"So mine would be different ... how exactly?"

"Well, for a start, there's almost no existing literature – I checked. Just some rather general stuff about serial killers and criminal psychopaths."

"Aren't all psychopaths criminals – at least potentially?"

"Oh, Bob, come on, you know better than that. How many times have you heard Peter talk about it? There are many social psychopaths out there, some of them very successful. Haven't you ever heard the phrase 'a successful psychopath'?"

"All serial killers are psychopaths, but not all psychopaths are serial killers, you mean?"

"Yes, exactly. But let's get back to this paper idea. I think it would really be quite simple. All you need to do is get hold of the numbers, make sure that they are all properly referenced, and then advance some alternative theories and choose your hypothesis."

"My hypothesis?"

"Yes, it's the theory which you choose to test in the paper. In this case you would advance your idea that the numbers cannot be explained except, at least in part, by there being a number of undetected serial killers active in the country at any one time. I haven't really given it too much thought, but I suppose what you'd do is look at other possible explanations and see if you can rule them out. You'd also want to state the various things which you believe support your point of view: the electronic signature stuff, for example."

"Well, I don't know. Do you really think I could do something like that? I'm not sure I've got it in me."

"Oh, Bob, don't be so negative. And don't forget that Peter would be happy to co-author it with you. He does this sort of stuff all the time."

He shook his head with a smile and looked again at his watch. At last it was a time at which he could just about justify clocking off.

CHAPTER 4

The following morning found Priya Desai knocking on the front door of Conrad Taylor's other neighbour, Jack Rowbotham. This was a much smaller house and did not boast a nameplate. Instead the number '26' featured neatly on a small blue plate to the side of the doorway. After some delay a shuffling noise presaged the arrival of a dark shape behind the small window in the door, which was then opened, but only a crack. Nor was the chain removed.

A man of about 60 peered bleakly at her. He was unshaven, his hair was dishevelled and she could not help noticing that he was wearing old-fashioned red carpet slippers.

"You're from the police are you?" he asked warily.

"Yes, Mr Rowbotham, I'm DC Desai. I phoned you from the police station, remember?"

"All right, well I suppose you'd better come in. Just wait there."

The door closed, the chain rattled, and then the door reopened.

"You can't be too careful, you know," he said conversationally. "I don't get many visitors."

"You live here on your own then?"

"Yes. I prefer it that way. Can't be doing with people. Come through."

He led the way into a living room which faced out onto the garden. In marked contrast to their proprietor, both were elegant and well-kept. She took the opportunity to gaze out through the window. Though she was no gardener, she sensed that it was Italianate in design, featuring flowerbeds, stone pathways, and flanked on each side by brick walls which were now pleasantly aged.

"Do you do the garden yourself?"

"Yes, though it pretty much looks after itself. I designed it that way. It's just a question of keeping the weeds under control and cutting everything back at the end of the summer. Do you like it?"

"Very much, though I don't really know anything about gardening. My dad used to do a bit."

"Doesn't he still? Why not?"

"Oh, he died," she replied, feeling a suddenly catch in her throat. It was ridiculous, she told herself fiercely, that she should still allow it to affect her in this way.

"I'm sorry to hear that. Won't you sit down?"

With old world gallantry he waited for her to perch herself on the edge of the sofa before sitting down himself in an armchair opposite.

"You said you wanted to ask me about my neighbour," he prompted.

"Yes. Have you known him long?"

"I've lived next to him for the last 20 years or so, but I wouldn't say that I know him. Not sure that anybody does. He's pretty much a total recluse you know."

"So you don't visit him then?"

"Now and then."

"How often?"

He gave a brief laugh.

"I've probably not been in the house more than a dozen times in all that 20 years or so. Once or twice because I had to – problems with the roof, guttering, that sort of thing – and a few times because he asked me."

"Really? I thought you said he was a total recluse?"

"Actually, I think I said he was pretty much a total recluse. He's strange; difficult to describe, but just strange. Every so often for no apparent reason he'll ring me up and ask me round for a mug of coffee. Just instant, you know, he never drinks anything else."

"When was the last time?"

"Oh, just about ten or twelve weeks ago I think. Not that I stayed long. Raj was there, and he's a cold fish make no mistake, so I didn't feel exactly welcome."

"Raj? Is that the Indian guy I've heard about? The one who lives there?"

"That's him, though I can't tell you very much about him. In fact I know almost nothing about him. He works in IT I think. I'm pretty sure I remember Conrad telling me that. But where I don't know. He certainly seems to spend a lot of time next door – during the day I mean – so maybe he works from home."

"What's he like to meet?"

Again, Rowbotham laughed.

"Bloody weird, to tell the truth. He hardly says a word. I've only actually met him a few times, though I've seen him coming and going quite a lot. That last time I was round there he just stared at me. It felt really hostile, as though he was making it clear he didn't want me to be there."

"Hostile? You mean sort of ... like scary?"

"Yes, a bit. You could tell Conrad was embarrassed by it. I think he hadn't expected him to be there. When I went round there were just the two of us, but then Raj came in through the front door after we'd been together for about ten minutes. He said 'hello' in a very stiff sort of way. Then just the silent treatment. After a bit I made my excuses and left."

"And that was the last time you saw Conrad, was it?"

"Come to think of it, yes it was. Not that I'd read anything into that necessarily. He hardly ever goes out of the house. I think Raj did all the shopping."

"What about Raj? When did you last see him?"

Rowbotham thought hard.

"Let me see. Not for a couple of weeks at least. I remember seeing him walking down the road one morning when I came back from the shop with my newspaper."

"You don't remember exactly when that was, do you?"

He thought some more.

"I remember that I had a delivery the next day: some books I'd ordered. So I suppose it would be possible to check. I could have a look the next time I switch on my computer if you like."

"Yes, could you do that please? It might be quite important. Here's my direct number."

She took out one of her cards and passed it across to him.

Then she carried on jotting things down in her notebook. He watched and waited for her to finish.

"So, to summarise, you were last in the house two to three months ago, and you haven't seen anybody go in or out for at least the last couple of weeks?"

"Yes, exactly."

"And that doesn't bother you at all?"

"You mean do I have any concerns for Conrad's safety?"

"Yes. Do you?"

He shifted uneasily in his chair.

"I assume you've been talking to Helen, and that's why you're here. She tried to persuade me to come with her to the police you know."

"Yes, I do know. Why wouldn't you?"

"Oh, I don't know. Partly because I thought she was making a bit of a fuss about nothing. And partly because I didn't really want to get involved, to be honest. I'm not a recluse like Conrad, but I do like to keep myself to myself."

"You think she's making a fuss about nothing? So you're not worried that there might be something wrong next door?"

"Now, now, don't get me wrong. I'm not unfeeling, or uncaring, or anything like that. It's just that I'm used to not seeing Conrad for long periods of time, though I must admit it's a bit unusual not to have seen Raj."

"Do you know how long he's been living there – Raj, I mean?"

Rowbotham puffed out his cheeks and raised his eyebrows.

"God, I'm really not sure. No, let me think ... A year or two, certainly."

"Say two or three?"

"More like one or two I suspect."

Priya made some more notes and wondered how best to phrase the next question.

"Forgive me, but this may be important. Do you have any idea what the ... well, the nature of their relationship is?"

"You mean are they a couple? I really haven't the slightest idea. I suppose I've always assumed so, yes. Bloody odd couple, though. There's a big difference in their ages for one thing. No, wait. Maybe that's not fair. Maybe I'm just letting myself be prejudiced by how I see Raj."

"Has Mr Taylor ever described Raj to you in any way? 'My partner', or 'the lodger' or anything like that?"

"No, not that I can remember."

"OK, thank you. I need to go away and work this up into a report. But before I do, I wonder if you can help me with any background? About Mr Taylor's family, for example?"

"There's certainly been nobody but him there for the last 20 years. I believe there was a family in residence around the time I bought this house, but I think they were gone by the time I actually moved in. The house stood empty for quite a while because I was having some building works done – including this room, and those garden walls incidentally – so it was 6 to 12 months before I could move in. I was getting divorced at the time as well, so there were all sorts of complications. You know, legal, financial, all that sort of rubbish."

"There are some references to a family called Schneider living next door. A family with two children, a girl and a boy."

"Like I said, that's probably before my time. If they were there when I bought, I'm pretty sure they weren't there any longer by the time I moved in."

"Can you think of anybody else I can speak to who might know any more? Any of the other neighbours for example?"

"God, no. Conrad and I are by far the most long-standing residents now, as far as I know. This road has changed completely, you know. When I bought this place the whole of Downshire Hill was family homes. Traditional family homes, I mean. The sort of places where people lived for generations. Ordinary people – well, pretty well off obviously – but nothing like today."

"So how is it today? What's different?"

"Pretty much everything. Except the church, that's the same. But everything else has changed beyond recognition. What used to be a nice old decent boozer down the road is now a gastro- pub – what a horrible phrase. And any time a house is sold now it's bought by an investment banker, or a hedge fund manager, like Helen's husband. Oh, nothing against them – Charlie's a decent bloke – but they've got no interest in Hampstead as a community, still less the spirit of the place. Oh God, that sounds very pretentious doesn't it? I'm sorry."

"Not at all, I'm interested. Let's see, Charlie, that's Helen's husband is it? Mr Barnes?"

"Yes, and he's a pretty typical specimen of what I'm talking about. No sooner bought the place than he and his builders were ripping the guts out of it. Even applied for planning permission for one of those bloody great basement extensions. Come to think of it, that's why I visited Conrad recently. We'd both objected to the planning application, and it got rejected. I think it's the only time I've seen Conrad really happy. Most of the time he seems pretty flat."

"So the basement isn't going to get built then?"

"Oh, I wouldn't be too sure about that. It's pretty routine around here that applications get rejected by Camden, but then granted on appeal. I have a horrible feeling that we'll wake up one morning to find earthmovers outside – you know, like in *The Hitchhikers' Guide*."

"What's that – a film?"

"It is, though I'd advise you to avoid it. Read the book instead, or books I should say."

"How many are there?"

"Five. It's a trilogy."

She stared at him in bemusement.

"You said a trilogy, right?"

"Yes, a trilogy in five parts, well six actually."

"I'm sorry, I'm not getting this. Am I missing something?"

He smiled.

"Well, if you haven't read Douglas Adams, then yes, I'm afraid you are."

Desai jotted down 'Douglas Adams' very neatly at the bottom of the page and then closed her notebook.

"Well, thank you very much, Mr Rowbotham. Do let me know when you've checked up on that date, won't you? Like I say, it could be important."

"I'll do it straightaway as soon as you've gone."

"Thank you. I may need to speak to you again, by the way."

"You'd be very welcome. Like Conrad, I don't get many visits, but unlike him I'm quite capable of enjoying them when they happen. Goodbye, Constable. I do hope we meet again."

CHAPTER 5

The following morning Collison rapped briefly on Metcalfe's door and went into his office.

"Morning, Bob," he greeted him, taking a seat.

"Morning, guv. Anything happening?"

"If you mean has anybody in North London been horribly murdered overnight then no, I don't think so. But there is this thing that Priya has been looking at. Have you had a chance to read her report? The full report I mean, after the interview with the second neighbour?"

"Yes I have. I'm really not sure what to make of it. What do you think?"

"I'm really not sure either. On the one hand it sounds a bit fishy and if something has happened to the old boy then we need to get in there and start investigating it as soon as possible. On the other hand, we're going to look pretty silly – which I suppose really means I'm going to look pretty silly – if we throw a lot of bodies at an investigation which turns out to be a wild goose chase, particularly if a real murder comes in while we're at it, and I have to start drafting in people from other nicks."

"Isn't that sort of what the new arrangements allow for?"

"Yes it is, but I'd rather not do it unless I have to. Things get a bit difficult if people are having to travel halfway across

North London all the time. Not to mention the ACC, who I'm sure would have something to say about overtime and the budget."

"Reading between the lines Priya seems pretty concerned."

"Yes, and not just reading between the lines either. I've been chatting to her about it. She seems to have a very strong instinct that something sinister has happened."

"Copper's nose? Not Priya surely. She's always so matter of fact."

"Well, I'd agree with you there, but she's really going out on a limb on this one. Don't knock copper's nose by the way. Tom Allen claims to have solved just about every one of his cases with it."

"Don't I know it. Where is Tom by the way? I haven't seen him for a few days now."

"He's up at Edgware investigating the suspicious death of a Women's Institute member."

"Really? Do they have a Women's Institute in Edgware?"

"A fair question: probably not. I believe the lady in question lived in Mill Hill."

"Oh, Mill Hill. That's different."

They both smiled. Everybody who lived in Edgware aspired to live in Mill Hill, just as everybody who lived in Mill Hill aspired to live in Totteridge. Perhaps only in Hampstead were the residents truly content with their lot: after all, just about everybody in the whole of North London aspired to live in Hampstead.

"But we digress, as I'm sure Peter Collins would say. What about this wretched recluse round the corner?"

"What does your copper's nose tell you, guv?"

"It doesn't seem to be working this morning, but I'm leaning in favour of backing Priya's instincts. I've known her for a while now and I think she's got good judgement."

"Me too. She's good. She knows what she's doing and she doesn't take 'no' for an answer."

"OK then. Set it up for this afternoon will you? Whistle up some uniform to break the door down."

"Who should I send from CID? Apart from Priya I mean? I'll go if you like. I've got nothing else on."

"By all means go if you're looking for something to do. Take Karen with you if you like. She was looking pretty bored too when I passed her in the corridor just now. Keep me informed of course. It might be an idea to warn the doctor and SOCO to be standing by as well, just in case you do find anything."

Metcalfe had cause to regret his keenness when he put his nose out of the door on Downshire Hill to encounter a steady drizzle.

"Oh damn," he said. "I don't have an umbrella with me."

"You can share mine if you like," Willis invited him as she pushed him out through the door onto the pavement.

"I can't be seen with that thing," he replied as she opened it with a quick snap, "it's pink."

"Actually it's magenta, and it matches my stockings."

"And there was me thinking that was just a coincidence, Sarge," Desai said innocently.

"Well it's a girly colour whatever it is," Metcalfe complained, "and I'm not going under it."

"Fine, get wet then."

"You can share mine if you like, guv," Desai offered. "It's black – which matches my trousers," she added.

Metcalfe tried huddling under Desai's umbrella as bidden, but it was small and anyway he felt ridiculous walking along with his knees bent. So he gave up, and strode on ahead, the rain beginning to soak his hair and jacket in what he hoped would be seen as fine manly fashion.

The two uniform officers were already waiting for them, looking bored and idly swinging the heavy ram which was used routinely on drugs raids.

"Afternoon, sir," they said as Metcalfe approached, having comfortably out-distanced the two women. "Ready to go are we?"

"Have you knocked?"

"Yes, guv, very loudly three times. No answer. The lady next door put her head out to find out what was going on, but we asked her to go back inside. You can see her peeping out of the window if you look carefully."

"Oh, never mind about her. OK then, go ahead."

As the two women walked up the path under their umbrellas the PCs swung the ram back and then forwards between them in a single smooth motion. The door yielded at the first blow, crashing backwards into the wall of the hallway.

"Police! Hello – is anybody there?" one of them shouted through the open doorway.

"You want us to go in, guv?" the other asked Metcalfe.

"No," he decided. "Let's find out what we're dealing with

first. Why don't you go back to the nick? We can call you if we need you."

They nodded and departed, doubtless in search of a cup of tea in the canteen.

The three detectives stood and looked at each other for a moment. Metcalfe surveyed what he could see from the front door. As Helen Barnes had described, a sea of papers stretched in all directions. The hallway seemed to lead into the kitchen at the back of the house. There was a single door on each side, both closed. He went inside and beckoned them to follow him, which they did, closing their umbrellas as they did so. They moved aside to allow him to close the front door.

"All right," he said. "Let's take one room each and try to disturb things as little as possible. Downstairs first."

"I'll go in here if you like," Desai offered, indicating the door to the right.

"OK, Priya, go ahead. Karen why don't you go through to the kitchen at the end? I'll take the door on the left."

He experienced some difficulty in opening the door. As he pushed harder it became apparent that it was being held in place by various old newspapers. He finally succeeded in opening it halfway, and edged around it into the room.

It felt a little like walking into a museum, although perhaps a junk museum. The walls were covered in dark wooden panelling and the room smelled musty, as though it had not been entered for some time. The floor was completely obscured by papers. On them, in one corner two or three old suitcases had been piled up. An old leather Chesterfield and two matching chairs stood isolated like islands surrounded by dusty and yellowing papers. He felt for the light switch and turned it on; it worked.

"Christ, what a mess," he murmured to himself.

Carefully, so as to disturb the surroundings as little as possible, he waded slowly across the room. When he reached the wall he turned and started back diagonally. He repeated this process two or three times until he had covered the entire room and was satisfied that there was nothing under the papers. It was as he was turning the light off again that he heard Desai's cry.

"Priya? Are you all right?" he called.

He and Willis reached the doorway to the other room at the same time and peered through it together. Desai was standing in one corner, very still, and with her hand over her mouth.

"I'm sorry," she said, "I didn't mean to call out like that. I think I've found Mr Taylor, guv."

She pointed downwards, to where something dark could be seen on the floor through the papers. It looked like the body of a man, lying on its side facing away from the door.

"Are you sure he's dead?"

"Very. I think he's been dead for some time. Oh, I'm sorry, I think I'm going to be sick."

"Don't contaminate the crime scene, for God's sake. Come out quickly. Get her outside, Karen."

He snatched open the front door once again. Desai just made it onto the pathway from where she was noisily sick into a clump of thistles.

"Hard luck, Priya," he said as he stood outside and

thumbed his mobile phone. "Looks like you were right, but I'm sorry it had to be you that found him."

While Metcalfe called the doctor, SOCO, and Collison, Willis pulled some tissues out of her bag and Desai took them with a tearful smile. It was still raining and by the time he had finished his calls the two women were once again standing under their umbrellas, Desai looking embarrassed.

"I'm so sorry, guv," she said again.

"Don't be," he said with a smile. "We've all done it."

"So what happens now?" Willis asked.

"Well, as I've just explained to the guvnor, all we know at the moment is that Taylor is dead. We don't know whether it's suspicious or natural causes. We'll have to wait for the doctor for that. I suppose we should really have searched the house anyway to find out if that Indian guy is in there too, but I think I'd rather not disturb the scene any more, just in case it does turn out to be suspicious."

"I agree," Willis nodded.

The rain was getting harder. Metcalfe's grey jacket was now almost black with accumulated water.

"Why don't you two go back to the nick for a bit?" he suggested. "I can give you a ring when it's OK to go in."

"No, let me stay, guv. I'm the junior."

"No thanks, Priya. You go off and get a cup of tea. I want to stay anyway to speak with the doctor and ask SOCO how we should approach the crime scene – if that's what it is. I'm damned if I know what we're going to do about all those papers."

He watched them start to walk back up the road, clutching

their umbrellas, and then tried to stand inside the little porch to shelter from the rain. This achieved only limited success, as a wind had got up which was driving the rain directly against the door. Since he was already very wet, he simply shrugged and waited.

Brian Williams, the forensic surgeon, was first to arrive.

"Afternoon, Bob. What have you got for me then?"

"Deceased male, whom we believe to be Conrad Taylor, the owner of the house. That's about it, I'm afraid. I got everybody out into the garden as soon as we realised what we were dealing with."

"Fair enough. Let's just hope SOCO don't take too long to get here. Would you like to share my umbrella?"

The doctor's umbrella was also colourful, but in a respectable golf club sort of way. It was also very large, and Metcalfe was happy to take shelter under it as Williams fought to control it in the strengthening wind.

About 10 minutes later Tom Bellamy arrived with his assistants. Metcalfe briefed him while everybody climbed into white forensic overalls and then hopped around awkwardly just inside the front door as they slipped the footwear equivalents over their shoes.

Once properly clad, Bellamy entered the room cautiously. Metcalfe noticed that he was treading deliberately in Desai's footsteps. He squatted and gazed very deliberately at the body.

"Not that there's any doubt about it," he called back over his shoulder, "but could you come in please, Doctor to certify life extinct?"

Williams carefully followed in Bellamy's wake. As he reached the body, Bellamy moved aside and Williams squatted down in his turn. After a moment he glanced at his watch.

"I certify life extinct at 1631," he said formally.

He stood up and gazed across the room at Metcalfe.

"Obviously I can't be sure until after the post-mortem, Bob, but I'd say he's been dead some weeks. Oh, and he appears to have been battered about the head. Looks like you've got a murder on your hands, doesn't it?"

CHAPTER 6

Simon Collison arrived on the scene about 10 minutes later under a black umbrella of impeccable plainness. There was a chorus of 'afternoon, guv' as he joined the small group clustered in the front doorway.

"Afternoon, everybody. So Priya was right then, Bob?"

"Yes she was, guv. It was she who found the body as a matter of fact."

"So, what do we have?"

"A bit of a poser actually. I'm not quite sure what to do so I'm glad you turned up when you did."

"If I could cut in, sir," Tom Bellamy said, doing exactly that, "the problem is this. The doctor has certified life extinct. Indeed, it's pretty obvious that the poor chap has been dead for some time – maybe weeks. And it looks like he's had his head bashed in. So we know we're dealing with a crime scene. But do we restrict our procedures just to that one room, or do we take on the whole house? You can see for yourself that would be a mammoth task: just look at all these papers scattered everywhere. They would all have to be collated, marked out on a floor plan, and catalogued. And that's just for starters. Once we've done that we'd need to make a full forensic investigation of every single room in the house. Do you have any idea how long that would take? I'd say a week at least, possibly two."

"I hear what you say, Tom, but I'm conscious that we may have another body in the house somewhere. We believe that Conrad Taylor – that's the owner of the house, whom I assume is our victim – was living with an Indian man called Raj. He hasn't been seen by the neighbours for some time, so I think we have to assume – at least for the time being – that he's still here somewhere."

"Yes, guv, so I understand."

"Well, that being the case, I really don't see that we have any choice, do we? We're just going to have to go over the whole house, no matter how long it takes."

"I don't have a problem with that, guv. I just want to make it very clear upfront how much work is involved. It's not going to look pretty on your budget. I'm a few bods short at the moment, so it may mean a lot of overtime."

"So be it, Tom. I'll authorise whatever you think you need. When can you start?"

"I'd like to make a start today – right now – but it's getting very dark outside and the rain is getting worse. If we're going to start from the front door and work inwards I'd like to get some really good lights rigged up, and that will take time. If you like, I could get it done overnight and we can start first thing tomorrow morning. I can secure the door and seal off the scene until then."

"Sounds good. Bob, could you ask uniform to arrange to have people here overnight, please? As soon as word spreads we'll have Joe public trampling all over the garden and trying to look through the windows."

"Already done, guv."

"Good man."

Collison became aware of Dr Williams patiently awaiting his turn to speak.

"Hello, Brian. Good to see you again."

"Likewise, Simon. I was just hanging around to ask if we could move the body. I'm assuming you'd like the post-mortem report as soon as possible."

"I do of course, but only if Tom is happy with that; the crime scene is his responsibility. Have you finished with the body, Tom?"

Bellamy pursed his lips and moved his head from side to side indecisively.

"Yes, I suppose so," he conceded at last. "I'd really prefer to wait until we have the really powerful lights available to take some more photos, but we've examined the floor and papers around the body in some detail so I'm not sure what more that would achieve. So yes, Brian, you can have the body. But please make sure your chaps disturb as little as possible."

"You can make sure yourself," Williams said briskly as he stepped outside and shook open his umbrella. "I'm off to my lair to make sure everything is ready for our guest when he arrives."

"Just before you go, Doctor," Metcalfe said. "Could you just repeat for Mr Collison what you told me?"

"Certainly. Death appears to have been caused by head injuries, apparently as a result of being struck at least once with a heavy blunt object. But obviously I can't say any more than that until after I've conducted the post-mortem."

As the doctor withdrew, Collison considered the situation. Given that the deceased had been dead for some time, there wasn't quite the usual urgency about the situation. It was important, he felt, that they should get everything exactly right, even at the expense of spending a little extra time.

"I'll leave you to it, Tom," he said, drawing Metcalfe to one side.

"I think we may as well go back to the nick," he said. "I don't see that we can do anything more here today. I suspected that might be the case, actually, which is why I didn't bring Priya and Karen back with me. I think we'd be better occupied setting up the incident room and pulling a team together. There's Timothy Evans for a start. Let's grab him. We know he's good."

Metcalfe pulled a face.

"Are you sure, guv? He scored a bit of an own goal on the last case, didn't he?"

Collison was silent for a moment as he spread his umbrella over them both.

"He did, Bob," he said quietly as they began to walk up the hill, "but he's young and you have to expect these things. I think he has the makings of a very fine officer, maybe not as much potential as Priya has, but he'll do OK, and it's important for us to show that we trust him. Important to show that we're not going to pillory him for just one mistake."

"I'll remember that, guv."

Collison took a few more steps, wondering if he had said enough.

"You know, Bob, it's none of my business whatever you've written in Timothy's file, but for my part I mentioned that I thought that it was the girl who made all the running. You can't really expect a red-blooded young man bursting with hormones to turn down an offer of sex with an attractive young woman, can you?"

Metcalfe smiled.

"Karen said much the same thing," he admitted. "And don't worry, guv, I went easy on him too. After all, he had no idea at the time that she was going to turn out to be such a material witness."

"Well, exactly. All right then, he's on the team. I'll leave you to pull together whoever else may be available. Don't look outside our own nick for the moment, not until we're certain what sort of manpower we need on this."

They reached the police station and went round to the front door; the side door only opened from the inside these days. As they went up the stairs Metcalfe glanced at his watch and was shocked to see that it was only 4:30. It felt as though several hours had passed. He moved his shoulders uncomfortably as his wet jacket clung to him.

"You'd better get out of that wet jacket," Collison said as though reading his thoughts. "Ah, Karen. How's Priya bearing up?"

"She says she'll be fine, guv, but I think she's pretty upset actually."

"That's entirely understandable. What you think – should we send her home?"

She shook her head.

"I think she'd take that badly. You know Priya. If she says she's OK then I think we just have to pretend that we believe her, and carry on as though nothing is wrong."

"All right. Then let's get together quickly in my office, shall we? Grab Timothy as well. Bob, will you press the button on setting up the incident room, please?"

"Already on it, guv," Metcalfe replied, picking up his phone. "If you want to go on ahead I'll be with you in a few minutes."

Collison sat at his desk and pulled a pad towards him. He unscrewed his pen, trying to marshal his thoughts, but before he had a chance to do much more than jot down 'Conrad Taylor' as a heading there was a brief tap on the half open door and Willis ushered Desai and Evans into the room.

"Sit down everyone," he enjoined them, waving at the various chairs which stood around the large, half-empty room.

"We'll just wait for DI Metcalfe, but for your benefit, Timothy, we found a dead body this afternoon at a house just round the corner in Downshire Hill. The doctor reckons he died violently: from a bash on the head to be precise. Other than that we know very little, apart from the fact that he seems to have been sharing the house with a young Indian lad called Raj, who hasn't been seen for some time."

"The killer, sir? Or another victim?"

"That," Collison said grimly, "is exactly what we need

to find out, Timothy. Ah, here's the Inspector. How are we doing with the incident room, Bob?"

"IT are making a start on it right now, guv. Should be ready to go sometime tomorrow morning, say about 11."

"All right. Let's start trying to get our thinking in order, shall we?"

Collison stood up and walked across to the flipchart where he liked to jot down things as they occurred to him. He had used it a lot during the preparation of his recent paper.

"Raj," he said, scribbling the name as he did so. "We need to find him. If we find his body at the house then that obviously strongly suggests that they were both killed by the same person. If we don't find his body, then we need to find him, and fast. He's an obvious suspect and needs to be eliminated."

"Our victim," he continued, as he wrote 'Conrad Taylor', "was the only other occupant of the house so far as we are aware. How much do we actually know about him? Not very much, it seems to me, despite Priya's excellent work with the neighbours. We need to dig a lot more deeply into his background. In particular, we need to find somebody who knows the truth about his relationship with Raj. Were they lovers? If not, what on earth was Raj doing there? And who is he, anyway? We need to find his full name ASAP."

"Maybe we'll find something in all those papers," Willis suggested. "Some recent post, for example."

"Yes, and I'm glad you mentioned that, Karen. It seems to me that this case may be similar to the one at Burgh House: you know, with lots of papers lying around which may or may not be relevant. I hate to do this to you, but you did such a good job on it last time, that I wonder if you'd take that on again? I suspect it may be pretty much a full-time job, but it's important. The lead we're looking for may well be stuck away in one of them somewhere."

"Of course, guv. I'd be happy to."

"What about the deceased's family?" Metcalfe queried. "I know he was a recluse, but he must have some relatives stashed away somewhere."

"Agreed, Bob. Priya, why don't you take that on? You've been the one gathering the background so far, and you really know your way around the computer system."

"Happy to do that, guv," she replied, "but it's only fair to warn you that I was here until late last night trying to do exactly that, and it's not going to be easy. Taylor's quite a common name and I wasn't able to cross-reference anything conclusive. I couldn't even come up with anything that might be the deceased's birth certificate. I reckon he was about 60, don't you? Well, I went back 80 years just to be sure and I couldn't find anything at all for a Conrad Taylor."

"Then maybe he was born abroad?" Willis asked. "Something else we need to find out about."

There was a silence while they all gazed at the flipchart.

"That's probably all we can do until we have a full team in place, and until we have the post-mortem and SOCO reports," Collison commented. "I know that Brian Williams will do his best to get the former to us as quickly as possible, but I think SOCO will be some time. They have the whole house to examine, and all those papers to go through. Karen,

I suggest you ask Tom Bellamy to let you have each batch of papers as they clear them and bag them, together with a note of where they were found."

Willis nodded and made a note on her pad.

"There's one other thing," Collison said. "As soon as we have a better idea of what may have happened here, I'd like to get Peter Collins involved. Could you have a word with him this evening please, Karen, and see what his availability is likely to be?"

Willis smiled.

"If there's a chance for him to get involved in another murder enquiry, guv, I think he'll be very available indeed."

CHAPTER 7

The incident room the next morning was in its usual state of induced chaos while IT set it up prior to handing it over to the investigative team. One terminal after another was plugged in and activated, its screen flickering into life; a technician would wait patiently for a login screen to appear before moving onto the next machine. Around the room, telephones rang in turn as their newly allocated numbers were noted and checked. With all this going on, Collison decided to defer the initial briefing meeting until 11 o'clock, by which time IT promised the room would be ready. In the interim, arriving team members sat down at a desk, logged in, and brought themselves up to speed on the background of the case. A few of the speedier ones then went for coffee or sat around aimlessly, waiting for order finally to reassert itself.

True to their word, IT handed the room over to Metcalfe just before 11, and he passed the word to Collison who duly arrived a few minutes later. The room fell silent as he walked in.

"Good morning, everybody. Good to see you all. I'll ask DI Metcalfe to brief us in a minute, but first I just wanted to welcome you all. I think I've worked with most of you before, and I'm looking forward to getting to know the rest of you. Thank you, Bob. All yours."

"Thank you, sir. OK, everybody, I think you all know who I am, but just in case I'm DI Bob Metcalfe. I will be in overall day-to-day command of the investigation, reporting to Mr Collison as SIO. DS Karen Willis – sitting over there – will be backing me up, although she will probably also have some specific responsibilities on this case, as you will hear in a minute."

He walked over to the big whiteboard where Willis had already assembled notes, together with some preliminary photographs which SOCO had sent over by email.

"Yesterday afternoon, acting in response to concerns expressed by some members of the public for the welfare of a Mr Conrad Taylor of Wentworth House, Downshire Hill – just round the corner in fact – I visited the property with DS Willis and DC Desai. When we were unable to gain any response, I authorised uniform to break down the door. We subsequently found a corpse, believed to be Mr Taylor, in the front room on the right-hand side of the house as you look at it from the street. We immediately evacuated the house to await the arrival of the duty pathologist and SOCO."

"It is the doctor's opinion – preliminary, of course – that death almost certainly occurred as a result of head injuries which have an appearance consistent with having been inflicted by a blunt object. In short, we are now treating this as a murder enquiry. After discussion with SOCO, Mr Collison took the decision that the entire house should be subject to detailed forensic examination. This will obviously take some time. It's quite a large house, and every room that we have seen so far appears to be littered with papers. That means that we're going to be receiving information from SOCO piecemeal as our enquiries go forward. Not very satisfactory, I know, but there's no way round it so we just have to live with it. Karen, why don't you bring it up to speed on what we know so far?"

"The short answer to that is not very much, at least not at the moment," she said, taking his place by the whiteboard.

"Our victim, Conrad Taylor, was a recluse. So much so that we don't even have a photo of him – of him alive that is – to show you yet. DC Desai has spoken to the neighbours on both sides of Wentworth House. Both had been inside it, though briefly and infrequently. Taylor was almost never seen outside, his shopping apparently being done by a mystery figure known to the neighbours only as Raj who was apparently living with Mr Taylor. One of the things we obviously need to do is to try to define exactly what the nature of their relationship might have been. Raj is missing, by the way, so we don't know at present whether to treat him as a potential suspect or a potential second victim. That's one of the things we'll be looking out for SOCO to discover: is there a second body at the house?"

"Excuse me, Sarge," Desai called out, "but I've spoken to both neighbours again this morning. Neither of them had any idea what Raj's full name might be, but Mr Rowbotham – he's the one who's been there the longest – says he thinks Taylor might have mentioned to him that Raj is a Tamil."

"Okay, well that's something anyway I suppose. One thing we've asked SOCO to let us have as soon as possible is any post they may come across. Hopefully that will tell us what we want to know."

"Thank you, Karen," Metcalfe said. "Just a bit more background for you all. We believe Conrad Taylor had lived at the house for at least the last 20 years or so. Before that there seems to be some record of a family called Schneider, which we believed to have comprised two adults and two children: one boy, one girl. At the moment, they seem to have vanished without trace. But it simply can't be possible for the trail to go completely cold like that. Somewhere, somebody knows what happened to them and where they are today. That's one of the things I'd like to find out as quickly as possible."

Collison walked into the middle of the room.

"As you can see, it's early days and there's a lot we don't know. We need to change that. First, there's the mysterious Raj. Who is he? On what basis was he living at the house? What does he do for a living? We understand from Mr Rowbotham that he works in IT, yet he seems to spend a lot of time hanging around at home. Where was he living before he pitched up at Wentworth House, and most important of all: where is he now? Is he alive, in which case he's an obvious suspect, or is he dead like Conrad Taylor?"

He waited while Willis jotted these questions down on the whiteboard.

"Then there's Conrad Taylor, whom we are assuming to be our deceased. We need to gather as much background on him as we can if we're to understand who might have killed him. Bob, we need to apply for a court order to identify and access his bank accounts. Let's also ask the Law Society to circulate his details. It would be good if we could find his lawyer. We also need to intensify our efforts to find his family. Even if he was living there alone – apart from Raj that is – he may have siblings, or even children. We need to find them."

He looked around the room.

"Any other thoughts, anyone? No? Then let me give you my initial analysis."

He thought deeply for a moment and then went on.

"First, there is always the possibility that he was killed by some random caller; a burglary gone wrong perhaps. What used to be called the passing tramp theory. Uniform haven't had any reports of burglaries in the area recently, but that doesn't mean we can rule the possibility out."

"Second, there is the alternative possibility that he was killed not by a stranger but by someone he knew. Here the fact that he was a recluse should be an enormous help. After all, he simply didn't know many people. So far, Raj is the only one we know about. There are the neighbours of course, but neither of them had any obvious motive, nor indeed any opportunity. So far as we know neither of them had a key to the property. We should check that though, Priya."

"Yes, guv."

"At the moment, all roads seem to lead to Raj. We need to find him, dead or alive, and we need to find out more about him. Well, I think that's it for the moment. You'll have the post-mortem report and ongoing information from SOCO as they become available. I'll leave DI Metcalfe to allocate responsibilities."

He nodded and left the room.

"Right, listen up," Metcalfe called. "DS Willis will be taking point on any papers that are found at the property as soon as SOCO are finished with them. It's quite possible this may turn out to be a huge task – I've seen the place and it's knee deep in some places – in which case we'll allocate more bodies to it in due course. The rest of you, come and take one of these task sheets and then get on with whatever you've been assigned. I think you've all done this before, so you know what to expect. We will meet in here every morning at 9 o'clock at which time you will bring the team up to speed on what progress you have made with your own particular responsibility. If you come across anything which you feel to be urgent, then you come and talk to me at once, or DS Willis in my absence. Clear? Good. Let's get on with it then."

He watched them all come forward and take a sheet off the pile. Then, with a quick smile to Willis, he left the room. He headed up the stairs, walked along the corridor, and knocked on the door to Collison's office.

"Come in. Ah, it's you, Bob. The troops all organised?"

"Yes, that's all OK, but there's something I wanted to ask you, guv."

"Sit down then. What is it?"

"Well, I was thinking overnight, and it's occurred to me again just now. We really need at least one more DS on this, particularly with Karen likely to have only limited time for day-to-day stuff."

"Sounds very sensible. So why not get one?"

"Well, that's a bit delicate. The ones I'd like are already allocated to other enquiries. A few are off on courses. That leaves only two, and to be honest I've worked with them both before and have no particular wish to again."

"You don't trust their abilities?"

"To be honest, no I don't."

There was a pause while Collison digested this. Then he gazed at Metcalfe..

"You wouldn't be bringing me this, Bob, unless you had some solution to propose. What is it?"

"It's Priya actually. What about making her acting DS just for this investigation? I think she's ready for it and I'd certainly trust her more than those other two goons."

"I think it's an excellent idea. I've been meaning to recommend her for promotion anyway, so a spell of acting up will look good on her file. Anything else? No? Then why don't you ask her to come up and see me and I'll break the good news."

A few moments later Desai, looking unusually nervous, tapped uncertainly on the door and found herself in her turn sitting before the Superintendent.

"Is something wrong?" she asked at once.

He smiled and shook his head.

"Not at all, Priya. The fact is that DI Metcalfe has asked for you as an acting DS on this enquiry. He thinks you're ready for it, and I agree. If you're happy to accept then I'll do it with immediate effect."

Desai gulped.

"Yes please, sir," she said simply.

"Good. Well, congratulations. I'll ask Bob to put out an email at once notifying the troops. I should warn you, by the way, that Karen is likely to have her time occupied mostly with all that documentation, so you'll need to organise your own time very carefully. You will need to delegate a lot of your own stuff to others so that you will have the time available for people to come and talk to. DS is a very important position on a team like this. If you miss something, then it gets missed full stop."

"That won't happen, guv. You can rely on me."

"I'm sure I can."

CHAPTER 8

"Morning, Sarge," Desai greeted Willis the next morning.

"Morning, Sarge, yourself," she replied with a smile, gesturing towards her computer screen. "Congratulations. By the way, in the circumstances I think you'd better start calling me Karen, don't you?"

"Oh, thank you, but I'm sure it's okay? After all, I'm only acting DS."

"I shouldn't worry about that. Provided you do okay on this one then I would have thought it's almost automatic, isn't it? They don't normally ask someone to act up unless they've already pretty much made up their mind to promote them."

"Well, let's hope so. I'm pretty nervous I don't mind telling you."

"Well, I'm here to help. Anything you're not sure about, just ask. Bob did the same thing for me. It's great to know there's someone watching out for you."

"Thanks, Sarge – I mean Karen. That's really kind of you."

Looking at her, Willis realised it was the first time she had ever seen Desai exhibiting anything other than total self-confidence. Today there was a hint of insecurity, perhaps even vulnerability.

"Is everything okay otherwise, Priya? No trouble at home, or anything like that?"

The question felt clumsy as soon she asked it. It was common knowledge that Desai was not in a relationship and still lived at home with her mother, her father having died recently. Perhaps it felt clumsy to her as well, for she gave Willis a sharp glance.

"Yes of course, why shouldn't it be?"

"No reason, no reason at all. Sorry, I was just trying ..."

Around in the room was filling up and Willis was able to fall silent without further embarrassment as Collison came through the door. The team was larger now, pretty much complete, and one or two new arrivals who had not worked with Collison before stared at him curiously. As Collison of the Yard, as some of the less weighty newspapers had dubbed him after a couple of high-profile successes, he had become the closest thing to a media celebrity that the Metropolitan Police possessed. He nodded to the room in general and went and sat at the back, as he often did.

"When you're ready, Bob," he called out as he sat down.

"Thank you, guv, and welcome to those of you who weren't here yesterday. Before we start, as you'll all have seen from Mr Collison's email yesterday, Priya Desai has kindly agreed to act up as DS to fill a hole in the team, so thank you and congratulations to her. I anticipate that she will be playing a very full role in this enquiry as DS Willis already has some specific responsibilities which are likely to take up most of her time. So, from now on, if there is anything you need urgently and I'm not around, please speak to DS Desai. Okay?"

Everyone looked at Desai, who squirmed a little and tried not to meet anybody's eye. It was the first time she had heard herself addressed by her new rank and it had given her a spontaneous little thrill of pleasure. Ridiculous, she thought angrily. Am I really that vain?

"Now to business," Metcalfe continued. "We have a new development. Karen, why don't you tell us about it?"

"Late last night," Willis said, speaking clearly, "I received the first package of papers retrieved from Wentworth House by SOCO. They were from the front hall, and of limited evidential value since various people have been trampling around there. There are a few old newspapers which I don't think amount to very much, but also some un-opened mail. It's mostly junk: circulars and so forth. However there is a bank statement for Conrad Taylor. It's dated about six weeks ago, which may help fix the date of death as well, unless he was in the habit of leaving his bank statements lying around unopened of course."

She picked up another plastic evidence bag.

"More interestingly, we have an envelope addressed to Rajarshi Subramanian, so it looks like we now know Raj's full name at least. It's dated just 10 days ago, but unopened like the bank statement. SOCO extracted the contents – they're here in this other plastic wallet – which was an invoice for a computer printer, apparently ordered over the Internet."

"So that suggests that Raj hadn't been at the house for the last 10 days, at least?" Evans proffered.

"Which would gel with what Mr Rowbotham said about not having seen him for a while," Desai nodded.

"So where is he?" Collison asked. "Finding him must remain our first priority."

"But apparently he's not at the house, guv," Metcalfe said. "SOCO did a preliminary sweep of the whole place before focusing on individual rooms, and they're certain there are no more bodies hidden under the papers. Of course he could have been concealed somewhere – under the floor or buried in the garden, for example – but they haven't got nearly as far as that yet."

"And if it was a double murder," Desai chipped in, "then why conceal one body but leave the other in plain view? It wouldn't make sense."

"I tend to agree," Collison said mildly. "Karen, have you run any checks on this – whatever his name is – that might help us find him?"

"Yes and no, guv. Yes, I've run the checks. No, they don't help us very much. There's nobody of that name on the electoral register anywhere in the country, nor registered for council tax. Nor do the tax authorities have any record of him. There is one reference which may be significant, though. Somebody with that exact name was granted limited leave to remain by the immigration authorities nearly 3 years ago. It was while the Sri Lankan civil war was going on, and he claimed asylum in the UK on the grounds that the Tamil population was being oppressed, and that it would not be safe for him to return. He was granted limited leave to remain so that his claim for asylum could be assessed, but nothing was heard of him again. It appears that he simply slipped away and went to ground."

"Curious," Collison commented. "So where has he been between absconding from the immigration authorities and pitching up on Downshire Hill? We need to try to pinpoint exactly when he started living at Wentworth House, and how he managed to do so without apparently generating any electronic paper trail at all. What did he do for money? Where did he live? Still, at least we know now who we are looking for."

He stood up and went to stand beside Metcalfe at the front of the room.

"It seems to me that right now Raj – DS Willis will circulate his full name – is our prime suspect in this murder enquiry, so we need to devote all our resources to finding him, and as quickly as possible."

"Excuse me, sir," Evans said, raising his hand as if in class.

"Yes, Timothy?"

"The invoice, sir. If we contact the website which supplied the printer, they should have a record of how it was paid for. Presumably it was done with a credit card. If so, whose?"

"Very good, Timothy. Why don't you get onto that yourself?"

"I've scanned both the invoice and the envelope, and they're on the system," Willis told him.

"We also of course now know where the deceased banked," Metcalfe observed. "I've already applied for a blanket order covering any bank. Hopefully I'll have that before close of play today, and we can ask for access to all relevant details."

"Good. Thank you, Bob. What else do we have?"

"In terms of finding out more about the deceased's history, sir, I think I've taken it about as far as I can with the neighbours," Desai said. "I think we need to widen the enquiry and find other people who might have lived around there over the last 20 years or so. For example, we could speak to the people who used to own the Barnes property."

"Yes, I agree," Collison replied. "It will be a long job I'm sure, but I don't see that we have any alternative. There's always the possibility that the key to this lies somewhere in Taylor's past. But don't you do it, Priya. You have line management responsibilities now. Delegate that, please, and make sure that the relevant people report back to you soon as they have anything."

"Will do, guv. As far as the family who live there before are concerned, I've drawn a bit of a blank I'm afraid. There's simply a reference to a "Mr K. Schneider" holding the property as sole proprietor, and the only address given is that of the property itself."

"Well, perhaps some of these other people might be of help us with that: some of the older residents."

Collison paused for thought.

"Actually, let's make that a priority too, Bob. I'd particularly like us to speak to whoever Helen Barnes and her husband bought their house from. Why don't we ask for the details of her solicitors? We can follow the trail from there."

"Excuse me, guv."

"Yes, Priya?"

"Sorry, I should have mentioned that; I checked the land registry. The people before the Barnes couple were only there for a short time themselves: about three years. The ones who sound really interesting are a couple called McKenzie, who seem to have owned the house from 1966 onwards. There's a McKenzie before that too, so presumably they inherited it from the husband's parents. There's a lady with the same name and address who's registered as having died about six years ago, so the dates match. Presumably the husband didn't want to stay on in the house by himself."

"Good work, Priya. Can we find him?"

"I'm trying, guv. No luck so far. His full name is Colin Arthur McKenzie, and I can't find anyone of that name and age registered as having died, so the good news is he must still be alive and out there somewhere."

"We need to find and interview everyone," Collison said. "This McKenzie bloke sounds really interesting. He and his wife must have lived alongside the Schneider family. He must also remember Taylor buying the house. He may even be able to tell us about when Raj arrived, and exactly what sort of arrangement he had with Taylor."

He looked around the room and noted with approval that most people seemed to be jotting things down.

"Well, we're making progress. We don't have much firm information yet, but we know what questions to ask and we've mapped out some lines of enquiry. Now that we know Raj's full name we can put out a nationwide alert for him. No photo though, Karen?"

"Not yet, sir, no. We'll have to wait and see what SOCO come up with."

"Very well. Any other thoughts, anyone?"

Desai half raised her hand and then, just as hesitantly, lowered it again.

"Yes, Priya?"

"I'm not sure, guv ..."

"Come on, out with it."

"Well, this may be nothing, but ... well, alright: if Taylor and Raj were living together then we're assuming that Taylor was gay, right? Well, as we all know there's a very active gay scene in Hampstead. There are gay pubs, and areas of the Heath where ... well, where gay guys meet. Why don't we see if we can tap into that circle? Somebody may just remember him."

"Taylor was a recluse, remember," Metcalfe said doubtfully.

"Yeah, well he might not always have been."

"You mean he might have ... dipped his toe in the water so to speak. Even if it was a little while ago."

"Yes, guv, exactly."

"It sounds like a great idea, Priya, and let's face it we don't have many other avenues of enquiry, do we? Let's at least investigate it and rule it out. How would you suggest going about it?"

"I think there's an LGBT liaison officer right here in the nick, guv. It shouldn't take too long to put the word out."

Some of the team cast surreptitious glances at their friends. Collison noticed it. Tread carefully, he thought. He was only too aware that there was still a lot of homophobia in the Met.

"Great idea, Priya, like I said. Let's leave that with you, shall we?"

CHAPTER 9

The forensic pathologist called Metcalfe later that day.

"Bob? It's Brian Williams. I've completed the post-mortem. I'm sending the report over to you to put on the system, but I thought you'd appreciate a quick update on the phone."

"Yes, thank you, Doctor. Was it as you suspected?"

"Yes, pretty much. Looks like a single blow to the head administered with some force with a blunt object. There's a pretty massive depressed fracture of the skull, but no sign of any skin puncture such as a blade or sharp edge might make. I'd be interested to hear what SOCO might find at the scene, but we could be looking at a ball hammer or something like that."

"So something quite clinical then, rather than a frenzied attack?"

"Yes, certainly not a frenzied attack. As to 'clinical' that rather depends whether it was premeditated or not, doesn't it? Your department, not mine."

"You say the blow was administered with considerable force. Does that rule out a woman, for example?"

"Not necessarily, if she was sufficiently fit and she had room enough to work up a sufficient swing of the arm. But I'd favour a man as our murderer."

"Did you find anything else?"

"Nothing significant, I'm afraid. No signs of a struggle. Nothing under the fingernails except normal dirt: household dust, that sort of thing. No sign of him having tried to protect himself either, which I suppose suggests that the attack was from behind and unexpected. I've had nothing back from toxicology yet, and I'll let you know when I do. As far as the stomach contents are concerned it looks as though he had eaten fairly recently before death. We found traces of bread or toast as well as coffee – instant, apparently."

"Toast and coffee would suggest breakfast, I suppose."

"They would certainly be consistent with it, yes," Williams replied cautiously.

"What about time of death, Doctor. Can we be any more specific about that now?"

"It's a difficult one. Usually we can use things like the life-cycle of the blowfly, but the room was closed and there's no sign of any insect or larvae activity. From the general deterioration of the body I'd go for somewhere in the range between 6 to 8 weeks. Sorry, but I can't be any more certain than that."

"Doctor," Metcalfe said hesitantly, "there's something else I'd like to ask you; something somebody here has brought up actually. Was there any sign of sexual activity, particularly homosexual sex?"

"Nothing I could see; I checked of course. But unless it was some combination of recent, forceful, or frequent then it wouldn't necessarily show up."

"I see, OK. Well, thank you very much for getting this

done so quickly, Doctor. I know Mr Collison will be very grateful."

As he rang off, he saw a new email slide into his inbox entitled 'Post Mortem Report: C.Taylor'. He looked around the room quickly to check that he was not needed and headed upstairs to see the Superintendent.

"Thank you, Bob," Collison said when he had finished passing on the pathologist's news. "I'm not sure it takes us very much further though, does it?"

"Well, not a frenzied attack anyway, guv, so perhaps that makes it less likely that it was a lovers' tiff."

"Not in the heat of the moment, certainly; I'd have to concede that. But it could have been some serious argument or disagreement that festered and grew into a cold-blooded, premeditated attack quite literally when the victim's back was turned."

"So you still fancy Raj for it?"

"I think we have to, don't we? At least until he's found."

"Well, I think we may have made a little progress there, guv. Karen's just had some more papers in from SOCO and there are a few photos among them, including one we think must be Taylor and Raj together. We're having them blown up, but it's unclear how useful they will be. They're old film and paper photos, not digital."

"It's something anyway, Bob. At least we've got something now we can circulate with the national alert for Raj, and something the liaison officer can use with the local gay community."

"Are you really taking that seriously, guv?"

Collison shrugged.

"It's a line of enquiry, isn't it? Hopefully we can eliminate it as quickly as possible and crack on with finding our suspect."

"There was something else interesting in the package of papers we got today. There was another envelope – empty and opened this time – but addressed to a 'G.Rajarshi'. Do you think Raj might have been using multiple identities?"

"God knows. But if he was, why do it using one of his own names?"

"Perhaps so that if mail came when he wasn't at the house, Taylor would recognise it as being for him, and therefore not throw it away."

Collison chuckled.

"You're clutching at straws now, Bob. Let's just find him, shall we? Then we can ask him ourselves."

"Talking of finding him, that mention of liaison officers has given me an idea."

"Yes?"

"Well, I'm just wondering if the Tamil community in London might be one of these tightknit groups where everybody knows everybody else. Perhaps I'm just clutching at straws again, but I wonder if there might be anybody we can talk to – a Tamil, I mean."

"Not a bad idea, Bob. I'll speak to the Yard. If they know anyone, I'll let you know."

"Right you are, guv. I'll press to get those photos back as soon as possible. We're really flying blind without them."

"Any luck on those neighbours, by the way?"

"We found the most recent ones, guv, and I'll send

someone to interview them. The McKenzie bloke may take a little longer, but we're following the paper trail from the respective lawyers' offices so it should hopefully only be a matter of a day or two."

That evening found Metcalfe at home with Willis and Peter Collins.

"I was hoping Lisa would be back by now," Collins commented, gazing absently around the room as though she might be hiding behind a sofa.

"Her mother rang," Metcalfe replied. "They want to run a few more tests. They're still worried about these headaches she's getting."

Willis and Collins exchanged a quick glance and then looked guiltily at Metcalfe to see if he had noticed.

"I must say," Willis said, changing the subject as smoothly as possible, "I'm looking forward to hearing what you have to say about this new case, Peter."

"There's really not much I can say at the moment. So far as I can see we know pretty much nothing about either the victim or the suspect – or whatever the relationship might have been between them, come to that."

"Very true."

"Do we know anything at all about his past? The deceased, I mean."

"No, and that's one of our real priorities. We know that he bought the house 20 odd years ago from a family called Schneider because it was previously registered in the name of K. Schneider and somebody has a dim recollection of a couple with two children. We are looking for them, of course, but no luck so far. After all, a lot can happen in 20 years."

Peter looked at her intently.

"Did you say Schneider?"

"Yes, what of it?"

He smiled that slightly superior smile which she often found briefly but intensely irritating.

"Then wherever you're looking, it may be in the wrong place."

"What on earth do you mean, Peter?"

"Try the German dictionary. Schneider is the German word for Taylor. Isn't it possible that K. Schneider, say Konrad Schneider, and Conrad Taylor are one and the same person?"

Metcalfe and Willis stared at him in amazement.

"Good God," Metcalfe said simply.

"But why?" Willis asked, struggling to think clearly. "Why would anyone do that? And if you're right, what happened to the family?"

"All good questions to which you need to find the answers, Harriet," Collins burbled in his Lord Peter Wimsey voice. "As to why, I don't know, but it's not uncommon in London you know. A lot of immigrants of German extraction anglicised their names around the time of the First World War. The first Sea Lord, for example, had a German name. He was Prince of Battenberg, and the king insisted that he change it to Mountbatten."

"In case you hadn't noticed, Peter, the First World War ended a hundred years ago."

"Just an example, Bob. It's happened right the way through

the last hundred years, for all sorts of different reasons. A lot of the Jewish emigrés who came over in the 30s changed their names, perhaps because they felt they would make them stand out, or perhaps because they were worried English people wouldn't be able to pronounce them. Who knows? But it happened a lot. Just take a look in the phone book – oh, I keep forgetting, there isn't a phone book any more is there? – but you know what I mean. See how many people in London are named Gold, for example. They might have been Goldberg, Goldschaft, Goldstein, or any one of a dozen other names."

"I see that," Metcalfe replied thoughtfully. "But there wouldn't have been any reason like that 20 years ago, would there? Or am I overlooking something?"

"No, I don't think so."

"So that would suggest – suggest very strongly – that whatever the reason for Taylor having changed his name, it's a personal one? Something to do with his private life perhaps?" Willis reasoned.

"It would certainly seem so, old girl. And it does seem a bit of a coincidence, doesn't it, that he seems to have changed his name at much the same time that his family – assuming they were his family -seem to have disappeared?"

"And despite your well-known views on synchronicity," Metcalfe said with a grin, "as police officers we don't like coincidence."

"It would certainly seem likely that the two things are connected, yes. And once we know what happened, and why, we can begin to build a psychological picture of our victim. We know he was a recluse, for instance. Was he always a recluse, or was this in some way a response to something that happened? Was he psychologically damaged by the experience, or did he just not like people very much?"

"We know that he did have some limited interaction with at least one of his neighbours," Metcalfe proffered.

"We also know from two different sources that Raj seemed very unhappy with that contact, and did his best to deter it," Willis added.

"All good stuff, *mes amis*, but you need to dig deeper – or more deeply, should I say. Whole families don't just disappear, after all."

"Bob, I remember the guvnor saying that something from the victim's past might be relevant to the murder. It looks like he could be right, doesn't it?"

"Now let's not get carried away here," Metcalfe said calmly. "Remember we do have a prime suspect who seems to have had it away on his toes and vanished without trace. Innocent people don't usually run, do they? Remember that vile woman who attacked Lisa; she ran out of the flat the second the deed was done."

"I take it that 'to have it away on your toes' means to run away, does it? Good, I must make a note of that."

One of Peter Collins's several current hobbies was the compilation of a dictionary of Metropolitan Police slang. Willis saw him reach for his notebook and sighed. The problem with Peter's hobbies, she knew, was that they tended to grow into obsessions.

"But let us also remember," Collins went on, having noted

the reference and closed his notebook, "that the most obvious suspect is never the criminal."

"In crime fiction perhaps, Peter," Willis said firmly, "but not in real life. In our job we normally have a pretty good idea right from the outset who the criminal is. It's simply a matter of proving it."

Metcalfe nodded his agreement.

"And, of course, in a case like this, finding them first."

"How do you go about that, as a matter of interest?"

"Well, some of it's very old-fashioned. We circulate his details to every police station, and the transport police at ports, airports, railway stations, and so on. Some of it is more up-to-date. For example, it's very difficult for anybody to do anything these days without leaving some sort of electronic signature behind them. Using an Oyster card on the tube, taking cash out of an ATM, that sort of thing. The problem is that we don't know at the moment which signature to look for. We haven't been able to trace any record of him having any credit or debit cards. It also seems that he may have been operating a number of different identities. But we'll get him. One way or another, we'll get him. And then we'll see what he has to say for himself."

CHAPTER 10

"So I think we're making progress," Collison said encouragingly at the morning meeting. "We now believe it's possible that the family who previously lived at Wentworth House was in fact that of the deceased himself, who seems to have changed his name – anglicised it anyway – at about the same time. It therefore becomes even more pressing that we find Mr MacKenzie and get him to tell us anything he might know about what happened at that time. We should probably re-interview Mr Rowbotham as well, and jog his memory as best we can."

He looked down at his notes.

"As you know we now have a photo of the deceased with Raj, who is currently our main – indeed our only – suspect. DI Metcalfe has had these blown up as best we can, so at least we have something to show to people. Priya, any luck with the LGBT liaison officer?"

"Nothing yet, guv, but it's early days. It didn't mean anything to him, but he's going to show it around in some gay bars this evening."

"OK. We have also asked the Yard if there is anybody, preferably somebody prominent, we could speak to within the Tamil community here in London. We've drawn a bit of a blank there. They have sent round their official Tamil translator, but I'm not sure how much she can actually help us. Priya, I'm sorry, I didn't really feel I could say no since the Yard probably believe they're doing us a favour, so could you see her please? It doesn't need to be a long interview."

"Right you are, guv. When's she coming?"

"10 o'clock, I said, so any time now. Anything else, Bob?"

"No, I don't think so, sir. As you know, people, we now have the post-mortem report which you will have seen on the system. It's pretty much as we expected. It looks like the deceased was struck from behind with a single blow, which killed him instantly. SOCO haven't as yet found anything which could be a murder weapon, but their examination of the house is ongoing."

Now it was his turn to consult his notes.

"Timothy, where are we with the invoice you are following up?"

"I'm expecting to hear something today, guv. I did stress it was a murder enquiry."

"Very good. While we are on the financial front, I'm also expecting copies of our victim's bank statements this morning. I'll go through them myself in the first instance, and see if there is anything which looks worth our serious attention."

He glanced enquiringly around the room and, when nobody said anything, said "right then, let's get on with it."

As the meeting broke up, Priya's phone rang. It was the desk Sergeant reporting that her guest had arrived. She thanked him and set off down the stairs. As she walked into the reception area he caught her eye, and nodded at a young woman who was sitting on one of the chairs along the side wall. She was slim, wearing a dark blue trouser suit, and looked Chinese. As Priya approached she looked at her, smiled, and stood up.

"Hello," she said. "I'm Sophie Ho. I'm the Met's official Tamil translator. My supervisor at the Yard said I might be able to help you with something."

"Well, you might that. I'm working on a murder enquiry and we believe our chief suspect to be a Tamil."

"And you want me to translate while you interview him I suppose?"

Desai shook her head.

"If only it was that simple. He's done a runner and we haven't caught him yet. I was hoping you might be able to tell me a little bit about the Tamil community, just in case it might give us any useful pointers to where he might be. Why don't we go somewhere where we can talk?"

She briefly considered the interview rooms, but was then struck by a thought.

"Why don't we go to my office upstairs? It's empty at the moment because while we're working on an investigation we use the incident room instead."

"OK, that sounds good."

"Would you like a coffee or something?"

"No thanks, I'm fine."

She scooped up her bag and looked expectantly at Desai, who turned and that the way upstairs.

"I probably should explain," the translator said as she sat down in front of Desai's desk, "that I don't actually know the

Tamil community here in London. I'm from Singapore you see."

"And you're a Tamil? Forgive me, but you don't look like one."

She laughed.

"I'm not. I'm actually part Chinese and part Malay. Singapore is a bit like Switzerland in that it has four official languages – English, Malay, Mandarin, and Tamil. But unlike Switzerland, where everybody speaks all four of the languages, in Singapore people tend just to speak their own, with English as a backup. If you can't speak English at all, that's pretty bad. You're pretty much excluded both socially and in the workforce. It happens with some of the young Malay men, and sometimes Chinese as well. They're called 'ah beng' and they tend to drift into crime, partly because they can't get any decent jobs. So if you can speak all four you're pretty useful to the police, which is what I did there: translating for the Singapore police. Then I had a chance to come to England and it seemed logical to apply to Scotland Yard."

"That's interesting, I never knew any of that. My family are originally from India, although I was born here and be honest I've never been there. I keep meaning to take a holiday. My mum keeps in touch with all my aunties and uncles of course, but I've never actually met them."

"Oh really? I can speak Hindi as well."

"Please don't," Desai said quickly. "I can't."

For some reason this struck them both as very amusing and they both went off into peals of giggles. Collison, who was passing in the corridor at the time, paused in mid stride and gazed at the closed office door in consternation. Was that really Priya in there?

"Well, of course I'll help you in any way I can," Sophie said once their giggles had subsided. "What would you like to know?"

"Well, there's this for a start," Desai said. "Can I show something on my computer?"

She brought up the scanned images of the two envelopes addressed to Raj. Sophie came around to her side of the desk and lent over her shoulder to peer at the screen.

"What am I looking at?"

"These are two envelopes that were found at the crime scene. As you can see, they both seem to be addressed to the same man, but in different names. Any thoughts?"

Just as Desai, who was very wary about her own personal space, became uncomfortably aware of just how close their cheeks were to each other, Sophie drew back and went round to her chair again.

"Oh yes, I can explain that very easily. You see, most Tamils don't actually have a surname, a family name in the same way that we do. Most of them use the form of name on that second envelope there, which is the initial of your father's name followed by your own. His name is Rajarshi of course, which is why it appears in both forms. Presumably his father's name began with a G."

"Gosh, doesn't that make life rather difficult? For the police, for example?"

"It certainly does. It's a problem here too with people like the NHS, or local authorities, or the tax people. The traditional form of Tamil name simply doesn't fit any of their forms or IT systems."

"So what happens then?"

Sophie shrugged.

"If people want you to have a surname but you don't have one, then you make one up. Subramanian is quite a common one actually, but there are lots of others. That may be one reason why you're having problems finding this bloke. That's almost certainly not the name on his birth certificate."

"Actually he wasn't born here anyway. With found a record which we're pretty sure relates to him, an immigration record. Apparently he's from Sri Lanka and he arrived here during the civil war, claiming asylum from the oppression of the Tamils back home."

Sophie looked sceptical.

"Did he actually have a Sri Lankan passport?"

Desai brought up the relevant entry on her computer and gazed at it intently.

"Yes, he did."

"Is there any record of immigration actually checking its authenticity with the Sri Lankan Embassy?"

"No. Why do you ask?"

Sophie laughed and crossed her legs.

"I wouldn't mind betting it's a fake. Southeast Asia is awash with them. It was a real problem in Singapore. A lot of the local Tamil population were buying them in the back streets for precisely that reason. Where did his incoming flight originate?"

Desai looked back at her screen and whistled.

"Singapore," she confirmed. "Well, what do you know?"

"And presumably he never turned up for any of his immigration interviews and just vanished into thin air?"

"Got it in one. So you've come across this before then?"

"Yes. Like I said, it's a pretty well-known racket. Normally they go underground within their own community and try to find some way to arrange a fake identity. But presumably he didn't do that?"

"We don't know what he did originally. We know that he lived for a while with our murder victim right here in Hampstead; just round the corner actually."

"And now he's disappeared again?"

"Yes. Any thoughts?"

"Well, for someone to vanish without trace and survive without leaving any sign of their existence, suggests one of three things: either he's dead, living under an assumed identity with all the proper paperwork, or he's being hidden by someone. But as to who that might be, I really can't help you. As I said, I don't know any of the local Tamil community here in London. I don't know many people at all actually; I've only been here six months."

"Well, at least you've sorted out the name thing anyway. Thank you for that, at least. Shall I show you out?"

"Where do you live in London?" Desai asked as they walked down the stairs.

"Earls Court. And you?"

"Oh, Colindale."

"Why do you say 'oh' like that? What's wrong with Colindale?"

"There's nothing actually wrong with it. It's just not very exciting, that's all. There's a big Indian community there and my parents felt comfortable being part of it I suppose."

They reached the door and turned to look at each other. Suddenly Desai became aware that there was a tension in the air, a tension which she couldn't identify. What was the matter? Had she said something out of place? She started to speak, to find the right form of farewell, but found that she couldn't think what to say.

"I don't suppose you'd like to go out for a drink one evening would you?" Sophie asked casually.

Desai heard a little girl somewhere say "Oh, yes, thank you, that would be very nice."

"Great. Give me a ring why don't you? Here's my card."

Then she was gone and there was only the door swinging gently behind her. Desai stood for a moment wondering what on earth had just happened. Then she shook her head and walked briskly up the stairs. She should have gone straight back into the incident room but for some reason she didn't. Instead she went into her office and stood uncertainly in the middle of it, gazing at nothing in particular. She looked at the white business card in her hand and then reached forward to slide it gently into her shoulder bag, which she had left on the desk.

As if from a long way away she heard someone ask "Priya, is everything all right?"

She came to with a start and saw Collison standing at the open door, a slight smile on his face.

"Oh, yes," she said, slightly flustered. "I'm sorry, guv, I was miles away. I was just thinking about something."

Knowing that she had recently lost her father, it was now Collison's turn to be embarrassed.

"I'm sorry," he said awkwardly. "I didn't mean to intrude."

"You're not," she said, shaking her head determinedly. "I'm fine. Everything is fine."

CHAPTER 11

Just as she was beginning to think about leaving for the day, Desai received a phone call on her direct line.

"Hello, Constable Desai? It's Jack Rowbotham."

"Actually it's Sergeant now but yes, it's me."

"Does that mean you've been promoted? If so, congratulations."

"Well, sort of, yes, but never mind. What can I do for you?"

"Well, you're not going to believe this but I think I saw Raj this afternoon and I thought I'd better let you know straightaway."

"Yes, of course, thank you. Where was this? And when?"

"Just outside Belsize Park tube station. I came straight home to call you – I don't have a mobile – so probably no more than about 20 minutes ago. He was away off in the distance and, although I hurried down the hill as quickly as I could, he'd gone by the time I got there. I had a quick look in the tube station but he wasn't in the ticket hall. Presumably he'd gone down to the trains."

"Well, thank you, that's very helpful."

"Wait, there's more. It suddenly struck me that he might have gone into the little corner shop there – you know the one that's open late and sells just about everything – because

I think that's where he does his shopping. I asked the man who runs it if Raj had been in. He asked who I meant and I remembered that he used to have a very distinctive old airline bag which he used for shopping. As soon as I mentioned it he said yes straight away. I took the liberty of giving him your card, which I still had in my pocket, and asked him to call you immediately should he come in again."

"That's extremely good of you, Mr Rowbotham. Thank you very much."

"That's all right. Always happy to help the police you know. Anyway, I lead a pretty boring life you know, and it's not everyday that one of your neighbours gets his head bashed in. How's it going by the way? Are you making any progress?"

"I can't tell you that I'm afraid. But while you're on the line I was meaning to ask if I could come and see you again. There's a lot we need to find out about what happened in the past – a long way in the past I mean – and we're hoping that we may be able to jog your memory a bit. It seems that the family who lived there might actually have been Conrad Taylor's own family, in which case we are naturally anxious to find out what has happened to them. He may well have changed his name at much the same time as they disappeared, which is odd to say the least."

"I'm very happy to extend an open invitation, Constable – or Sergeant, I should say. But I'm really not sure how much help I'm going to be able to be to you. Like I said, I don't remember there being a family next door when I moved into the house. It's always possible there was when I bought it, but it was empty for quite a long time while all the work was being done. I was living somewhere else."

"Where was that?"

"I was renting a small flat in Clapham."

"I see. Well perhaps I could come round tomorrow if that would be OK? Maybe about 10:30?"

"Please do. I'd be delighted to see you again."

She put the phone down and called across the incident room to Metcalfe.

"We have a development, guv. One of the neighbours has just seen Raj down the road in Belsize Park. They reckon he ducked into the underground, in which case he could be anywhere by now. But apparently he'd just been to the local convenience store there, which suggests that's where he's still doing his shopping. The neighbour very kindly left the card which I'd given him, and asked the proprietor to ring should Raj go in again."

"Good news!" Metcalfe said, jotting down a note. "I'll ask uniform to go in and reinforce the message."

He glanced up at the clock.

"Why don't you nip off home, Priya? Things are likely to get very busy around here in the next few days, so it would be good to get some rest while you can."

"I was just thinking the same actually, guv. Thanks, I will."

She closed down her computer, picked up her bag, and left the room. Without really knowing why, she turned right rather than left and walked into her office, closing the door behind her. She opened her bag, took out Sophie's card, and dialled the number.

"Oh hi, Sophie, it's Priya. Priya Desai from Hampstead nick," she said awkwardly. "I'm glad you're still there. I thought you might have left for the day."

"I was just about to actually. But what about that drink? When would you like to meet up?"

"Well, I'm not sure how much time I'm likely to have over the next few weeks. You know, the investigation…"

"Don't worry, Priya, it's OK. Just ring me sometime when you're free, if you like."

"Oh no, you don't understand. What I meant to say was … well, might you be free this evening? Like I say, things could get pretty hectic around here any time so I was thinking -"

"Say no more. This evening would be great. Why don't we both head out now and meet up somewhere?"

•

That evening Lisa Atkins made a welcome return to the house in Frognal. When Peter Collins walked into the living room it was to find her and Metcalfe in a companionable embrace on one of the sofas.

"Peter!" she exclaimed, jumping up and kissing him on both cheeks, "how lovely to see you."

"Likewise, old fruit, but how are you? How did the tests go?"

"Oh, don't let's talk about all of that," she said with a pout as she sat down again. "If I have to see another doctor or sit inside another machine I shall go mad, I swear I will. But where's Karen?"

"She's upstairs having a shower I think. I'm sure I heard her come in."

"Yes, we walked back together," Metcalfe said. "I'm afraid she's had a very boring day sifting through old papers."

"Oh yes, is this the new case you're both working on? Is it that old man who was found murdered in Downshire Hill? It is, isn't it? I read about it in the Standard. I say, how thrilling. But they didn't say how he died. Was he strangled and left with a hideous grin on his face? Go on, do tell."

"Now, you know I can't talk about it, darling," Metcalfe said gently, "so please don't ask me. I spoke without thinking. I was just trying to explain that I think she felt a bit grubby having been handling dusty sheets of paper all day."

"Beyond dusty," Willis said as she walked into the room, "some of it was actually mildewed and I'll swear that there was some pretty strange fungus on those old book proofs. Ugh! I needed a good scrub."

Her hair was still pinned up damply from the shower and she was wearing a simple T-shirt, Capri pants and a pair of pumps.

"You look like a 1950s film star," Metcalfe said admiringly.

"In that case," Collins said quickly, "a cocktail is clearly in order."

He crossed to the drinks cabinet, opened the doors, and contemplated its contents: bottles in neatly serried ranks. Lisa gave a little squeal and clapped her hands.

"Oh goody! A cocktail is exactly what I need after the last few days. How clever of you, Peter. You are wonderful."

"I am indeed," he murmured as he came to a decision and reached out for Cointreau and Tequila.

"I believe I have some lime juice in the kitchen," he said. "So how does a Margarita sound?"

"It sounds wonderful, Peter," Willis replied. "Let me get the ice."

"No, you stay there, Harriet. I can manage perfectly well myself."

As went, Willis gazed fondly at Lisa.

"So how are things really, Lisa? What was the point of all these wretched tests?"

"I'm really not sure. I think it was just Mummy worrying about nothing. I had a couple of really bad headaches you see, and I'm supposed to tell the hospital as soon as something like that happens, so I did. But they couldn't find anything wrong. Probably just a virus or something, I reckon."

"Then a Margarita is just what you need," Willis replied. "All that alcohol and vitamin C will do you the power of good. Better than an anti-viral drug, and much more fun."

"Talking of fun," Lisa said, "I was looking at one of those vintage websites while I was away, and they're doing a tea dance at the Waldorf hotel in a few weeks. Shall we go?"

"We should definitely go," Collins concurred gravely as he walked back into the room carrying a bucket of ice and a jug of lime juice.

"Oh, wonderful! It will give me a fantastic opportunity to buy a new outfit – well, a new vintage outfit anyway."

"We might be able to find something to fit you in my wardrobe," Willis suggested.

"There again, maybe not," Metcalfe said quietly.

They all laughed, even Willis, though the joke was at her

expense. Her vintage outfits were tailored very precisely to her personal measurements and designed to show off her magnificent figure.

"Actually, Lisa, your mention of a new outfit reminded me of a thought I had the other day," Collins said as he began mixing the jug of Margaritas.

"Really? What?"

"Well, I got to thinking. We all enjoy these vintage events, but it's really quite difficult to keep finding new outfits, and jolly expensive too. What if somebody was to actually manufacture outfits today that were based on the old designs we love so much, but were actually completely new?"

"Oh, Peter, that would never work," Willis cut in briskly. "There wouldn't be enough demand for it. It's a lovely idea of course, but there just aren't enough of us vintage enthusiasts to make it worthwhile."

"I suppose you're right," he said sadly. "Oh well, I did have this other idea too. Hasn't it struck you how lovely it would be if someone were to open a 1950s style nightclub ...?"

"Peter, darling," Willis said gently as she walked across the room and took the first two glasses of Margarita from him, "you're hugely intelligent, but no businessman I'm afraid. Why don't you leave the entrepreneurial ideas to other people?"

She gave her two glasses to the occupants of the sofa and then took the one which Collins handed her.

"However," she conceded after an appreciative sip, "you do make a wonderful Margarita."

•

Down the road in Camden Town Sophie Ho and Priya Desai were by coincidence also drinking margaritas, though in their case as an accompaniment to a Mexican meal. Sophie had ordered a jug, an idea with which Desai concurred, though she rarely drank. Perhaps because she was unused to alcohol she was already feeling the effects, though Sophie seem to be too as they were spending a lot of time squealing with laughter and putting their arms around each other's shoulders.

Finally the time came for paying the bill and walking to the underground, which they did merrily though slightly unsteadily. They went through the barrier and down the escalator, Sophie standing on the step below and talking upwards to her, though it was almost impossible to hear what she was saying. They came to the platforms, where they paused, as Desai was heading north and Sophie south.

They gazed contentedly at each other but for the first time that evening Desai found herself unsure what to say.

"I've had a wonderful time," she managed finally.

"I'm glad."

Sophie leaned forward and kissed her gently on the lips. Desai should have been surprised, shocked even, yet somehow was not. Sophie's lips lingered on her own, but just as she started to respond the other girl pulled away with a shriek of laughter and disappeared into the crowds on the southbound platform, her shout of "bye-ee" fading into the roar of an approaching train.

CHAPTER 12

"Quite a bit of progress yesterday, one way and another," Metcalfe reported in the incident room next morning.

"First, I received the statements I requested from the deceased's bank. Very interesting. Conrad Taylor carried a pretty much permanent bank balance of about £50,000, which he topped up from a deposit account every so often. The deposit account contained about 10 times that amount and seems to have represented his store of capital. Until about seven weeks ago he'd been spending very small amounts of money every week or so – presumably on shopping – and paying his utility bills, but that's about it. As I say, all that changed about seven weeks ago. Since that time someone has been withdrawing £500 from the account every few days using a cash card. Most of the withdrawals have been from outside the same bank in Belsize Park."

"So let me get this right, Bob," Collison said. "We believe that our victim has been dead for at least six weeks, and yet somebody has been withdrawing money from his bank account? When was the most recent occasion?"

"Yesterday, guv. Which brings us to the other piece of news which everyone will have seen: Raj was spotted in Belsize Park yesterday by the neighbour, Jack Rowbotham.

So it seems highly likely that it's him who's been drawing the money out of the account, and it also seems reasonable to assume that this pattern more or less fixes Taylor's date of death."

"Yes it does, doesn't it? What are we doing about the cash card, by the way?"

"I was going to ask you about that, guv. I was just about to tell them to cancel it and set it up to fire an alert the next time he tried to use it, but then I got to thinking."

"Yes?"

"Well, as I said, all of the withdrawals to date have been from the same ATM just down the road in Belsize Park. Believe it or not, they're mostly also made at about the same time of day, namely early afternoon. It seems like Raj is a creature of habit. So might it not make more sense to leave the cash card alone and stake out the ATM instead? That way if we don't catch him for any reason at the first attempt, or if he uses a different ATM for once, he won't be alerted to the fact that anything is wrong, which gives us more chance to nab him when he does finally return to his favourite venue and find us waiting for him."

"I see what you mean. He does seem to be a creature of habit, doesn't he? Very well, let's try that, starting today. We should have enough resource here within the team to keep the machine under observation between, say, 1300 and 1600. Let's try it for the next three days, at least."

"I'll set that up, guv. Priya, where are we with re-interviewing Jack Rowbotham?"

"I have an appointment for 10:30 today, guv."

"Good, I might come with you if that's OK. Rowbotham seems to be the only serious witness we have, at least until we locate Colin McKenzie. Timothy, where are we with the invoice?"

"A bull's-eye, guv. The goods were paid for online right enough, with a credit card issued to our victim. But the date's wrong for it to have been him that did it: only about four weeks ago."

"OK, so where are we?" Collison asked the room at large. "It seems that we have clear evidence that Raj has been operating Taylor's bank account and credit card since the time of his death. We also know that he was living with Taylor at the house, although as yet we're unsure for exactly how long. I suppose theoretically it's possible that somebody else might have stolen the cash card and credit card, but there's no evidence that Taylor had been mugged recently – after all, he never went out – and no sign of a break-in at the house. Anyway, they would have needed the pin number, or password as appropriate, and how would they have got that?"

"So Raj is our man, sir?" Willis asked.

"Looks like it, doesn't it? In which case the big question is 'why'? Why should someone who's been living with Taylor, perhaps for a year or two, suddenly brutally murder him? Let's catch him and find out."

As the meeting broke up, Collison wondered slowly towards his office. As he walked along the corridor, he met a uniformed constable coming in the opposite direction.

"Just been looking for you, sir. Message. Can you phone the ACC please?"

"Right, thank you."

He closed the door, sat down, and dialled the ACC's office. He was put through at once.

"Simon? I've just had Philip Newby on the phone. It seems like there may be a slight complication with this Downshire Hill case of yours."

"Oh yes?" Collison asked warily.

Commander Newby was in charge of Special Branch, the department of the Met which cooperated with the security services.

"Probably nothing, but I want to make sure you're properly briefed. Can you pop over here this afternoon? Might as well bring Metcalfe with you. After all the two of you already have security clearance, so we may as well make use of it. 1500 OK with you? Good. See you then."

Despite having been summoned to the august presence of one of the Met's most senior officers that afternoon, Metcalfe reckoned that he would still have enough time to attend the interview with Rowbotham, so it was that he stood beside Priya Desai as she knocked on the door of his house at precisely 10:30. The Jack Rowbotham who answered the door was no longer wearing carpet slippers and, indeed, seem to have smartened himself up considerably.

"Oh," she said with evident disappointment as he caught sight of Metcalfe.

"Mr Rowbotham, this is DI Metcalfe. We'd like to talk to you together if we may."

"I can't tell you how grateful we are for all the assistance you're giving us, Mr Rowbotham," Metcalfe said as they were led through into the living room at the back of the house.

"You're very welcome. If it was Raj who killed Conrad then I want him caught. To be honest, I've never liked the little creep anyway. Gives me the willies, he does."

"We were wondering," Metcalfe went on after they were seated, "if you could cast your mind back to when you first bought this house. We really are very keen to find out as much as we can about the family who were living next door at that time. Can you think of anything that might help us, anything at all?"

Rowbotham shook his head helplessly.

"I wish I could. I've been wracking my brains since your colleague here first raised the issue with me. Do you know, I think I can remember there being a family next door, but only vaguely – in the background as it were. You see I wasn't actually living here for some time because there were pretty major building works going on. So I was just popping in at odd times – usually after work in the evening – and taking a quick look at what had been going on. But yes, I do remember a family. I think I remember being aware of seeing a couple of children in the next door garden one evening. A boy and a girl, I think."

"Well, that's some progress at least, sir. Do you remember their names by any chance?"

Again Rowbotham shook his head.

"No, I'm sorry to be so useless about this but I don't remember having any actual contact with them at all. I was usually just in a hurry to get home to Clapham. There was nothing here, you see. No furniture or anything like that. For a while there wasn't even any plumbing, because I was having new bathrooms fitted."

"This may seem a strange question, but I think DS Desai has already explained the background to you. Do you remember Conrad Taylor being here, as part of that family?"

"I honestly didn't notice either the man all the woman at all. To tell you the truth, I'm not particularly sociable myself. Oh, not a complete misanthrope like Conrad, nor a recluse either, but I keep myself to myself. I don't like to get involved in other people's affairs. I'm quite happy to go through life enjoying my own company."

"Oh well," Metcalfe said in resignation. "I suppose it was a long shot. But should anything suddenly come to mind, please contact us won't you? The slightest little thing. You never know, it might turn out to be important."

"Actually, there is something I remembered just before you arrived, but it's something different, not about the family."

"Go on."

"Well, a few months back I noticed some bloke hanging around the front door of Wentworth House. I think he'd been knocking but got no answer. So he walked back to the gate, sort of hesitated and looked around, and then came up my path and knocked on my door. Asked if I knew where Conrad was."

"Can you remember exactly what he said?"

"He asked if Conrad still lived there. Naturally I wondered who the hell he was. He didn't show me any ID, so I don't think he was there on official business. I was a bit nervous, to be honest, and just got rid of him as quickly as I could."

"Can you describe him?"

"He was white, not young but not old – maybe about 40? – and quite powerfully built. I told him Conrad did still live there but that maybe he was out visiting someone. That was a joke, of course. Conrad never went out to visit anyone. But I just wanted to get rid of him. He scared me a bit. There was something about him."

"And he just went away? He didn't tell you why he was looking for Conrad Taylor?"

"No, he didn't."

"Why didn't you tell me this when I was here before?" Desai asked.

"I'm really sorry, but I'd completely forgotten about it. Is it important do you think?"

"Might be," Metcalfe said noncommittally. "Well, if you do remember anything else, Mr Rowbotham, please do give us a ring won't you?"

"You know what?" Rowbotham suddenly said as he led them back through the hallway. "I should have thought of this before. You should get hold of Colin McKenzie. He is likely to have a much better idea of what went on next door than I do. He and his wife were next door – in Helen and Charlie's house that is – just about for ever, I think."

"Thank you, we've already thought of that actually. You wouldn't have any information that might help us find him might you?"

"No, I'm sorry, Inspector. We weren't close you know.

Just passed the time of day occasionally. But I think he knew Conrad better than most people – not that that's saying very much."

"Did Conrad ever talk to about his family?" Metcalfe asked as they paused on the doorstep. "Did he ever mention any children, for example?"

"Do you know, there was something, just once. It was before Raj arrived on the scene, so it must have been several years ago. I was having a cup of coffee with him in his front room and I happened to mention children in some context or other. He said something like 'damn children, they just bring you pain and trouble' and then clammed up. I asked him what he meant, of course, because naturally I was intrigued. But he just changed the subject and made it clear he didn't want to talk about it anymore."

"I see. Well at least that suggests he did have children, at least."

"Yes, I suppose so. I wonder if we'll ever really know the truth about him?"

"We usually get to the truth sooner or later, sir," Desai said reassuringly.

"I do hope so, Sergeant, and do feel free to call again won't you?"

"I think you have a bit of fan there, Priya," Metcalfe said as they walked up the driveway together.

"Oh don't be silly, guv," Desai replied, determinedly reaching out to open the gate herself before he could do so for her, "he's old enough to be my Grandad."

"Doesn't stop a man from dreaming, Priya. I said he was a fan of yours, not the other way round."

"Well, in that case I wish he wouldn't be."

"I shouldn't worry about it too much. It happens to Karen all the time."

"That's different. She's different."

"Different? How do you mean?"

"Just different, guv. That's all."

CHAPTER 13

"Hello, Simon, come in. Afternoon, Bob."

The ACC held open the door and waved them expansively into his office.

"Now, you both remember Commander Newby, don't you?"

"Of course, sir."

They both shook hands with the powerfully built man who rose to greet them. Metcalfe winced slightly as a result, while Collison showed more stoicism.

"Well, sit down everyone. Now, as I said on the phone, Simon, there may be some security implications about your current case in Hampstead. Philip, why don't you go ahead?"

"Thank you, sir. Well, I should tell you straightaway that nothing about this seems very straightforward. Part of what I'm about to tell you is stuff we know for certain, but quite a lot of it is conjecture."

"Understood," Collison nodded.

"When your alert about this Rajarshi character went into the system it flagged up a reference to something we've been asked to look at both by Interpol and by our colleagues in the security services. It revolves around the issuing of fake passports – particularly Sri Lankan passports – and their use by criminals or, and hence the interest of the security services, terrorists."

"It seems that the man you know as Raj was living in Singapore, not Sri Lanka. It's possible that he may have family connections with Sri Lanka; after all there's a big Tamil community there as you know. At the time we're talking about they were engaged in a civil war with a government which largely represented the Sinhalese majority. But there's nothing to suggest he ever even lived there, let alone that he was born there."

"Somehow he was connected with the police in Malaysia – Kuala Lumpur to be exact. It's possible that he was a police informer there, but that's conjecture on my part. Whatever the case, he seems to have been recommended by the Malaysian police to their counterparts in Singapore as someone who might be trusted to go undercover and infiltrate this false passport network. He was to hold himself out as wanting to get into the UK. To get into the UK illegally, that is, by claiming asylum on the false premise that he was from Sri Lanka and that to send him back there might be a danger to his life."

"And to do that he needed a Sri Lankan passport," the ACC commented.

"Exactly, sir. And he must have been very convincing in the role because he seems to have been accepted as a genuine customer with no trouble at all. The problem was that he probably *was* a genuine customer. The Singapore police now believe that he had no intention at all of following through with the sort of deep level penetration they had in mind, but simply to get himself into the UK for his own purposes. This was embarrassing, not only for themselves and their counterparts in Kuala Lumpur, but also because they had already tipped off our security services that they would be running this operation on our territory. They asked for our cooperation, which we were happy to give since we knew that if someone like Raj could enter the UK in this way then so could a genuine terrorist pretending to be someone like Raj."

"But Raj simply disappeared when he got here?"

"Yes he did. And there's one angle of which you should be aware."

"Yes sir?"

"Before Raj left Singapore his handlers were getting distinctly twitchy precisely because they were suspicious he was using them for his own ends and would simply do a runner as soon as he got into the UK – which is of course precisely what happened. So they put him under pressure, threatening to cancel the whole thing and send him back to Kuala Lumpur unless he gave them a detailed report on everything he'd found out to date."

"And he did?"

"Yes, he did. Furthermore, his handlers believe that he was sufficiently alarmed at the thought of being left hanging in the wind that his report is almost certainly reliable. They made it clear that they were proposing to check up on everything he told them, and everything they *were* able to check seemed to make sense. So, reluctantly, they allowed the operation to go ahead."

"What was in the report?"

"A lot of useful day-to-day stuff; the names of the contacts who had sold him the passport, that sort of thing. But they were after a few of the big names behind it, while this was all strictly low grade stuff. With one exception. There was something he told them which shocked them rigid. It seems that there was a small group of police officers right there in Singapore who were somehow implicated in all of this. Whether it was simply being paid to look the other way, or something more sinister, we're not sure because the chaps in Singapore are playing their cards very close to their chest. But there's something else."

Newby paused to drink some tea, and then continued.

"As you can imagine, a key undercover operative like this was being handled very much on a 'need to know' basis, and that group of people was a very small one. However, just after Raj left for the UK there was an unauthorised access to some details on the police computer system which would have disclosed both Raj's identity, and the full scope of his undercover activities."

"Including his allegations against police officers?"

"Yes, I'm afraid so. The hack was traced to a fairly junior person in the IT department. He'd pulled the old trick of asking someone for their password so that he could do some work on their computer. The IT bloke never showed up for work again and seems to have vanished into thin air. But another informant, who was also identified in the stolen files, was found murdered two days later."

"So you think Raj may be in danger – even here in the UK?"

Newby shrugged.

"Who knows? I've given you everything I know, Simon, because I thought you needed to have it. From this point on, your conjectures are as good as mine. There's one other thing you should know, though. As you can imagine from the moment the alarm was raised in Singapore the police there have been keeping a very close eye on certain people's movements. One of the people who may be implicated – and it's only 'may' mind you, simply because she had some sort of contact with the passport enquiry – is one of their official translators who recently gave up a job in Singapore for no apparent reason and moved here to the UK. Her name is Sophie Ho. Unfortunately, without us being aware of it, she has already been brought into contact with your investigation."

"But as I understand it we have nothing concrete against her?"

"Nothing at all. But probably better to be safe than sorry, eh?"

"What would you recommend, sir?"

Newby considered this for a moment.

"Nothing that may give her cause to suspect that we're onto her. Of course she may be entirely innocent, but if she isn't we don't want to scare her off. Properly handled she could still lead us, and our associates in Singapore, to someone important. Just make sure that she doesn't get access to any of your lines of enquiry. In particular, please keep away from Raj if and when you catch him."

"And for the record, sir, I assume all this is classified?"

"Yes, absolutely. Which means that, as before, you can't share it with any other member of your team. If you find yourself in a situation where you need to investigate something which has any bearing on Sophie Ho then please give me a ring and we'll arrange to give you access to the services of some of our people who have the necessary clearance."

"Thank you, sir, I appreciate that."

"Don't mention it. Happy to help."

"I think I should tell you that one member of our team has already had contact with this young woman. Priya Desai, an acting DS. She's a very fine officer and I can vouch for her absolutely. Can I bring her within the Chinese wall?"

"No, I don't think so. Sorry. Just try to find out as discreetly as possible anything she might have told her or shown her. Then let's talk again."

•

Had they but known it, the object of their concern was at this moment in telephonic contact with Desai, who had gone to her office to take the call.

"Hey you," Sophie said.

"Hey you yourself."

"I thought I'd give you a ring to check that you got home OK last night."

"Yes, of course. Colindale's not exactly the Wild West you know. And you?"

"Yeah, no problem. So, did you enjoy yourself then?".

"Yes, you know I did, it was great. Thank you for suggesting it. I was all ready to go home for an evening of watching telly with my mum."

"Boring or what?"

"Yeah, well ..."

"So how's the investigation going then. Any new developments?"

"You know I can't tell you that."

"Oh, come on, Priya, don't be so stuffy. I'm in the Met too, remember."

"Yes, but you're not a member of the team, are you? So I can't tell you anything about the investigation."

"You already have."

"I showed you something as a possible witness, someone who might be to help us, that's all."

"Oh all right, have it your own way. I couldn't really care less anyway. I was just trying to show an interest."

"I'm sorry, Sophie ..."

"Forget it. It really doesn't matter. Now, when can I see you again?"

"Well, that would be lovely but I'm likely to be quite busy the next few days."

"But you do want to, don't you? To see me again?"

"Yes, of course I do. It's just I'm not sure when I'll be free."

"Well, I'm here and I'm not going anywhere. Just ring me any time when you think you may have an hour or two to spare and I'll come running."

"All right, that's great. Wonderful."

"OK. Bye then."

"No, wait. Sophie ..."

"Yes?"

"Last night. Tell me ..."

"What about it?"

Now there was a laugh lurking behind her voice, almost teasing.

"Well, was it ... well, a date I suppose. Was it a date?"

"What do you think?"

"I don't know. That's why I'm asking you. Please tell me, Sophie. I'm all messed up here."

"I'm sorry, honey. Sorry to be making fun of you. Messed up how?"

"Well, I've never ... well, I've never been on a date with a woman before. That's what I wanted to say. And that's why I feel completely messed up inside. So please tell me, Sophie, because I need to know. Was it a date?"

There was a pause, and again that tension, which this time seemed to increase as the pause lengthened. Then, like a distant crackle of electricity, the voice at the other end said quietly but firmly "you bet your life it was".

CHAPTER 14

"OK, so how shall we play this then?" DC Susan Godwin asked Timothy Evans.

The two of them had just arrived at the junction of Haverstock Hill with Glenloch Road and were hovering uncomfortably outside the bank, trying not to look conspicuous. This was difficult, since Godwin was tall, and powerfully built as a result of frequent weights sessions at the gym, and Evans looked exactly like a plainclothes police officer.

"Well, I suppose we could always stand over there on the other side of the road and have a snog," he suggested. "That would look pretty natural, wouldn't it?"

Just for a moment she gave him a look of such utter disdain that he could not help but wonder if she and Desai somehow shared some common genetic material.

"For three hours?"

"Well, you know, we could sort of start and see how we get on."

"Bring a box, did you?"

"A box? What would I need a box for?"

"To stand on. How are you going to reach otherwise?"

Evans laughed and tried to make it sound convincing.

"Yeah, right. Good one."

"Forget it, Timothy. It's not going to happen, except maybe in your dreams that is."

"All right then, wonder woman, what do you suggest?"

They stood and looked around. Godwin could see that across the road, just up the road from Belsize Park tube station, there was a coffee shop and a couple of fast food restaurants, all of which seemed to offer a much more attractive prospect than standing in the open for three hours.

"What do you reckon?" Evans asked, following her gaze.

"Dunno," she said dubiously. "All this traffic means you couldn't have the ATM under constant observation, particularly when a bus comes up the hill and stops just here. It also means you can't just run straight across the road to nick him, either. Not without risking getting run over anyway. It seems like there's an ambulance along here every few minutes with its blues and twos going."

"Yeah, well the Royal Free's just around the corner, isn't it?"

Evans looked around closer to home. On one corner was a carpet shop.

"I suppose we could always ask the bloke in there if we could pretend to be customers, or even sales assistants. See, it's got a big window that looks straight out on the front of the bank."

"OK if he just comes and uses the cash machine without a care in the world. But suppose he's on his guard and checks out the area first? Mightn't it look a bit fishy if we were just sitting in there for so long?"

"Oh, I don't know," Evans countered. "We'd be all right I reckon."

"Tell you what, Timothy. See that service road just here behind the shops? You could stand round there out of sight – behind those bins, say – and I could be in the shop pretending to look at some samples. As soon as I see him I'll give you a quick call on the radio and you can nip round the corner and grab him. I'll be here on the other side of the road if he tries to make a run for it."

"Yeah, all right then. Let's do that. But be quick. It's nearly 1 o'clock."

The man who ran the carpet shop – after experiencing the surprise and momentary panic of having someone show him a Metropolitan Police warrant card – was very agreeable to the idea of Godwin sitting beside him for the next three hours, and insisted on making her a cup of tea. Evans, taking up his position in the service road, suddenly realised that Godwin's proposed arrangement of them changing places every hour would result in her spending two hours in relative comfort compared to his one. As if to punish him for not having been quicker on the uptake, a distant peal of thunder heralded the approach of rain.

•

"Priya," Collison said carefully, "I'm in a bit of a difficult situation. I need to ask you something, something which may seem rather strange, but I can't tell you why. Will you bear with me?"

"Of course, guv. What is it?"

"I need to know whatever you may have told or shown Sophie Ho – anything to do with the investigation that is."

"Well, I told her most of what we knew to date about Raj, which wasn't very much at the time. Just that we thought he'd been living at Wentworth House, that he'd gone missing, and that we were looking for him. I was hoping that she might know some people within the Tamil community in London who might be able to help us."

"Yes, I know. Did she?"

"No, she didn't. It turned out she'd only been in the country about six months. She used to live and work in Singapore, for the police actually."

"Did you show her anything?"

"Yes, I showed her the scans of the two envelopes SOCO found at the house, the two addressed to Raj. I was hoping she might be to throw some light on why he seemed to be using two different names. She could, as it happens. It seems that Tamils don't really have surnames the way we do, so they often use their father's initial and then their own first name."

"And you're sure that's all you showed her?"

Priya looked puzzled, and a little distressed.

"Yes, of course I'm sure, guv. Is something wrong? I wish you could tell me what this is all about."

"Believe me, so do I. But you must understand that there are times when certain members of the team can't share everything they know with other members. It happened in that Burgh House case if you remember."

"Yes, I do remember. But that was Special Branch, wasn't

it? Surely there aren't any security implications to this case are there?"

"Like I said, Priya, I really can't say any more. But I need you to do something for me."

"Yes of course, guv. Anything you want."

"Well, I need you to be very careful not to share anything about the case with Sophie. You haven't done anything wrong at all. It was my idea that you should meet with her, and it was quite right that you should show her anything you thought appropriate for her to see if she could help, but things have changed now. We need to enforce very strictly the rule about not speaking to non-team members. OK?"

"Yes, of course. Er, guv ...?"

"Yes?"

Priya seemed flustered.

"There's something you should know. I've seen Sophie, socially I mean. We've been out for a drink and a meal together and I've sort of arranged to see her again."

"No reason why you shouldn't, Priya, no reason at all. You can be friends with anyone you want. You just have to be careful not to discuss the case, just like I have to be with my wife, or Bob Metcalfe has to be with his fiancée."

"Yes, I will of course."

Collison looked at from moment.

"Since you've spent time with her, tell me this. What's she like, do you think? What sort of person is she?"

"She's really nice, guv. I like her a lot. I can't believe she's mixed up in anything dodgy, if that's what's being suggested."

"I didn't say anything like that."

"No, but I mean ... well, you know."

"I really am sorry, Priya," Collison said as he rose to leave. "I wish I could tell you more, but I can't. Though please don't let any of this affect your friendship with Sophie. I just need to take a few precautions, that's all."

•

The rain was getting harder now, and the windows of the carpet showroom were misting up. Godwin rubbed a patch of glass clear for the umpteenth time and peered through the hole at the pavement on the other side of the road. She tensed as somebody scuttled up to the ATM largely hidden under an umbrella. She reached for her radio and nervously stroked the transmit button. Then, as the figure turned and revealed itself to be that of a middle-aged woman, she relaxed again.

"Who you watching for exactly?" the salesman asked curiously.

"Can't tell you that, I'm afraid. But it's serious. We're on a murder investigation."

"How about another cup of tea? And I've got some biscuits in the back if you fancy one."

"That would be great, thanks. Hello, what have we got here ...?"

This time the figure on the rain-swept pavement opposite was definitely that of a man. Godwin tried to get a look at his face, but his features were hidden as he bent over the machine. This time she pressed the transmit button.

"Timothy? You there? Standby. I think we've got a possible."

"Roger," Evans replied amid a brief burst of static.

He was by now shivering, very wet, and very miserable. He had tried placing a flattened out cardboard box over his head but this seemed to have achieved little apart from attracting some very curious glances from two passing schoolchildren, safely huddled inside hooded jackets. He moved out from behind the bins and started to trot towards the end of the service road. As he approached it, his radio crackled again.

"Timothy, it's him! I'm sure it's him. I'm coming out of the shop now. Move in."

As Evans turned left from the service road onto Glenloch Road the man was just moving away from the cash machine. The tall figure of Godwin was stepping off the curb outside the carpet shop and moving in his direction. Needing to make ground quickly, Evans broke into a run. This sudden movement attracted the man's attention. He looked briefly over his shoulder and then started off down the hill, also running. Godwin tried to grab him as he went past her, but missed. Nothing daunted, she set off in pursuit. Quickly overhauling him, she launched herself from behind and brought him crashing to the ground outside a funeral parlour, with her substantial frame pinning him to the pavement. Evans arrived a few seconds later, panting.

"Who are you? Let me go!" the man shouted, clearly panicked.

He bucked and writhed, attempting to unseat Godwin. However, as she had most of her weight pressing down on the small of his back, he was unsuccessful.

"That's enough of that – you're nicked!" Evans shouted, thumbing his own radio.

Godwin reached deftly backwards into the waistband of her trousers and extracted the handcuffs which had been digging into her well-muscled body uncomfortably ever since she had begun the afternoon's observation. Since she already had his arms pinned behind his back it was the work of a moment to slap these into place around his wrists. By this time, despite the rain, a curious group of onlookers had begun to gather on the broad pavement, some clutching supermarket bags full of shopping.

"Rajarshi Subramanian," she said, stumbling slightly over the pronunciation, "I'm arresting you on suspicion of the murder of Conrad Taylor. You do not have to say anything, but it may harm your defence if you do not mention, when questioned, something which you later rely on in court. Anything you do say may be given in evidence."

She felt the man go limp beneath her. She got up, dragging him to his feet too, his hands restrained awkwardly behind his back. Seeing that she was in control of the situation, Evans had been on the radio for a patrol car, and was now scanning Haverstock Hill up and down for the first sign of approaching blue lights. Within a couple of minutes the sound of a siren heralded the arrival of a white police van, which double parked and then disgorged four uniform officers.

Completely silent now and unresisting, the man was dragged into the van and pushed down onto one of the bench seats between two constables. He was staring straight ahead of him as if dazed.

"Give you a lift if you like," the driver said, gazing dubiously at Evans's soaked jacket and trousers.

"Yeah, nice one. Thanks a lot," he replied, and then sneezed loudly twice.

CHAPTER 15

Metcalfe knocked briefly, and put his head around Collison's door.

"We've got him, guv," he announced excitedly. "Godwin and Evans nicked him outside the bank when he turned up to use the ATM. They're bringing him in now. Would you like to sit in on the interview?"

"I would very much, but unfortunately I have a ton of things to do. Anyway, it's probably appropriate for you to do it. Why don't you ask one of the arresting officers to sit in with you?"

"OK then, I'll go and tell the troops."

"I'll come with you."

As they walked together towards the incident room they met Godwin and Evans at the top of the stairs.

"Hey, you two, well done!" Collison exclaimed.

"Susan's collar, guv," Evans informed him. "I just stood around and radioed for the cavalry."

"And got very wet by the look of things. You'd better go and get changed, Timothy. Do you have any spare clothes in your locker? If not, you'd better borrow a uniform from someone. Well done again. And well done to you, Godwin. Since you made the arrest, I'd like you to sit in on the interview with DI Metcalfe."

"Well, thank you, sir."

There was a momentary hesitation at the doorway. Collison knew he would never feel comfortable with going through a door ahead of a woman, but equally this was the Met's way: rank came first, and he had to respect that, so he led the way into the room. A hush fell instantly, though whether it was his presence or the fact that the news of the arrest had already spread was unclear.

"Good news, everybody," he said. "You've probably heard this already, but thanks to Godwin and Evans we have Raj downstairs in custody."

A little cheer ran around the room, though everybody knew this was probably just the beginning, not the end of the investigation.

"I going to ask DI Metcalfe and DC Godwin to lead the interrogation. But perhaps somebody could update me on where we are with everything else."

"I have some news myself, sir," Desai replied at once. "I was just about to go and look for DI Metcalfe to tell him."

"Well tell us all."

"Gladly, sir. I've located Colin McKenzie; I managed to trace him through the lawyers who acted for him when he sold his property. It took a bit of time as they had to get the file back from their archiving service. He lives in Luton now. I've contacted him and he's very happy to talk to us."

"Well done, Priya. Well, since he could be a very important witness, I'd suggest that you go and interview him yourself. Don't you agree, Bob?"

"I do indeed, guv. Why don't you go tomorrow, Priya?"

"Happy to, but I don't have any transport. Could I draw a car from the pool at Kentish Town?"

"Yes, no problem. Let me have a chit and I'll sign it."

Collison cleared his throat as if he had something else to say, as indeed he did.

"Good, well, while I'm here there's something I wanted to make everybody aware of. DI Metcalfe and I have been made aware of various facts – no not even facts, really – which may or may not have some bearing on the case. I'm sorry to be so vague and mysterious and I really wish I could tell you more, but I can't because there are security implications."

Everyone looked at each other in bewilderment.

"Security implications, sir?" Godwin asked before she could stop herself, "in a house in Downshire Hill?"

"Yes, I know it sounds a bit improbable, but there you are. The reason I'm telling you is that should either DI Metcalfe for myself come to the view that there may be something in what we have been told, and that it may have some bearing on the case, then we have been instructed to call in officers from Special Branch, who have the necessary security clearance to investigate these matters. So, all I'm really trying to say is that should at any time you get a request for information from Special Branch then you should go ahead and share whatever information they asking for. OK then?"

He nodded and left a now heavily confused incident room.

As a uniformed constable from downstairs looked into the room uncertainly.

"DI Metcalfe, sir? The sergeant says your man can be

interviewed whenever you're ready. He hasn't asked for a brief – not yet, anyway."

"Thank you. Please tell the sergeant I'll be down in a few minutes with DC Godwin."

"Very good, sir."

Godwin appeared unbidden at Metcalfe's desk clutching a notebook. He stood up and looked at her for a minute.

"Have you ever done anything like this before?"

"Not on a serious case like this, sir, no. Burglary and drug busts were more the sort of thing at Wood Green."

"Wood Green? Was that where you were before?"

"Yes, not quite the same as Hampstead is it? To tell the truth, I was very happy to get the transfer."

"All right, well basically just sit there, operate the tape machine, and don't say anything unless I ask you to. Obviously the tape will give us a full transcript to put on the system, but feel free to make notes of anything you think significant. OK?"

"Yes, sir. Understood."

The uniformed constable brought Rajarshi into the room and sat down opposite them. Godwin put two tapes in the machine, switched it on, and made the usual announcements.

"Now then, Mr Rajarshi, as you've just heard I'm Detective Inspector Metcalfe and this is Detective Constable Godwin. DC Godwin cautioned you when she arrested you and I want you to understand that you are still under caution now for the purposes of this interview. Do you understand that?"

Raj stared at him, said nothing, but gave a barely perceptible nod.

"You've also been told your rights by the duty Sergeant. In particular I want to remind you that you have the right to ask for a lawyer at any time. Now, let's get started shall we?"

He made a show of consulting his notes.

"To start with, could you tell us how long you lived with Mr Conrad Taylor at Wentworth House?"

Raj gazed at him but said nothing. Metcalfe tried again.

"Mr Rajarshi, you're not obliged to answer any questions which I put you but remember what it says in the caution. If you try to raise something in court which you had an opportunity to talk about here, but didn't, then the jury are allowed to take that into account when considering your case. Now, as I'm sure you're aware, Conrad Taylor has been found dead at Wentworth House. He was murdered, and you are currently a suspect for the murder. If in fact you are innocent of the crime then I would very much like to be able to eliminate you from our enquiries, which means it is in your interest to answer any questions I put to you."

He looked at Raj to see if any of this it had sunk in, but there was no sign one way or the other.

"So, shall we start again? How long have you lived at Wentworth House?"

"You say I'm a suspect. Why am I a suspect? I haven't done anything."

"If you haven't done anything then let's try to prove it. We're the police. We have to deal in evidence, not just what people tell us. But, since you ask, you are a suspect since at the moment we believe you may have been the last person to see Conrad Taylor alive, and since you have been drawing money out of his bank account even after his death. Did he know you had the details to his bank account?"

"Of course he did. I often had to pay for things, pay for him I mean. Things he needed. Shopping and stuff. That's why I had the PIN for his cash card, so I could draw money out of the machine."

"All right, well let's come back to that later. When did you start living at Wentworth House?"

"About two years ago I guess."

"And how did that come about? How did you meet Mr Taylor?"

"I visited him to ask about a book he was writing. Someone had told me he was looking for someone as a researcher. When he heard I didn't have anywhere to live – nowhere proper anyway – he said I could stay with him as part of the deal. That was all I got really, apart from a bit of pocket money."

"And that was all there was to it? That you were allowed to stay at the house while you were doing research for him?"

"Why, what else would there be?"

"Well, an obvious question would be whether you and Conrad Taylor were lovers."

"No, we weren't. There was nothing like that. Anyway, I'm not gay."

"Do you know if he was?"

Raj shrugged.

"Who knows? It's not the sort of thing you ask someone, is it?"

"Not even someone who asks you to live with him? Wouldn't you be even a little bit curious, or even concerned?"

"No."

"What were the sleeping arrangements?"

"I had a bedroom at the back of the house. He said it used to be his wife's. He slept at the front. Quite a small room. Never quite sure why he chose that one."

"Did he say what had happened to his wife? And did he ever mention any children?"

Again Raj shrugged.

"They used to be there, but they're not there anymore. That's all I know. I didn't pry and he didn't encourage questions about it. I assumed he'd got divorced and she'd taken the children to live somewhere else."

"And was the house always like it is now? Awash with papers, I mean?"

"It was like that when I moved in, so I suppose so, yes. They were his papers, not mine. He would never throw anything away. He was strange like that."

"Talking of 'strange', do you remember him occasionally having visitors from his neighbours on either side?"

"From time to time, yes. Why do you say that's strange?"

"Well actually, it was you who was described as strange, and by both neighbours. They say that when they visited, you just sat and stared at them and made them feel unwelcome."

"They were unwelcome. Conrad never wanted visitors, never wanted anybody in the house. He was just too weak to send them away sometimes."

"Had he always been like that, do you know?"

"How should I know? I'd never met him before two years ago."

"All right, well we can come back and revisit all these matters later in more detail, but at the moment I'm trying to cover as much ground as possible so we can get an overall picture, as it were. So why don't you tell me how Conrad Taylor came to die?"

"I don't know. He was dead when I found him."

"And when was that?"

"One day about six weeks ago. I've been out during the day and when I got back he was in the front room with his head bashed in."

"Can you remember exactly what time of day that was?"

"Sometime around 5 o'clock I think. Late afternoon anyway. I was doing a job for someone in Willesden – fixing their computer – and I think I left there about 4:15."

"And you found him dead when you got back?"

"Yes, I just said that."

"Was there any sign that anybody might have broken into the house?"

"Not that I could see."

"So that whoever murdered him must have had a key with which to let themselves into the house?"

"Or he let them in himself."

"Quite, but you just said he didn't like having people in the house."

"He didn't like it, but it happened from time to time. You said so yourself."

"So what did you do – when you found him, I mean?"

"I realised I couldn't stay there because there was going to be trouble, so I packed my bag and left. I got a room in a guesthouse in Camden. I've been living there and just coming up to the ATM when I needed cash."

"So, to be clear, you were drawing cash from Mr Taylor's bank account even though you knew him to be dead?"

"Yes, what of it? He didn't need it, did he? And he probably wouldn't have minded anyway. It's not like he had anybody to leave it to, is it?"

"But why did you just pack up and leave? Surely an innocent person would just have called the police and waited for them to arrive?"

"Like I said, I didn't want any trouble. I didn't want to get involved in anything."

"But surely you could see that he'd been murdered? That it wasn't a natural death?"

"I suppose so, yeah."

"So, I ask you again, it was nothing to do with you why didn't you simply call the police?"

"I didn't want draw attention to myself."

"Why not?"

"Because your security people wouldn't like it. I work for them, you see: MI6. You ask them. They'll tell you. I'm doing an important job for them and I'm supposed to be keeping a low profile."

Godwin gave Metcalfe a startled sidelong glance, which he ignored.

"I think it's best if we end things there for a while," he said, trying to pretend that this was the sort of thing that happened every day of the week. "Interview suspended at 16:48," he announced, looking at the clock on the wall. "Mr Rajarshi, I'll arrange to have you taken back to your cell."

CHAPTER 16

Desai drove up the M1 to Luton the next morning. As usual, the section following the junction with the M25 was ridiculously busy, with traffic pretty much at a standstill. However, since she had left plenty of time for her journey she was only a few minutes late as she drew up outside the small house on a modern housing estate.

When Colin McKenzie opened the door she guessed he was probably about 70. From the way in which her arrival prompted twitching curtains in the surrounding houses she also guessed that he probably didn't get many visitors.

"Come along in, please do," he said as if reading her thoughts. "I don't get many visitors you know."

When they were seated in the living room with tea and biscuits, he gazed at her keenly through eyes that were still sharp and intelligent.

"So what do you want to know about Conrad? I warn you I may not be able to help you very much. After his family left he became pretty much a recluse. Even I couldn't get in to see him very often."

"Ah, so that was his family then? We were wondering about that. The change of name and everything..."

"Yes, I was never really sure what was behind that."

"Why don't you just tell me what you can remember Mr McKenzie? About the family I mean."

"Well, it all seems a bit bizarre in retrospect. One day they were there, the next they weren't. I asked Conrad what had happened to them and he just said that they had gone away. I assumed that he and Judith – that was his wife – had split up and that she had taken the children with her. She was a strange one, Judith. I never really got to know her at all. Highly strung is probably the best way to describe her. I used to hear her shouting at him and the kids day after day."

"The kids? That would be a girl and a boy would it?"

"Yes. When last I remember them being there I guess the boy was about 16 and the girl a few years younger. Johann and Elizabeth they were called, although they usually went by John and Liz. They were a bit strange too, particularly the boy."

"So, just to be clear, Conrad never explained to you exactly why the rest of the family had left home, or why he had changed his name?"

"No, he didn't. He was a very private man you know. He didn't encourage anybody to stick their nose into his affairs."

"Didn't he ever say anything at all about them: the family, I mean?"

Not really. There was just once, in a sort of unguarded moment when he said something like 'families really screw up your life'. I wasn't sure what to say, but I pushed him a bit and asked him if he'd enjoyed having a son, at least. He looked really angry for a moment – you know, sort of what you might call suppressed rage, as if there was something bubbling away inside – and said 'my son was a vicious little bastard'. I've always remembered that."

"And did he seem like he was serious?"

"Absolutely serious. I changed the subject and never raised it with him again."

Desai jotted down a few notes, and then went on.

"Up until the time you left Downshire Hill, did he ever have anybody living with him do you know?"

"Not so far as I'm aware. I was surprised to hear that he'd been sharing the house with some young lad. Like I say, he was a very private person."

"Talking of that, did he ever give you any indication that he might be gay?"

"Not as such, no, but there was something I heard one night in the pub. That he'd been seen hanging around on the Heath. That part of the Heath where ... well, you know."

"When was that?"

"I don't know exactly. I heard about it a couple of years before I left – my wife was still alive I think – so that must have been five or six years ago now."

Desai scribbled rapidly in her notebook.

"Do you remember who it was who told you that?"

"No, just some bloke down the pub. You know what it's like."

"Hm, OK. What more can you tell me about the family?"

"Well, like I said, the wife had an evil temper on her. She and Conrad never seemed close. I had the idea she was the sort of person who always has to find fault with something.

You know what I mean? Someone who's always discontented, no matter how good their life may actually be."

"And you used to hear her shouting?"

"Yes, a lot. Sometimes you could hear somebody shouting back, usually the son."

"Yes, now what about him? Did you know him at all?"

"Only to say hello to in the street from time to time, though he was a difficult child as you probably know."

"How do you mean?"

"Well, didn't he have a criminal record or something?"

"Really? Nothing has shown up in our searches. But then we weren't sure exactly what his name was. Do you know something?"

"Well, he was big for his age, and maybe a bit physically advanced as well. He and some of his mates used to hang around after school in that service road behind the shops on Haverstock Hill. You know the one? If any of the girls from the school used the service road as a cut through they used to give them a bit of a hard time."

"How do you know this?"

"Rather sad really. A mate of mine who used to drink in the same pub – he's dead now – used to have a little flat above the shops which looked down at the back. He used to stand there watching them most days. I think it used to give him some sort of thrill. He invited me round to watch with him a few times, but I only went once. Poor bloke was a bit strange, I think. He'd been on his own a long time."

"When you say the boys used to give the girls a hard time, what do you mean exactly?"

"Not all the boys, just this small group – a gang, maybe you'd call it – led by John. He was bigger than the others, more like a man really. So he used to tell the other lads what to do and they'd pretty much go along with it. But there was apparently one day when one of them stood up to him, and he punched him really hard in the face a few times – broke his nose I heard."

"Go on."

"Well, you can get to the bus stop or the tube station perfectly easily by going round by the main road, see? That's what pretty much all the girls did, because they knew John and his mates hung around in the service road and they didn't want to get involved with them. But some of the girls either didn't know better because they hadn't done it before, or just didn't care. They took a shortcut and the boys used to gather round and call out things to them. Then they'd make them give them a kiss or something to let them pass. I don't want to turn this into something it wasn't, you know. Times were more innocent back then and it was basically just boys and girls having fun together, but John used to go a bit far sometimes."

"How do you mean?"

"Well, I got the impression that John was that bit more advanced than the rest of the gang – sexually, I mean. To be honest, I think most of the boys were just as embarrassed as the girls when they had to kiss. It was just a quick peck and that was it. But John used to give them a really long kiss, much more like an adult, and his hands would be all over them."

"And the girls used to put up with this?"

"Pretty much. Like I say, it wasn't like they didn't have a choice. They chose to walk that way, and they must have known pretty much what was going to happen because most of them did it more or less every day. There was one girl in particular, though, who definitely used to enjoy it. Or at least, that was the impression she gave."

"Can you tell me anything about her?"

"Yes. I suppose in a way she was the female equivalent of John, although she wasn't as old as he was. She was probably more Liz's sort of age: say 14 or maybe 15. But she could look older, much older. My mate's flat used to look out not only over the service road but also the approach to it, and I saw for myself that this girl used to actually prepare herself before she ducked behind the shops. She stopped and rolled up the waistband of her skirt to make it really short, and she shook out her hair and brushed it. She was what my mother would have called a tease. She used to stroll up the service road as though butter wouldn't melt in her mouth, but you could tell that she knew everyone was looking at her, and that she was happy about it."

"Did John treat her any differently to the others?"

"Yes, very much so. He wouldn't let any of the others touch her. That was what the fight was about, I heard. She was flirting with one of the other boys, sort of daring him to kiss her. He did, and John hit him. That was the story I heard from the bloke in the flat, anyway."

"Who was she? Did you ever hear her name?"

"No, but like I say she was very different from the others. I used to see her around during the holidays and at weekends and if you hadn't seen her in her school uniform already you would never have known she was a young girl. She used to dress much older, and wear high heels and make-up. My mate said she used to hang around by the shops trying to pick up older men. I didn't believe him at first, but then one evening she called out to me as I went past. "

"Really? What did she say?"

"Something like 'like to buy me a drink, Mister?' I think. I've always remembered it, to be honest, because I found it so shocking – a young girl like that behaving like some sort of street tart."

"Where was this – do you remember?"

"I'm pretty sure it was in Downshire Hill. Yes, it was, and more or less right outside my house as well."

"You said John got into trouble with the police. Was that when he punched the other boy in the face?"

"He might have got into trouble for that, but that wasn't what I had in mind, no. There was a time – in the summer, I think – when John and his friends started jumping out on women as they went past and ... well, groping them I'm afraid. I heard they did it for a dare and thought it was just a bit of fun, but naturally the women didn't share that opinion. They had the police come down to the school and set up an identity parade, and John was one of the boys who got picked out. I can remember the police coming to the house to speak to Conrad and Judith. She went ballistic, needless to say."

"Did you ever see any sign yourself of him being aggressive?"

"Only when I used to hear him shouting back at Judith. They were a fine pair, they were."

"Do you know if Conrad ever heard anything from his family after they left?"

"If he did, he didn't tell me, but like I say he became almost a total recluse, so it wasn't easy even to get to see him, let alone have a conversation with him."

"And you didn't ever see the family again, or hear anything from them?"

"No I didn't, though that's hardly surprising. We were never close and to be honest I thought Judith was a bit of a nutter. She picked a couple of arguments about nothing very much with my wife, who was a very gentle soul. No, Judith was the sort of person who could have got into a fight with a complete stranger just for the fun of it."

"You say that you weren't close with the family. What about the neighbour on the other side?"

"I seem to remember that house being empty quite a lot of the time around then. I think Jack Rowbotham had bought it, but he wasn't actually living there as he was having a lot of building work done. I used to see him dropping in in the evenings on his way home, presumably to check on progress. But come to think of it, I don't think he actually moved in until later, after Conrad was on his own."

"Did you know Jack Rowbotham well?"

"We were neighbours for quite a few years. We used to pop round occasionally, have a drink in the pub together, that sort of thing. But I wouldn't say we were particularly close."

"Do you know if he was ever married himself?"

"Yes, I think he was in the process of getting divorced when he bought the house. I'm sure I remember him telling me that."

"Did you ever hear him say anything about having any children?"

"No, I can't say I did. I don't see him with children somehow. He's a bit of a recluse himself to tell the truth. Oh, nothing as extreme as Conrad, don't get me wrong. But definitely a bit ... what's the word? ... curmudgeonly, that's it."

CHAPTER 17

"So we have quite a few new developments," Metcalfe told the team the next morning.

"First, we have Raj in custody but so far he has denied any involvement in the murder. He claims that he found Taylor dead, and effectively panicked and ran off. We can form our own views about how credible he may be as a witness. We do know, of course, that he has been drawing money out of Taylor's bank account. He claims that this was with his consent but even if that is true, that consent would presumably have come to an end when he died."

"Excuse me, guv, but what are we planning to do about Raj?" Evans enquired.

"The logical thing is to apply for him to be remanded in custody. Given that on his own admission he fled the crime scene, and that he has no fixed place to live, *and* that he's in the country illegally, I don't see that being a problem."

"Could I just cut in for a moment, Bob?" Collison asked.

"Of course, sir."

"I just wanted to say this. You will all have seen a claim which Raj made at the end of his interview yesterday. DI Metcalfe and I will be taking this matter up with Special Branch. We may or may not be able to share their response with you. But in any event, you will please all be even more careful than usual not to share any of this with anybody outside the team. Strictly speaking, we have already breached security since only DI Metcalfe and I have the appropriate clearance, but let's not make matters any worse than they need to be."

He looked around the room and was pleased to see nods of understanding.

"Carry on please, Bob."

"Thank you, sir. The other news is that the neighbour, Colin McKenzie, has given some useful background on the family. It seems that the son, proper name Johann but commonly referred to as John, has some previous, but curiously nothing showed up in our initial searches. Have you been able to track anything down, Priya?"

"Yes, guv. Nothing about the alleged attack on one of his schoolmates – perhaps that never got reported – but there was something on the sexual assaults. Mr McKenzie was right about the police attending the school and holding some identity parades but in the heat of the moment they didn't follow PACE guidelines. It was even worse than that, in fact. They let two of the complainants actually see John Schneider on his own before the parade took place. It was accidental, not deliberate, but very careless nonetheless. So without any identification evidence which would stand up in court, it was decided not to prosecute."

"So that's why nothing showed up. Well, even though there's nothing formal on record I think we know enough to suggest that John Schneider was aggressive, particularly towards women, and quite capable of physical assault."

"If I could cut in again, Bob, I'd be very interested to get a read on this from Peter Collins. Perhaps Karen could mention that to him?"

"Yes, of course," Willis agreed.

"But what we still don't know is why the family suddenly left," Metcalfe continued. "Both McKenzie and Rowbotham assumed there had been some complete marital breakdown, but that's just supposition. As far as we can tell at the moment they might just as well have disappeared into thin air."

"What about a television appeal, guv?" Godwin suggested. "There must be somebody out there somewhere who knows where they went, and why."

"A very good idea," Collison acknowledged. "I'll speak to the ACC and see what can be arranged."

"There's something else that has recently come to light," Metcalfe said. "It seems that a man called on Jack Rowbotham shortly before Taylor's death. He had been knocking on the door of Wentworth House without success, and came round to ask Rowbotham if Taylor still lived there. Now we have no idea who this man may have been. It seems pretty certain that it wasn't an official enquiry since the caller didn't show Rowbotham any ID. But who was he? He may have been something as innocent as a door-to-door salesman, but in that case why didn't he try to sell Rowbotham anything?"

"It's difficult to know where to start on this one," Collison commented. "Any thoughts would be welcome."

"Karen, has anything come to light in all those papers?" Metcalfe asked.

"Nothing much that I can see. I'm pretty much finished

now by the way. In particular, there is absolutely nothing which might throw any light on why the family went, or why."

"I'm just waiting for SOCO's final report," Metcalfe observed. "Unfortunately what we have so far doesn't help us very much. They found five different DNA patterns in the front room. Three have been identified as Helen Barnes, Jack Rowbotham, and DS Desai. So it seems likely that the remaining two are Taylor and Raj, but we're checking that. Interestingly there are very faint traces of a possible sixth person, but it's faint and corrupted so it's possible we may never get a definite match. I suppose it could be old DNA from Colin McKenzie, but that's just conjecture on my part."

"Excuse me, guv, but there was one more thing," Desai interjected. "Colin McKenzie apparently heard gossip in the local pub to the effect that the deceased had on at least one occasion frequented the gay area of Hampstead Heath. I've passed this on to the gay liaison officer, but he hasn't been able to turn anything up. He has been showing the photo around local pubs, but with no result."

"Is that everything, Bob?"

"Yes, sir."

"All right, well we have Raj in custody and I think we must continue to treat him as our prime suspect. We have only his word for how he discovered the body, and the fact that he fled the crime scene and continued to draw money out of the deceased's bank account may be more than enough to support a prosecution. We can take advice on that in due course. But we need to try to sort out these loose ends. Is there a mystery about the disappearance of the Schneider family? If not, if someone comes forward to explain what happened to them and where they are today, then fine. But if we can't track them down then we have to ask ourselves if there might be some connection between their disappearance and Taylor's murder, even separated by a couple of decades."

"Right, folks, please check your assignments with DS Desai. I think that's everything."

"Let's go upstairs, Bob," Collison said as he passed him. "I want to call Philip Newby."

•

"Good morning, sir," he began the conversation, "this is Simon Collison. I have Bob Metcalfe with me."

"Good morning, good morning. Yes, now then, I've been looking at this transcript you sent over. It's unfortunate, to say the least."

"Yes, I know. I'm beginning to think I should have conducted the interview with Bob, at least until we knew what Raj was going to say."

"On balance I think you should, but let's not cry over spilt milk. I suppose this transcript went on the system in the usual way, so that the whole team have access to it?"

"Yes they do, but there are under strict instructions to be even more careful than usual about maintaining absolute confidentiality."

"Well, I suppose that's the best we can hope for. But anyway, I suppose you want to know whether any of this stuff is true?"

"Yes please, sir."

"Well, this is all slightly embarrassing, but the basic answer is no. One of our chaps did meet briefly with Raj when he first came into the country. The context was that, as you know, we had been asked to provide assistance if necessary to the Singapore police who wanted to run Raj as an undercover agent within the UK end of the passport racket. Five were supporting the request because they were worried the same route could be used by terrorists to get into the UK."

"May I ask if the Special Branch officer was alone at this meeting?"

"No, he wasn't. He was accompanied by someone from the Singapore embassy in London. Officially he was on a temporary posting as a trade attaché. In reality, he was a Singapore police officer who specialises in running undercover agents. Well, the long and short of it is that our Branch chap was unconvinced by Raj. He found him insincere and evasive. He brought the meeting to an end so that he could discuss his concerns with our friend from Singapore. They arranged to see Raj again a few days later, but that second meeting never took place as he absconded from his hostel and was never seen again."

"I see. And how much of this could actually be made public, sir?"

"Absolutely none of it. HMG could never admit to allowing overseas police forces to run undercover operations in the UK. Nor could either Five or ourselves allow any suggestion that Raj was somehow an agent of ours. He wasn't, of course, he was part of the Singaporean set-up."

"That could be tricky, sir. Right now Raj is our prime

suspect in a murder enquiry. What happens if it goes to trial and he tries to repeat these allegations?"

"I've been discussing that with a chum of mine with the Attorney General. He seems confident that we could persuade the judge to hold parts of the trial *in camera*."

"*In camera*, sir? A murder trial?"

"Of course, I was forgetting," Newby said dryly. "You studied law didn't you?"

"Yes, I did, and I'm not aware that any murder trial in the UK has ever been held *in camera* before."

"There's a first time for everything, Simon. When national security is at stake you'd be surprised just how amenable a judge can be. Anyway, let's cross that bridge when we come to it. The important thing is that at the moment he's just making vague statements which we can easily refute. What will be interesting to see is if he starts to get into any of the specifics of the passport operation. Personally, I doubt he will. After all, he jumped ship on his mission and his handers, so it wouldn't show him in a very good light now would it?"

"There's something else, sir. One of the neighbours has told us that just before the time of Taylor's murder he had a mysterious male visitor who had already tried to gain access to Taylor's house before going round to the neighbour and asking if Taylor still lived there. Is there any way you could check at your end to see if that visit was prompted either by you or your Singaporean friends?"

"I'll do what I can. Off the top of my head I would say the answer is almost certainly 'no'. They say they had no idea where Raj was living, and I'm inclined to believe them."

"If you could just double check, sir, I would be very grateful. As I'm sure you'll understand, we are trying to eliminate this man from our enquiries."

"Yes, of course. Well, I'll do what I can, Simon. Best of luck with it now."

As Newby rang off Metcalfe and Collison looked at each other. Collison shrugged his shoulders. As he did so, there came a tap on the door.

"Beg pardon, guv," Desai said as she came in uncertainly, "but SOCO has just come up with something which I wanted to share with you both immediately."

"Yes, Priya, what is it?" Collison asked.

"Well, they decided to put a dog in. One that's trained to sniff out human remains. They thought it would be easier than taking all the floorboards up. Anyway, they drew a blank in the house but then decided that since the dog was there anyway they may as well give it a try in the garden, the back garden that is."

"Yes?"

"Well, they took it all over the garden with no success but then just as they were about to call it off, the dog suddenly went ape-shit – sorry, sir, but that's how they described it – barking and scrabbling away at the side fence. The fence that divides the garden at Wentworth House from Mr Rowbotham's garden. So they went round to ask if he would let them in, but he was out."

"So, let me get this right. The dog seems to think that there is a corpse buried in Jack Rowbotham's garden?"

"Yes, that's right, guv. And I got to thinking about

something he told me. He said that while the building works were being done there was quite a long period with no fence between the gardens, so anybody from next door could have walked in – at night, say – and have done whatever they wanted, because Rowbotham wasn't there to see them. He wasn't living at the house, you see."

There was a pause while the three of them looked at each other.

"Are you thinking what I'm thinking?" Metcalfe asked.

"If you mean that we may have found the family, yes I am," Collison replied grimly. "Priya, get hold of Rowbotham anyway you can. We need access to that garden – and tell uniform to bring some shovels."

CHAPTER 18

It was a sombre and slightly sinister group that assembled in the garden of Jack Rowbotham's house the next morning. First the dog was allowed to run free in the garden. After sniffing every part of it quickly it ran instantly back to the side flowerbed and started barking determinedly. The dog was then called off by its handler and dispatched to the front of the house and put back in its van while SOCO erected a tent over the whole of the flowerbed. Four uniform officers stood by with shovels. Rowbotham himself had been banished to the house but was gazing curiously out of the window. Collison shrugged; he could hardly order a man not to look out of his own living room.

"OK, guys, we're ready for you," one of the white-suited SOCO personnel called out, and soon the rhythmic sound of spade on London clay began to be heard. Collison, Metcalfe, Willis, and Desai stood uncertainly on the patio trying hard to look as though they witnessed a scene like this every day of the week. Fortunately they did not have to try for very long, as a shout from inside the tent prompted a cessation in the shovelling efforts. Uniform emerged from the tent, their shovels and boots encased in wet clay. Tom Bellamy followed them, and now approached Collison, removing his mask.

"It's a corpse right enough, guv. Too early to be specific

because there's still a lot of earth that needs to be moved, but we need to do that gently by hand from now on."

"OK, thank you, Tom. How soon do you think you'll be able to let me know any more?"

"Difficult to say. Some hours certainly. As soon as we expose the body properly I'll call Brian Williams."

"All right. Sounds like there's not much point us hanging around here then?"

"I'd say that's right, sir. I'll keep you posted of course."

Collison considered briefly how best to proceed.

"I think I'll get back to the nick, Bob. Some of us clearly need to stay here and re-interview Rowbotham, but I leave it to you to decide how best to do that."

"Well, Priya and I have had the contact with him so far, guv, so probably best to play it that way again."

"Fine. In that case Karen and I will slip away."

Metcalfe knocked on the back door. Rowbotham let them in at once, his face ashen.

"Have they found something? They have, haven't they?"

"Yes, I'm afraid so. I think we'd better sit down, Mr Rowbotham, if that's all right."

"Yes, of course."

They sat down in the living room, Priya balancing her notebook on her knee.

"It's too early to be specific, Mr Rowbotham, but we have unearthed what we believe to be human remains in your back garden. In the circumstances I am obviously obliged to ask you if you know anything about how they might have got there."

Desai smiled to herself at the thought of how Metcalfe was steadily beginning to sound more and more like Collison.

"No, I have absolutely no idea. Who is it? Who was it, I should say?"

"As I said, it's too early to be specific. Now, just to confirm my own impressions, Mr Rowbotham, is there any access to the garden other than through this house?"

"Not now, no. There is access round the side of the house but I had a security gate fitted when I had my building works done and I've always made sure to keep it in good repair; we get a lot of burglaries round here as you probably know."

"But that hasn't always been the case, has it?"

"If you're talking about the period before I actually moved in, no it wasn't. The side gate was one of the last things to be done, as the builders were using it to move things in and out of the house. And for a while – quite a long while actually – there wasn't even a fence closing off the garden from the house next door."

"So there was a period when pretty much anybody could have sneaked into your garden – perhaps at night – and there would have been nobody here in the house to observe them?"

"Yes, exactly."

"I see. Well, I'm sure we'll want to talk to you again, Mr Rowbotham, particularly when we've managed to identify whoever that is in your flowerbed out there, but for the time being I think we can leave it there."

As they rose to leave, and Priya put her notebook back in her shoulder bag, Metcalfe remembered the mystery visitor.

"I don't suppose," he asked without much hope, "that

you might have remembered anything more about that man who came calling on you about the time of Conrad Taylor's death?"

"No, I'm afraid I don't."

"And he didn't say anything except to ask if Conrad Taylor still lived next door?"

"I wasn't exactly keen to engage in lengthy conversation," Rowbotham said with a smile. "To tell the truth there was something menacing about him that made me nervous. He was a big man, you know, and I live on my own here."

"Do you have a burglar alarm as a matter of interest?"

"I do. I had to get one for the insurance company, but I keep it switched off. Naughty, I know, but I'm terrified of the thing going off in the middle of the night."

"I see. Well, thank you very much."

•

"I don't mean to pry," Collison said as they walked back up Downshire Hill, "but how are things with Bob and Lisa?"

"If you mean how were things romantically, they're fine; they're very happy together. If you mean how were things as regards Lisa's health, I'm not too sure. She seems to be going for test after test without them finding anything specific wrong. Peter and I are both quite worried about her, as a matter of fact. One of his friends is a neurosurgeon and he says that a fractured skull can have effects – sometimes way in the future – that nobody really understands. You know she developed epilepsy?"

"Yes, Bob told me about that."

He paused, unsure of how to express what he wanted to say next.

"Do you think that Bob perhaps..."

"Feels guilty for what happened? Of course he does. How do you expect him to feel? He'll never be able to get away from the thought that if he'd taken some backup with him the attack wouldn't have happened. Silly, of course. The way he describes it there wouldn't have been time for anybody to do anything, no matter how many people had been in the room."

"Yes, I agree. Rotten business, isn't it?"

"Funny," she said, but in a way which was far from humorous, "that's exactly the phrase Peter uses about it."

There was an awkward pause as they completed their brief journey.

"So what have you got on today?" Collison enquired as they reached the side door.

"I'm waiting for Bob to reassign me to something, actually. I finally finished all those papers, I'm happy to say. By the middle of each day I was already starting to feel really itchy with the amount of dust that was still on them. And at the end of it all, what did they tell us? Absolutely nothing."

"Well, that's police work for you. Most of our efforts come to nothing. It's just a matter of eliminating that and then moving onto the next possibility."

"Yes, I suppose that's right. Not quite so glamorous as it seemed before we joined, eh?"

He was about to say 'not as glamorous as you, certainly'

but stopped himself just in time. Even with someone he knew as well as he did Karen you couldn't be too careful these days.

"Tell you what," he said instead, "when Bob and Priya get back why don't we convene in my office, just the four of us, and review where we are?"

•

"So," he commented an hour or so later, "a rather dramatic new development."

"Dramatic indeed," Metcalfe agreed. "By the way, I spoke to Tom Bellamy before we came away. He said purely unofficially that he's pretty sure it's the body of a young woman. She doesn't seem to have been wrapped up in any way. A pink material which they originally thought might have been a bag or something turned out to be a raincoat. Because it was made from some synthetic – nylon, they think – it's survived in the ground pretty much intact."

"If she wasn't wrapped up," Willis observed, "that suggests she hadn't been carried any great distance. Which in turn suggests that she was killed close to where she was buried."

"Agreed," Collison said, "which in turn suggests that she may well have been killed in or around Wentworth House and then buried in Rowbotham's garden by someone who took advantage of the fact that the fence had been taken away."

"Are you suggesting, guv," Desai asked, "that the body could be that of Elizabeth Taylor, or Schneider I should say?"

"I think it seems a sensible assumption to be making, until we know more," Collison said cautiously.

"But in that case what about the rest of the family?" Willis asked. "Surely the wife and son wouldn't just up and leave knowing that the girl had been murdered? Wouldn't they have gone to the police, or at least have confided in someone? One of the neighbours perhaps?"

"All good questions, Karen. It does sound weird and no mistake. To be honest, I was rather expecting to find three bodies in the garden, not just one. But you saw the dog's reaction. It was definitely interested in that spot and no other."

"And it didn't show any interest in the garden of Wentworth House itself," Desai pointed out, "so we can rule out them having been buried there."

"All of which suggests that the mother and son left Wentworth House alive," Collison mused, "and presumably voluntarily."

"You mean there's the chance they might have been abducted?" Metcalfe ventured.

"In theory, yes, but it's all a bit far-fetched isn't it? Anyway, we know the son was a strong and fairly violent lad. It's difficult to imagine him going quietly. No, there's something that doesn't make sense here, and we need to find what it is."

He looked at the others and they nodded, but no further suggestions were forthcoming.

"All right, then. Let's try to summarise where we are in terms of working hypotheses. Number one, and seemingly the most likely one at the moment, is that Raj murders Taylor and then runs away in panic. Perhaps Taylor has discovered that Raj has been systematically looting his bank account and Raj sees killing him as the best way to keep it quiet. Perhaps

Taylor and Raj were lovers, and this is a lovers tiff gone wrong. Maybe both of the above. Who knows? But either way, Raj remains our prime suspect."

"In which case," Metcalfe said, "just for the record as it were, there would be no connection between the two murders, would there? Wouldn't that be quite a large coincidence, two corpses being found in such close proximity to each other?"

"Yes, it would. And that's what makes me uneasy. It might seem that we have a very strong case against Raj for the murder of Taylor, but assuming that this young girl was killed when the fence was down then there's no way that Raj could have been involved with that. I know we've dealt with coincidence before, but there's something about this I don't like."

"And, talking coincidence," Willis proffered, "what about Rowbotham's mystery visitor? We know that almost nobody ever tried to visit Taylor. So isn't it very strange that somebody should have been so very keen to see him just before he died? And it's difficult to see that Raj could have had any connection with this character, whoever he may have been."

Collison and Metcalfe looked at each other quickly.

"Let's assume that's the case for the time being," Collison said carefully. "In which case, do we have a hypothesis that can accommodate our mystery man? Perhaps he returns, unobserved by Rowbotham this time, gains entry to the house, and kills Taylor. But if so, why? What possible motive could he have? Of course it's difficult to guess at that without knowing who he is, but what might it be?"

"Perhaps he was a gay lover, who picked up Taylor when

he was on the Heath? It which case the lovers tiff angle might operate again," Desai suggested.

"Perhaps, but it's a bit tenuous isn't it? We know that Taylor didn't welcome people to the house, and Raj positively discouraged him having visitors, so if Taylor was having a relationship on the side where was it happening? And anyway, how could someone gain access to the house? There's no sign of a break-in, which means that Taylor would have had to know his attacker and let him into the house."

"And, once again, it would assume – presumably – that the two murders were unconnected."

"Yes, unless this mystery man was someone from Taylor's past, and again we simply don't know enough yet to be able to make that call."

"So our third working hypothesis," Metcalfe said slowly, "would be that Taylor killed his daughter, for reasons as yet unknown , buried her body in the next door garden, and was then killed himself twenty years later perhaps by someone seeking vengeance? Again, it all seems rather far-fetched, doesn't it? But perhaps it's the only possible explanation which makes sense of the connection between the two killings."

They all sat and looked at each other. This was always a difficult stage in an enquiry, Collison reflected, that period when the truth was gradually starting to emerge, but was capable of fitting several different scenarios.

"Well," he said firmly, "the one thing all this shows very clearly is that there is still a lot we need to find out. Good news, though. I've got permission to do a televised appeal tomorrow evening. Let's see if that flushes something out of the woodwork."

CHAPTER 19

Since the team were going to be in action that evening, Collison had called a break in the middle of the day and had told people they were free to go home if they wished, and to reconvene at the television studio at 5 PM. Rather than head back across London himself, he had gladly accepted an invitation from Willis and Metcalfe to spend some time at the house in Frognal. He was now happily ensconced in a large leather armchair, a cup of tea handily placed at his elbow.

"Now give me your professional opinion, Peter," he said. "Based on what we know so far, what do you make of Johann Schneider from a psychological point of view?"

"It's difficult to say," Collins replied, "because I don't have a lot of information to go on. But if it's true about his aggressive sexual activity as a teenager then that does strike a chord."

"I thought it might."

"Well of course you know this as well as I do, but attacks of a sexual nature during the early or mid teens are one of the common characteristics of a psychopath who may develop into a serial killer. So are acts of cruelty against animals, or damage to property; it would be interesting to find out whether anything like that went on. So, incidentally, is the lack of a proper relationship with either or both parents. Here, from what we know so far, he had a very difficult relationship with his mother and was then physically separated from his father. Separated, moreover, in what seemed to have been very mysterious circumstances."

"Yes, my thoughts exactly. Is it possible – and this is just a hypothesis, no more – that what we might be looking at here is the first victim of a serial killer, namely Johann Schneider? And if that's right, where do we start looking for later victims?"

"Well, wherever he went, presumably. But I should sound a note of caution. Serial killers rarely murder family members, not initially anyway. Christie killed his wife of course, but that was in rather different circumstances."

"So if the victim does turn out to have been Elizabeth Schneider, as we suspect, that would make the hypothesis less compelling?"

"Decidedly so, in my view."

"Sorry, guv," Willis said with a smile.

"Well, it is rather a pity isn't it? It would be a theory that would at least offer some connection. That's what baffles me about this case, at least so far. Is it really credible that two murders, committed in or around the same house, separated by 20 years or so but both discovered within the last few days, could really be completely unconnected?"

"Synchronicity," Collins murmured.

"Yes, I know all about synchronicity, Peter, and I'm very sympathetic to Jung's views as you know, but dammit I'm a copper, and coppers don't like coincidence. No, there's something missing here, something we don't know yet, or do know but haven't realised the significance of."

"Well, maybe the TV appeal will throw up something," Metcalfe suggested. "I've been talking to a mate of mine who did one a few years ago and they had a fantastic response: 40 or 50 calls within the first hour or so, including one with a lead which led them straight to their man."

"Let's hope so," Collison said fervently, "because, to be honest, I'm starting to run out of ideas."

•

On arrival at the TV studio it transpired that most of the team had contrived during the afternoon break to get dressed in their smartest clothes and generally make the best of their appearance. Willis strongly suspected that Godwin had even been to the hairdresser. Collison was whisked away by the presenter while the rest of the team were assigned to desks which had already been set up with telephones answering to the number which would be given during the appeal. There was now an awkward period of inaction while they waited for the program to air. The hot drinks from the studios vending machine were sampled, and pronounced to be even worse than those on offer in the canteen at Hampstead nick.

"Have you ever been on television before, Timothy?" Metcalfe asked Evans.

"Can't say I have, guv. And yourself?"

"Not so far as I'm aware, no. Still, I don't think people will see much of us. The focus will be on Mr Collison."

Evans seem disappointed to hear this.

"Hope not, guv," he said anxiously, "my mum's got

the whole family round to watch. She's recording it and everything."

As the transmission time approached the team were ushered back to their desks. Collison appeared in the seating area together with a well-known celebrity who was fronting the program. It looked suspiciously as though both men were wearing make-up. Metcalfe looked around curiously. He had never been in a television studio before, and was struck by how very few people were involved in the process. All the electronics seem to be handled remotely, while the cameras themselves were on robotic dollies and moved around the room like Daleks. As he watched, the producer counted them down and the program began.

The front man smiled engagingly into the camera and began by explaining the context of the appeal before introducing Collison.

"A few days ago," Collison began, "police officers discovered the body of a man in a house on Downshire Hill in Hampstead. His name was Conrad Taylor and he had been murdered some weeks previously. This is an unusual appeal in that we already have a suspect in custody charged with his murder, but there are many aspects of the case which we do not yet fully understand, and it is in the hope that somebody out there can help us unravel some of these mysteries that we have asking now for your help."

The photos first of Wentworth House and then Conrad Taylor over which he had been speaking faded from the screen. He went on.

"First and foremost, we believe that until about 20 years

ago Conrad Taylor lived at Wentworth House with his family, comprising his wife and two children: a son Johann, who also used the name John, and a daughter Elizabeth. I should also mention that we believe at that time not only the deceased but his whole family were using the name of Schneider. With the exception of Conrad Taylor himself, the entire family seems abruptly to have vanished from the scene. We are very anxious indeed to hear from anybody who may know of their past or present whereabouts."

"Second, we have very recently indeed discovered some human remains in the back garden of the neighbouring house. No formal identification of these remains has yet been possible, and it goes without saying that we are also anxious to hear from anybody who may be able to throw any light on this discovery. It seems that at about the time the family disappeared from Wentworth House, the fence between the two back gardens had been removed during the course of building works, so that it would have been possible to access either back garden from the other, or indeed from the street since one of the side gate had also been removed. We are for the time being treated these two crimes as connected."

"Third, we are anxious to trace a man who called at Wentworth House some weeks ago and, unable to gain any response, went next door to speak to one of the neighbours, asking if Conrad Taylor still lived at the property. He is described as about 40 years old, white, tall, and strongly built. We are very anxious to eliminate this man from our enquiries and would appeal to him to come forward and identify himself. We would also like to hear from anyone who may be able to explain why this enquiry was being made, and by whom."

The camera cut back to the presenter.

"As the Superintendent says, this is an unusual case for us to feature. Normally we are asking for your help either to identify a suspect or to locate their whereabouts. In this case, as the police readily admit, they have a suspect already in custody. But please don't let that stop you from coming forward if you know anything at all that you think may be of relevance to this enquiry. A telephone number is now being shown on screen, will be shown again at the end of the programme, and is featured on our website. If for any reason you are unable to get through, you may if you wish speak to your local police station. If you do know anything, no matter how unimportant it may seem, please do get in touch."

He waited for the notification in his earpiece that the programme had moved onto the next item, and then turned and nodded to Collison.

"Well done. You can relax now, the mics and cameras aren't live anymore."

Collison thanked him and wandered across to where the team were waiting self-consciously at their desks. There was an eerie quiet. He remembered the old joke about 'first nothing happened but then nothing happened'.

Suddenly, about 10 minutes after the item, the phone rang and Metcalfe picked it up. Slowly it was joined by others until most of the team were busy talking and making notes. Collison wandered around, looking over people's shoulders.

Nothing jumped off the page at him, except that Evans had been doodling excessively.

At the end of the programme there was a brief roundup by the presenter, who remarked that many phone calls had already been received on the Conrad Taylor enquiry. After about an hour more the calls petered out entirely, and Collison called a halt. The only officer still talking was Desai, who had just begun a new conversation.

"Hello, you're speaking to Detective Sergeant Desai. Thank you for calling. How can I help?"

"Well, it's that piece I just saw on television. About the house on Downshire Hill."

"Yes, I'm working on that investigation. Who's calling, please?"

"Do I have to give my name?"

"Not if you don't want to, but it's much better if you do. We might not be able to use whatever information you have if it's given anonymously."

"Well, I'd rather not get involved. It's just I know something about that family."

"OK, what can you tell me about them?"

"The three of them – the mother and the two kids that is – packed up and left one night and went to Canada."

"Canada? Now that is useful. Do you know whereabouts, or how we might contact them?"

"Somewhere near Toronto. The mother died a year or so back."

"How do you know all this?"

"Never mind that. I just do."

There was a pause and Desai sensed that the caller was fighting the impulse to hang up.

"Please don't go," she said quickly. "You only have to tell me what you want to tell me. I won't press you for anything else."

There was another long silence.

"Why do you want to know all this?" the voice asked finally.

"Because we want to know who killed Conrad Taylor, and we want to find out the identity of whoever it was that was buried next door. We'd be really grateful for any help you can give us with either question."

"You think it's the daughter, don't you? The body you dug up. Elizabeth Schneider, I mean."

"I can't comment on that, but obviously it's a possibility, yes."

"It's not. It's not her."

"Who is it then?"

"I don't know, but it's not her."

"And how do you know all this?"

Desai had a sudden premonition what the answer might be, and started waving her free hand, still holding a pen, to attract attention. The others gazed at her curiously.

Again there was a silence, but then the answer came.

"Because I'm Elizabeth Schneider."

CHAPTER 20

"You did well, Priya," Collison said the next morning.

"Do you think so, guv? I was gutted that I couldn't get her to tell me where she was, or agree to a meeting."

"She did say she'd call back," Collison replied, "and you gave her your number here at the nick."

"Yes I know, but will she?"

"Of course, it could be a hoax," Metcalfe pointed out. "It happens a lot, doesn't it? Remember the Yorkshire Ripper enquiry. That was completely derailed by a hoax caller they took seriously."

"Yes, Peter had an idea about that," Willis said. "He suggested that if she does call back we tell her exactly that. Namely, that unless we can talk to her in person and verify her identity then we can't be sure that she's on the level. In other words, we hint very strongly that if she's just a voice on the end of the phone we will probably have to assume she's a hoaxer."

"That sounds like good advice," Collison observed. "If she was keen enough to get in touch with us then surely she'll also be keen enough for what she has to say to be taken seriously."

Metcalfe looked at his watch. It was already 9:30 and the morning meeting would normally have been taking place, but had been delayed until 10 o'clock to allow the team, who had been at the television studio until quite late, a little extra time in bed.

"Can I suggest that Priya goes and sits by her phone? If she does call then we don't want to miss her."

"Yes, good idea, Bob. Priya, off you go. Now then, you two, before the rest of the gang arrives let's have a little think about where we go from here. We obviously have two alternative possibilities: either the body in the flower bed is Elizabeth Schneider, in which case last night's call was just some sort of sick joke, or it's not. I must say that I rather like the second alternative since it keeps alive the possibility of this having been the first victim of a serial killer, namely Johann Schneider."

"I was proposing to detail some of the team to investigate any reports of young women having gone missing locally at about that time," Metcalfe said. "I'm also going to ask people to investigate local dentists to see if anybody might have Elizabeth Schneider's dental records. It's a long shot of course, since it was a long time ago."

"Good, I see we're thinking along the same lines. If it isn't the Schneider girl, then of course that opens up all sorts of other possibilities apart from Johann. We know from Rowbotham that pretty much anybody could just have wandered in off the street, though whether they would have done so carrying a body must be open to question. And if it isn't the Schneider girl, then what on earth prompted the sudden disappearance of the rest of the family? Unless the death and the disappearance were entirely unconnected, which seems hugely unlikely."

"And it's even more complicated than that, isn't it?" put in Willis. "We don't know for certain that the family's disappearance was connected with the murder of Conrad Taylor. On the contrary, we have a suspect in custody who cannot have any connection with the disappearance at all. So we're not really talking about two possibly unrelated events, but three."

"True, all too true I'm afraid," Collison murmured. "More and more I find myself thinking that there's something we have yet to find out, something that will make everything fall into place and make sense. If only we knew where to look for it."

"And there's the other thing we shouldn't forget about," Metcalfe said with an awkward look at Willis, "the thing you and I know about, guv, but aren't allowed to mention to anybody else."

"You mean that this still could have been either a botched attempt to murder Raj, or a deliberate act to put the frighteners on him, or a deliberate act to frame him for murder?"

"Exactly, guv, and in any one of those three cases then we're talking about a third party, as yet unknown."

Collison shook his head helplessly.

•

It was shortly before midday that Priya finally received the call she had been waiting for.

"Listen, Elizabeth," she said after an awkward round of hellos, "we really need you to come in and see us. We need to know that you're for real."

179

"How do you mean? Are you saying you don't believe me?"

"No, I'm saying that we can't just accept your word for who you are. I'm sorry but after any appeal like that there are always a lot of calls which turn out to have been hoaxes. We really want to believe you, but we need to see you face to face and find some way of being sure that you really are Elizabeth Schneider."

"I'm not coming to any police station."

"It doesn't have to be at a police station. It could be anywhere you like, just so long as I can come and bring a colleague with me."

"Nice try, but it could be a trick just so you can arrest me."

"Why on earth would we want to arrest you? You haven't done anything wrong, have you? We just want to speak to you as a potential witness, that's all, to get some background on two different murder cases. We couldn't arrest you, even if we wanted to."

There was another of those silences. Desai tried again.

"Listen to me, Elizabeth. There's obviously something you want to tell us very badly, since you made the effort to call us, which we really appreciate. But it's no good for anybody unless we can take seriously whatever it is you want to tell us. We can't go around making allegations against people or deciding how to conduct an enquiry just on the basis of a voice on the end of the telephone. Do you understand that?"

"Yes, I guess I do. I just didn't think it would be this complicated, that's all."

"It has to be a bit complicated, Elizabeth, these are serious matters we're dealing with here. But if we can arrange to see you it can be at a location of your choosing, somewhere public if you like, and I promise that you'll be free to go whenever you like."

"But you know who murdered my dad, don't you? I heard on the telly that you've already got him banged up."

"We have a suspect in custody on suspicion of murdering your father, yes. But that enquiry is ongoing; we have no wish to put an innocent man behind bars if there is fresh evidence out there that might clear him. But there's this other murder to consider now as well, and that's the one I sense you can help us with. Come on, Elizabeth, there's a young woman just been dug out of a back garden in Hampstead. Whoever she may be, don't you want to see her killer brought to justice?"

A pause again.

"All right, I'll agree to a meet."

"Great. When and where?"

"Do you know Berkeley Square?"

"Yes, of course. What time?"

"Be there at 3 o'clock. Sit on one of the benches."

"OK. How will I know you?"

"You won't. Tell me what you'll be wearing and I'll find you. But if I think anything is wrong – that it's a trick, like – then I'll just walk away and you'll never see me again. Understood?"

"OK, understood. Look, I'm just wearing a black trouser suit, so nothing very distinctive. But I'll bring another female officer with me. Hang on, I'm just looking across to see what she's wearing today. OK, good, she's wearing stockings that are a sort of light blue colour. That good enough for you?"

"OK."

"And, Elizabeth, if there's anything you can bring with you that will help to prove your identity, then please do, all right?"

By this time everyone in the incident room and fallen silent and was listening openly. As Desai replaced the receiver a ripple of relief and approval ran through the team.

"Do I understand we have a date?" Willis asked with a smile.

"Yes, just you and me. Berkeley Square at 3 o'clock."

"It's a good choice on her part," Metcalfe noted. "Completely open, and with easy exits on all sides. It won't be easy to mount any surveillance, particularly not at such short notice."

"Oh please don't, guv. I sense that she's really jumpy. If she spots anything at all she'll just slip away and then we may have lost her for ever. Let's just play it really straight and try to win her trust."

"I agree," Willis nodded.

"OK, then," Metcalfe conceded reluctantly. "It doesn't sound like we have much choice."

•

Willis and Desai arranged themselves on a bench in Berkeley Square a little before the appointed time. It seemed very quiet. The lunchtime rush of sandwich eating office workers was over, and it was coming on to rain a little, with a sudden chill in the air. Desai huddled into her scarf, while Willis buttoned up her raincoat, but then crossed her legs and made sure the bottom part of the coat felt open so that her stockings were prominently on display. Then they waited.

"You think that's her?" Desai asked.

Careful not to point, she nodded in the direction of the Bentley showroom, towards a nondescript woman with mousy hair.

"No, I don't think so. Look, she's just walked straight past the entrance."

"Yes, but that's the second time she's walked round the square, and I could have sworn that she was looking at you, clocking the blue stockings."

"They're not blue actually, they're lilac."

"Yeah all right, whatever. But I'm betting she carries on and turns into the next opening – that one over there by the traffic lights."

"I hope you're right. I'm getting chilly."

They both tensed and held their breath as the woman continued her progress. At the next entrance point she paused uncertainly but then came into the square and started walking around the path towards them. They both exhaled in silent relief, and watched her approach while trying not to make it obvious that they were doing so.

She stopped in front of them. She was clearly very nervous.

"Are you the coppers then?"

"Yes, I'm Priya Desai. We spoke on the phone. This is Karen Willis."

"I didn't know coppers dressed like that," she said, staring dubiously at Willis.

"Some of us do. Just because we're in plainclothes they don't have to be … well, plain."

"Why don't you sit down and we can chat?" Desai suggested.

The two of them moved apart and she sat down between them, moving stiffly and pressing both her arms and her legs together in front of her.

"I know this can't be easy for you," Desai said, "but we really need to hear everything you can tell us about what happened."

Without answering, the woman plucked at the clasp of her bag and extracted a Canadian passport, which she handed wordlessly to Desai. She opened it and gazed quizzically first at the photograph and then back at the woman. She passed it across her to Willis, who repeated the process and then nodded and placed it back in the woman's almost nerveless grasp.

"OK, so you're Elizabeth Schneider. Thank you. It's really helpful even to know just that. We were worried that you might have ended up in a flowerbed in Downshire Hill."

"No. Like I said, that was someone else."

"Do you know who?"

"No, I haven't the slightest idea."

"Did you know that someone was buried there?"

"I've only known for a little while. My mum told me just before she died."

"Do you know what happened?"

"Only that my dad killed her."

"And how do you know that, Elizabeth?" Desai asked, trying to sound calm despite her suddenly pounding heart.

"Because she saw him burying her, that's how."

CHAPTER 21

"So what happened then?" Collison asked.

"We made it very clear that she would need to come in and give a formal statement which she would have to sign," Willis explained, "but we didn't have any possible grounds for arresting her, so all we could do was try to persuade her. I think Priya did a really good job of that, by the way."

"What's your feeling, Priya?" Metcalfe enquired. "Will she come in?"

"I really don't know, guv, but I have to say yes. I reckon her motivation for coming forward was to see that someone knows the truth about her father. I don't see how she could be satisfied about that if we weren't able actually to use whatever she told us."

"Well, let's hope you're right," Collison said. "Wow, it's a real turnup for the books isn't it? We go public asking for help with a 20-year-old murder, only for our supposed victim to turn up in person very much alive."

"And making allegations against somebody else," Willis pointed out.

"You must be happy, guv," Metcalfe said with a grin. "According to Peter this means that your serial killer idea is still up and running."

"It's only one of several hypotheses, remember," Collison

said slightly defensively. "Actually, I'd have been very happy to be able to eliminate it. We seem to have altogether too many possible solutions already for my liking."

"Well, now that we know the corpse in the back garden wasn't Elizabeth Schneider, does that make it more likely that these two murders were connected I wonder?" Willis conjectured.

"I suppose that if they really were murderer and victim then a connection makes sense, though who on earth would be coming back to seek revenge 20 years later?"

"Somebody who's been in prison for a long time perhaps?" Desai suggested.

"How about somebody who's been a long way away – say, Canada?" Metcalfe countered. "If Taylor was the girl's killer then how about this for a hypothesis: Johann Schneider knew the girl, finds out at the same time as his sister that Taylor murdered her, and comes back to take revenge."

"Yes, that thought had occurred to me too," Collison agreed. "It might also make sense of Rowbotham's mystery caller: it could have been the brother asking whether the father still lived in the same house. Oh dear, yet another hypothesis to put on our list."

"It seems like everything is riding on Elizabeth Schneider," Willis observed. "If she has the guts to come in and make a formal statement we can ask her where we might be able to find her brother. If she doesn't, then we're whistling in the dark again."

Suddenly the phone on Collison's desk rang. They all tensed. At the beginning of the meeting, the phone system had been set to divert all calls for Desai to this number. Collison lifted the handset, listened for a moment, said "just a minute, please", and passed it to her.

"It's for you," he said softly. "A woman's voice."

"Hello," Desai began, but then, after a pause and more awkwardly, "oh, I'm sorry but I really can't talk right now. I'm in a meeting with my guvnor and I'm also expecting an important call ... Yes, later will be fine. I'll call you."

"Sorry, guv," she said, handing back the phone. "It was nothing."

Willis and Metcalfe glanced quickly at each other. They had never seen Desai flustered before, yet flustered she clearly was.

"No problem," Collison said. "Now, where are we with everything else, Bob?"

"We've pulled some files on girls – young women I should say really – who went missing around the same time and were never found. There were six of them, believe it or not, all in the space of a year or so. Ages range between 14 and 19. We've cast quite a wide net in terms of geography. Two of them lived right here in Hampstead – or close anyway – and the others were from Golders Green, Muswell Hill, West Hampstead, and Kentish Town."

"What about the two closest to home?"

"Susan Barnard, age 15, reported missing by her mother on a Sunday morning. She hadn't come home the previous night. Initially the mother wasn't worried as she sometimes slept over with a girlfriend from school on a Saturday if they'd been out somewhere together, but when she rang the next morning they said they hadn't seen her. There were the usual enquiries – school, friends, family – but no widescale search. The officers in charge took the view that it was probably just another young woman who had run off with a man somewhere, and that sooner or later she would get back in touch."

"But she never did?"

"No, she didn't. We mustn't be too critical I suppose. Resources were an issue back then just as they are now, and teenage girls do have a habit of disappearing and then turning up again."

"And the second?"

"Janet Winston, age 16, also reported missing by her mother. She went to school one morning but never came back. Enquiries revealed that she had never turned up for class that day. Since she was 16 and technically an adult, even less was done in her case than with Susan Barnard. Again, it was assumed that she'd run off with some man, but, like Susan, she was never heard of again."

"Any connection between the two, do you think?"

"There's nothing obvious from the file, guv. Susan Barnard was from a white middle-class family; her father worked for a bank in the City. Janet Winston was black and from a single-parent family; her mother was a nursing sister at the Royal Free. They went to different schools and would have had different daily journeys. There's no evidence that they knew each other."

"There is one thing I spotted when I went through the files," Willis proffered, "well, two actually."

"Yes?"

"Both girls were described by their mothers and their schoolmates as looking older than they really were, particularly when they got dressed up to go out. Also, in the case of Janet Winston she'd been arrested once on suspicion of prostitution. She was interviewed as a juvenile with a social worker present, but released for lack of evidence. For the record, she maintained her innocence; said it was all a mistake."

"Yeah, isn't it always?" Metcalfe asked cynically.

"Well there we are, anyway," Collison said. "I don't suppose there's anything convenient on file such as dental records or distinguishing features?"

"No such luck, guv. One thing, though. Tom Bellamy told me unofficially that he thought the victim was white, blonde, and about 15 or 16. So that would rule out Janet Winston. I'm hoping to have the formal post-mortem report tomorrow morning, by the way."

"Well, we shall see what we shall see," Collison mused. "I must say I'm a bit shocked that so many young women should have gone missing in such a short time in such a relatively small area. Are these numbers unusual, do we know?"

"Actually, I've been doing a bit of research on this recently," Metcalfe replied. "They are striking, but not necessarily completely unusual. A lot of young people go missing every year, particularly in large metropolitan areas. And a surprising number of them are never heard of again. But the fact that their bodies are never found suggests that a lot of them really do just want to run away, disappear, get away from troubles at home perhaps. Presumably they manage to assume a new identity."

"Much more difficult today though, wouldn't you say? How could you get work without a National Insurance number? Or open a bank account without a passport or driving licence? And how could you get a passport or driving licence without a birth certificate? And, as Raj found out to his cost, it's almost impossible to move around now without leaving some form of electronic footprint behind you."

"True. Shall I follow up on Susan Barnard? There's nothing in the file since the enquiry was closed down 20 years ago. It's always possible that she might have turned up some years later and nobody bothered to notify us."

"Yes, please do, Bob. It might be an idea to do the same thing with the other four as well, just in case. We need some DNA specimens from family members too."

"OK, I'll get some of the troops onto that straightaway."

"Diplomatically of course, Bob. We're going to have to reopen some old wounds here, so please let's tread carefully."

The phone rang again. Once more Collison listened and then passed it across to Desai.

"Hello, Elizabeth? Thank God, I'm so glad you called, I was really hoping you would. How are you? ... Yes, I know this must be very difficult for you, but we really need you to make a formal statement, like we said yesterday. We really can't do anything without it ... Yes, it can just be me and Karen again if you like, you don't have to see anybody else ... Well, we will have to tape record our interview ... Yes, and then later we'll need to see you again so you can sign your statement."

She listened intently and then put her hand over the mouthpiece and said "tomorrow morning all right?" to Collison, who nodded emphatically.

"Yes, Elizabeth, tomorrow morning will be fine. 10 o'clock? OK. Now, you know where we are, don't you? We're just on the corner of Downshire Hill. You must have walked past the police station many times when you were young. OK then, we'll see you tomorrow, and thank you again; I really appreciate this."

As she replaced the handset there was an audible sigh of relief from the others.

"Let's hope she doesn't get cold feet at the last minute," Metcalfe said.

"I think she'll be okay, guv. She sounded quite calm; not as twitchy as she was yesterday."

"I think it's right that it should be just you and Karen who see her," Collison said. "You've clearly built up some sort of rapport with her and we don't want to do anything which might alarm her. But I think we need to plan this interview very carefully. Let's draft a list of the points we need to raise and then you can use that as a checklist tomorrow morning."

He pulled a pad towards himself and started jotting items down as they occurred to him.

"Feel free to throw out your own suggestions, anyone, but it seems to me we need the following. First and most importantly, exactly what did her mother tell her before she died? Exactly what did she see and how was she able to see it? It was night, remember. Was there a full moon? Was a light on, or was a torch being used? We need to know."

"It's a long shot," Metcalfe interjected, "but we should also ask if she has any idea at all who our victim might be. If she didn't, then it's unlikely the brother did either."

"Yes, and what about the brother?" Collison enquired. "Did they come back from Canada together? If so, where is he now and how can we get in touch with him? And what's he been doing all this time? He must be in his mid-30s by now. Does he have a job? Has he been in any trouble with the police?"

"I've got an enquiry out to the police in Canada," Willis commented. "I'm waiting to hear back from them."

"Good. Now, what else? Exactly what can she remember about the disappearance from Wentworth House? Whose idea was it? And why did they just up sticks and leave at a moment's notice, for goodness sake? If the mother has only told them the truth recently, then what did she tell them at the time?"

His pen paused as he glanced around the room for inspiration.

"Anything else?"

"It would be good to see if she can remember anything about her brother's time at school. In particular, can she corroborate anything we were told by Colin McKenzie?" Desai suggested.

"Yes, good, thank you, Priya. I'd be very interested to know that myself."

"There's something else," Willis said, "something quite fundamental I think. What can she tell us about the man we know as Conrad Taylor? Why should somebody who seems to have been a normal law abiding person suddenly murder a helpless girl? It doesn't make sense. But if anyone can tell us, then she should be able to. After all, the father /daughter relationship is a very special one."

CHAPTER 22

"Now then, Elizabeth," Desai said, "why don't you start by telling us about how you, your mother, and your brother came to leave Wentworth House?"

Elizabeth Schneider gazed at the blinking light on the tape recorder. It seemed to unnerve her somehow. Desai smiled and nodded encouragement.

"Well, at the time we didn't know anything about it – John and me that is – it was only later when we found out, much later."

"What can you remember about that time?"

Elizabeth stared blankly straight ahead, as if reliving the events in question.

"Mum came into my bedroom during the night. She was trying to be quiet but she woke me up as she opened the door. I said "what's wrong?" or something like that. She knelt down beside my bed and told me that we needed to pack very quietly when we got up in the morning, just a few things which we could carry on a bag, and that we were going away on an adventure."

"Didn't that seem a bit strange? Coming out of the blue like that?"

"Yeah, of course it did. I asked what was going on but she just repeated that we needed to get away. You have to understand that she was always a bit strange, my mum. She'd often come out with stuff like that, needing to get away and so forth. I think the truth is that she and my dad hadn't had much of a marriage for quite a long time. They slept in separate rooms, you know. I guess I just went back to sleep and assumed that by the morning she'd have forgotten all about it. She often used to wander around the house talking to herself. My mates at school used to think she was really peculiar."

"But she didn't – forget about it I mean?"

"No. She came back into the room once it was light and went mental that I hadn't packed anything. She started throwing things in a bag for me and kept saying that we needed to get away. But she was speaking very quietly, and when I asked her why, she said she didn't want dad to hear. So I said "isn't dad coming with us?" or something like that, and she said no, he was staying but we had to go right away without saying goodbye to him."

"And again, didn't that seem a bit strange?"

"Yeah, in fact I tried to sneak along the landing to his room but she saw me and belted me round the ear. I'll never forget the look on her face that morning. She was like a wild animal that's being hunted. She hissed in my ear that if I wasn't ready to go in 10 minutes she'd drag me out of the house in just what I was wearing, and with an empty bag if necessary. Then she pretty much threw me back into my room, and went off to get John."

"So presumably she'd had the same conversation with him already?"

"Yeah, and it was strange because normally they'd be going at each other hammer and tongs, but that morning he was real quiet. He just looked at me and told me to do what mum said. I found out later that he thought dad had died during the night and that mum was trying to get us all out of the house without knowing about it."

"So you all just left – just like that?"

"Yeah, that's about it. I can remember walking up the path and looking back at the house over my shoulder, but then mum grabbed me and pulled me through the gate. We went up the road – past this police station of course – and down to Belsize Park tube station."

"Where did you go?"

"I don't remember exactly. It was somewhere in West London: Hammersmith maybe? Mum checked us into a little hotel and told us to stay there while she went off to make some calls. John and I watched telly for a few hours and then when she came back she told us we were going off on a trip to a cousin of hers who lived in Canada. By this time John had told me he thought dad was dead. Naturally, I was upset, but when mum asked what was wrong with me he shook his head at me behind her back and I just said nothing was wrong."

"And did you go to Canada straightaway?"

"Yeah, we went to the airport and got on a plane and that was it. Next thing I knew we were in Canada. We landed in Toronto but it turned out aunt Molly lived in a place called London. Funny that, we thought."

"So your mother had taken your passports with her when you all left the house?"

"Yeah, though to be honest I'm not sure I had a passport of my own that stage; I might just have been on mum's."

"So you all made a new life in Canada?"

"Yeah. We went to school there, and then to college. John dropped out of college almost at once and went off to work in a garage, but he kept getting into trouble and never held onto a job for very long. Eventually he found a job in a hardware store. It was being run by a widow whose husband had just died, and she needed a man to do all the heavy lifting. I think she was sweet on John. I used to joke that he was ... you know, having sex with her."

"And you think he was – really?"

She shrugged.

"Who knows? Probably, yeah. He's obsessed with sex, you know. Oh, I know all men are, but I mean really, really obsessed. I can't imagine him ever saying no."

"Now you told us earlier that your mother died quite recently, but that before she did so she told you something about the night you left home. Could you tell us about that again, for the tape?"

"Mum died about a year ago. She'd been ill for some time. Finally they told her it was cancer and there was nothing they could do. So she had about three months at the end when she knew she was dying. I'd gone through college and qualified as a nurse and I was working at the local hospital, but once she had her diagnosis I gave up work and stayed at home to look after her. There was one afternoon when John was there too, and she said she had something to tell us; something important."

She stopped and took a sip of water. Again, Desai nodded encouragingly.

"She just came straight out with it. She said that night she'd been looking out of her bedroom window. There was bright moonlight and she could clearly see someone digging in the back garden of the house next door. Obviously she thought this was a bit funny, someone digging in the garden at 1 o'clock in the morning. So she looked a bit more closely and realised it was dad. Then she saw him put the shovel down, turn around, and pick up a body."

"Was she absolutely sure that's what it was?"

"I asked her that as well. She said yes, she was absolutely certain it was a body. She could see the legs hanging down from dad's arms. Bare legs, she said, and very pale in the moonlight. He put it in the hole he had dug and started filling in the Earth on top of it. She waited for him to come in and go to bed. Then, once she heard him start snoring, she came to our rooms and told us we had to leave."

"And how did you take the news? You must have been deeply shocked."

"John was really quiet and just went out of the room. Then I heard the front door close as he left the house. I didn't know what to think. I wanted to be glad that dad was alive after all, or at least that he might still be alive. But then there was what mum had said she saw, which meant he was a murderer. Nothing seemed to make sense. It still doesn't."

"What did you do then?"

"Nothing at first. I decided to concentrate on looking after mum in her final weeks. I tried to talk to John about it, but he was just really strange and silent. Then, once mum had gone, we decided that we'd both come to England and see if we could find dad. Confront him, John said. Me, I wasn't so sure. After all, we hadn't seen him for 20 years. Suppose he didn't want to see us? Suppose he just wouldn't talk to us? What were we going to do then? Come to you guys with some stupid story about something our mum said she'd seen 20 years ago?"

"But you did come?"

"Yes. It took time. We didn't have any money, John or me, so we had to wait for the lawyer to settle mum's affairs. There wasn't much money left over after all his fees, but it was enough. It gave us the few thousand dollars we needed to buy plane tickets and book somewhere to stay for a while."

"How did you end up having Canadian passport by the way?"

"I'm not sure, though I expect the lawyer could explain it. There was some sort of rule that if you'd lived in Canada with relatives for certain number of years you were eligible for citizenship. Mum arranged it all. It was never really an issue actually, because we'd neither of us ever wanted to travel before."

"So you came here together? What happened then?"

"I was getting more and more nervous, to be honest. I really wasn't sure that I wanted to see dad again. I mean, how can you see your father for the first time in decades and ask him straight out if it's true he's a murderer? But John went over to the house to have it out with him. He went a couple of times and banged on the door but couldn't get any answer.

The second time, he went next door and spoke to one of the neighbours. This guy told him that dad still lived there. So John said he'd go back again, but he never did."

"Why was that?"

"John is what they call bipolar. Sometimes he's very up, but a lot of the time he's very down, and those times are pretty bad. He usually just lies in bed facing the wall and won't talk to anybody. This would have been a week or two after we arrived in Britain, and John had run out of his medication. I went to a big chemist near Marble Arch and tried to explain what I needed, but they said we had to see a doctor and get a prescription. That was a problem, of course, because we weren't registered with a doctor here. It took me a few weeks to sort the problem out. It was only a couple of days ago that I finally managed to get a doctor to come and see him and prescribe what he wanted."

"So John never went back to the house after that last time when he saw the neighbour?"

"No, not so far as I know. That's when he got bad, like I said."

"So you know where he is now?"

"Sure I do. He's back at the hotel where we've been living. To tell the truth, I've been at my wits end these last few days. You see, our money's about to run out. I guess we can't get jobs here without British papers and so far as the law is concerned we seem to be Canadian now."

"Elizabeth, we really need to see John and ask him some questions. Is he well enough to be interviewed, do you think?"

"I really don't know. He's been very bad this time, what

with being without his pills and everything. What do you need to ask him about? Can't you ask me instead?"

"We are very grateful for any help you can give us about anything at all, but we will need to speak to John as well, if only to corroborate what you're saying."

"I'd really rather not involve him if at all possible. He doesn't like the police and he can get very aggressive. If you don't really understand him, the way he thinks, you might get the wrong impression."

"Does that mean he's been in trouble with the police – perhaps back in Canada?"

"Yeah, and not just in Canada. There was something that happened before we left here."

"Yes, I think we know about that, although we'd be very interested to hear your take on it."

"It was just some stupid dare between him and some of his mates at school. They had to run out into the street when a woman was passing, touch her up, and then run off again. It was all supposed to be just a bit of fun. But some of the women overreacted and went to the police. Of course the police had to be seen to do something, so they turned up in the school and started making trouble for John. In the end nothing happened, he was in the clear."

"Just so you know," Desai said, struggling to keep her voice calm, "some of those women were very badly affected by what your brother did to them. Also, he wasn't cleared. I'm afraid that some of my colleagues back then messed up the ID parade so they couldn't proceed against John. But what he did was completely unacceptable, and I have to say I'm surprised that you, as a woman, should treat it so flippantly."

Willis frowned; that had been clumsy. She saw a look of shock and then anger flit across Elizabeth Schneider's face. Fearing that she might simply get up and leave, Willis glanced meaningfully at Desai and cut in quickly.

"Elizabeth, I apologise for asking you this out of the blue, but have you ever heard of a girl called Susan Barnard?"

She stared at Willis.

"Sue? Christ, that's all a very long time ago. What's she got to do with any of this?"

"So you do know her? Or at least, used to?"

"Yes of course. We used to go to the same school. Why?"

Willis and Desai looked at each other and then back at Elizabeth.

"Susan Barnard was reported missing by her mother at much the same time as the three of you left Wentworth House," Willis informed her. "The same day, in fact."

She stared at them blankly.

"Missing?"

"Yes, and she's never been found."

Again she stared, as though struggling to comprehend what they were telling her.

"Elizabeth," Desai asked, "did John know Susan too?"

"Yes, of course he did," she said faintly. "She was his girlfriend."

CHAPTER 23

"So what can you tell us about Susan Barnard?" Desai asked after a significant pause.

"Not a lot really. We weren't in the same form you see, not even in the same year. She was older than me. She went round with two or three girls who used to go and mess about with John and his mates after school."

"Yes, we've heard a little about that, but why don't you tell us whatever you can remember?"

She shrugged.

"There's not much to tell. It was just silly kid's stuff really. John was bigger than most of the guys at school; stronger too. So the boys used to be a bit scared of him and either avoided him altogether or tried to be big mates with him. As for the girls, most of them fancied him, though they pretended they didn't. After school John and some of the others from his class used to hang around behind the shops in Belsize Park. Some of the girls used to go home that way. They didn't have to, they could have got the bus from out on the main road. So if they went that way it was because they chose to. They wanted to mess around with the boys."

"What you mean by 'mess around' exactly?"

"Well I don't know for sure because I never went that way myself, but nothing very much I expect. I used to hear some of the girls talking about it, and it sounded like the boys would sort of block their way and the girls would have to kiss them to get past. We were pretty innocent back then, you know. Things were different. Most of us had no real idea what sex was."

"But what about John? Was he innocent too?"

"It was always difficult to tell with him because he was always telling stories and you never knew whether to believe him or not. For example, he used to call Sue his girlfriend, but I'm not sure anything actually ... happened between them, know what I mean?"

"Are you sure about that? We have a witness who used to watch what went on in that service road and he seemed to think that John knew exactly what he was doing. In his words, John used to have his hands all over the girls."

"Oh, he used to feel them up, yes. But all the boys did. Sooner or later they'd all put their hand up your skirt if they got a chance. But Susan was different, I think. A lot of the girls used to talk about her. They used to say she was a tease and a bit of a tart, always leading the boys on."

"We understand that John used to protect Susan from the other boys, wouldn't let any of them touch her, that sort of thing."

"Yeah, I think that's right. I seem to remember there was some sort of fight one day, but it wouldn't surprise me if it was Susan who caused it. The last thing she needed was to be protected from the boys. More like the other way round, I'd say."

"Apart from that fight he got into – and we understand he

broke the other boy's nose by the way – can you think of any other examples of violent behaviour by John?"

Elizabeth took in a quick breath and stared at them one after another.

"Here, what's all this about? You surely don't suspect John of anything, do you? He's been in Canada for the last 20 years."

"We're just trying to build up as full a picture as possible," Willis cut in smoothly. "Every little bit of background helps us understand the context."

"Well, I'm not telling you any more about John. If you have any questions about him then you can ask him yourselves."

"So you will then let us see him then?"

Elizabeth hesitated, running one hand nervously up and down the other arm.

"Like I said, he's not well."

"But you said that he's back on his medication now. So surely he'll be on the mend, won't he?"

"Maybe. I don't know."

"Elizabeth, you've been doing really well, and we are incredibly grateful to you for all your help, but this is a murder enquiry and we have to speak to anybody who may be able to tell us anything – anything at all – that might just be relevant. Surely you can understand that?"

"Yes, I suppose so. All right then, you can see him tomorrow, but not here. Like I said, he's not good with the police. You'd better come to the hotel. It's the Palmerston in Earls Court."

"Okay, thank you. Would 10 o'clock be all right?"

"Yeah, that would be fine."

"All right, thank you, in that case I think we can call it a day. But we may need to speak to you again once we've had a chance to interview John. So please don't go away anywhere without telling us, OK?"

•

The team sat and looked at each other in the incident room as Desai finished her report of the interview.

"By way of an update," Metcalfe said during the pause, "we now have a DNA match. Our victim in the back garden is indeed Susan Barnard."

Collison nodded, and then asked "thoughts?"

"Should we put John Schneider under surveillance, guv?" Evans suggested. "We know he's been in trouble with the police before, and there's always the chance he might do a runner when the sister tells him we want to see him."

"It's a good question, Timothy. Bob, what do you reckon?"

"It can't do any harm, sir. After all it's only until tomorrow morning."

"Very well. You organise that, will you?"

"Right you are, guv."

"Now in terms of other enquiries which may be suggested by the interview with Elizabeth," Collison went on, "it seems to me that we really need to find someone who knows the full story about Susan Barnard. Of course we can ask the parents, but I fancy they've already told us everything they know, and I'm reluctant to put them through it again."

"Excuse me, sir," Desai said, "but if Susan Barnard was getting up to things with boys then she's most unlikely to have told her mother about it anyway. I think what we need is one of Susan schoolfriends, somebody who knew her well, somebody in whom she might have confided."

"Right," Godwin agreed.

"Very well then. Let's think about how we might be able to do that. Bob, why don't you see if we can get hold of the class list for Susan Barnard's last year at school, and we can try to trace any of the girls from that."

"We can try," Metcalfe replied dubiously, "but it won't be easy. Most of them will have changed their names at least once since then."

"Well then, let's see if we can find the form teacher. They may know what's happened to some of the class. You never know, they might even have stayed in touch with one or two of them. But somehow, we have to find someone who can tell us what Susan Barnard might have been doing during the last few days of her life. Schoolgirls don't just end up buried in flowerbeds for no good reason."

"On a different point, guv," Willis said, "we could get a photo of John Schneider and see if Rowbotham recognises him as the mystery caller."

"No," Collison said slowly, "I don't think I want to do that. I'd rather keep alive the chance of a formal ID parade, just in case we need it."

"But we know now that it was Conrad Taylor who killed Susan Barnard, don't we?" Evans asked, sounding confused. "Which means that John Schneider can't be a suspect for the first murder."

"No, but he could still be a suspect for the second,"

Collison replied. "Granted we don't know the exact date of Taylor's death, but it seems almost certain that the Schneider brother and sister were back in the country by the time it happened."

"But if Schneider was the mystery caller," Evans persisted, "then doesn't that mean that he hadn't managed to get to see his father? In which case, how could he have murdered him?"

"Well, put it this way, Timothy. If you had managed to gain access to someone's house and murder them, might you not then go round to the neighbour and say you haven't been able to get in?"

"Yes, of course. Sorry, guv," Evans said, abashed.

"Don't be sorry, Timothy. These are good points and we should never be afraid to question what we're doing."

Collison looked around the room.

"Anybody have any other suggestions? No? All right then, so we interview John Schneider tomorrow morning, we concentrate on finding someone who knew Susan Barnard – knew her well – and we bring that person in for questioning. OK, Bob, carry on please, and when you have a moment, can you pop upstairs?"

•

"Was there something, guv?"

"Yes, shut the door please, Bob. Now, come and sit down. Listen, I had Philip Newby on the phone earlier, but I couldn't say anything in front of the others. There's been a bit of a development."

"Yes?"

"News from Singapore. The police there are pretty certain

that the passport gang dispatched somebody to the UK to take care of Raj. Nothing specific, and we don't know exactly when. But we do know they were prepared to murder that other informant."

"So that means that someone may have turned up at Wentworth House intending to eliminate Raj – some sort of professional killer presumably – and ended up killing Taylor instead?"

"Exactly. Either because Taylor disturbed him, or maybe to put the frighteners on Raj, or maybe deliberately to implicate him as a murder suspect."

"There was no sign of a forced entry. Would Taylor have let this person in? We know he hated visitors."

"I thought about that, and I popped down the road to have a look at the front door myself. It's a standard Yale lock with no security flap or anything. I managed to open it myself with a strip of plastic, and I'm no professional housebreaker. So access would not necessarily have been an issue."

"Then I guess we have yet another working hypothesis to consider."

"Yes, it looks like it, doesn't it?"

"So what we do – to follow this up, I mean?"

"Nothing at all. We can't, you see, without breaching security to the rest of the team. Special Branch are going to follow this up themselves. They will let us know if they come across anything relevant to our enquiry."

"Well, good luck to them. It sounds like looking for a needle in a haystack. One person in a city the size of London?

When you have no idea what they're called, where they live, or what they look like?"

"Actually, they do have a specific suspect."

"They do?"

"Yes. Oh God, Bob, this is damned awkward. They're taking a look at that translator woman, Sophie Ho."

"Really? Well, OK, but how is that awkward? We never actually got her involved in the case, did we? We didn't need to. So what's the problem?"

"I have to tell you this, Bob, because we're the only two people inside the Chinese wall, but don't for God's sake mention this to anybody else, because it bears directly on the private life of a member of the team, and I'm desperate not to infringe on that whatever happens."

"A member of the team? Who?"

"Priya Desai. You see, it turns out that the Branch have had Sophie Ho under discreet surveillance for a while now. Well – and now you'll understand just how awkward this is – it seems that Priya and Sophie have been going out together."

"Well, that's OK, isn't it? So they meet up for a drink now and then, so what? Oh, wait a minute, surely you don't mean ..."

Collison got up and strode to the window, staring out at the street beyond.

"Yes, I do mean that," he said without turning around. "The Branch are convinced that Priya and this woman are *really* going out together: that they're having a relationship. Apparently Priya has stayed overnight at Sophie Ho's flat."

"Wow! I would never have thought ... well, you know."

"Yes, I know what you mean. It came as a shock to me too, though thinking about it I'm not sure why. Perhaps I've allowed myself to succumb to those ridiculous male stereotypical images of gay women. I hope not, but if so then I'm ashamed of myself."

"Well look," Metcalfe replied, floundering for something sensible to say, "Special Branch are a suspicious bunch, we all know that. They've probably picked on this poor woman just because she seems an obvious link with Singapore. As soon as they look into her more deeply I'm sure they'll realise they've made a mistake. After all, she's a translator, isn't she? Not a contract killer."

"That's the worst of it I'm afraid, Bob. Singapore is a very regulated environment. One of those regulations requires you to register with the police once you reach a certain standard in any martial art. It turns out that Sophie Ho is a second dan in karate."

CHAPTER 24

As Desai and Willis arrived outside the front door of the Palmerston hotel they hesitated. Desai glanced at her watch.

"It's only 9:45," she said. "What you want to do?"

"Why don't we go and sit with Timothy?" Willis suggested. "He's over there in the coffee shop – look."

Desai followed her glance and saw Evans, once again struggling not to look like a plainclothes policeman. She frowned, and then sighed in resignation.

"Oh, all right. If we have to."

They crossed the road and sat one on either side of Evans, who was perched on a stool looking out onto the street.

"Is he still in there?" Willis enquired.

"Well, I came on at six, Sarge, and he hasn't come out since I've been here. I haven't seen either of them."

"Good. Now, do we have time for a quick coffee?"

As she spoke her phone started ringing inside her bag.

"I'll get them," Priya said, and headed towards the counter while Willis fished out her phone and answered it.

It was Metcalfe.

"Karen? I'm glad I caught you. Listen, we've had a report in overnight from the police in London – London, Ontario, that is – and there's something you ought to know, both of you. They've had five or six unexplained disappearances of girls around the age 15 to 16 in the last 10 years or so. They've said straight out that they think they may have a serial killer on the loose."

"And is Schneider a suspect?"

"No, they don't have any suspects. But they've indicated that they would be eager to interview him should we end up being able to link him to the Barnard murder."

"Are there any similarities?"

"Well, the Barnard post-mortem report – which also came in this morning – says her hyoid bone was broken, so she was almost certainly strangled. The bodies they've found over there were strangled too. Other than that, there's nothing obvious."

"OK. Thanks, Bob. We're in a coffee shop over the road from the hotel and we're heading over there in a few minutes."

"Please be careful, Karen. I don't like the idea of you and Priya cooped up with him in a small hotel room. I think you should try to persuade him to go somewhere else: the coffee shop maybe. I'd be happier to know that you were somewhere public."

"Yes, I think so too. Don't worry anyway, Bob. We can look after ourselves."

Desai was by now waiting for the drinks at the end of the counter, and Willis went over and passed on the news. When the drinks arrived they headed back to Evans.

"Wow," he said when Willis told him what Metcalfe had told her. "So are we going to pick him up and take him back to the nick?"

"We can't do that unless he consents," Willis said at once.

"We've got no grounds at all to arrest him. And, by the way, from what Elizabeth said yesterday he's not likely to agree to come with us voluntarily. No, I think the best thing we can do is try to persuade him to come over here. At least that way we'll have you lurking in the background as backup."

Desai muttered something which sounded suspiciously like "huh".

"Hold-up, Sarge," her backup said suddenly. "Isn't that the Schneider girl? There, by the front door?"

The two women stared across the road. Elizabeth Schneider was standing in the doorway of the hotel looking around nervously.

"Yes, it is," Desai said. "I think she's looking for us. Come on, we'd better go."

Leaving their drinks behind, they darted across the road. Elizabeth saw them coming and took a few steps towards them as they arrived.

"Thank goodness you're here. Look, I told him you were coming and he didn't like it a bit. He had a real go at me about coming forward like I did. He really hates having anything to do with the police. He wanted to leave the hotel last night and not come back. I had a hell of a job getting him to stay."

Desai and Willis glanced at each other. So the surveillance had been a good idea after all.

"How is he now?" Willis asked.

"He's in one of his angry moods. Is there any way we could put this off? Do it another day?"

Willis shook her head determinedly.

"No, I'm sorry. We absolutely have to see him. If he won't

215

see as voluntarily then we may have to consider taking him into custody."

She waited anxiously. Would the woman know she was bluffing?

"No, don't do that. All right then, you can come upstairs with me. But please try not to upset him, will you?"

"Perhaps he'd be happier meeting outside the hotel?" Willis asked as she followed Elizabeth up the grubby stairs of what was really quite a seedy establishment, even by the standards of Earls Court.

"Where?"

"Oh, I don't know. What about that coffee shop across the road? We were just in there ourselves and it seems quite nice."

"That might work. He likes coffee – real coffee, I mean."

They came to a door and stopped. Elizabeth Schneider rapped on it quickly and then opened it with her key. She stepped back to allow the officers to go in.

"No, you go first," Desai said.

They moved in after her. The room was very small, uncomfortably so with four people crowded into it, one of whom was glowering angrily.

"Hello," Willis said calmly, "you must be Johann, or is it John? I'm very glad you felt able to speak to us. I'm Karen Willis and this is Priya Desai."

"And you're both cops?" the man asked antagonistically, his Canadian accident much more pronounced than his sister's.

"Yes, we're both Detective Sergeants, and we are

investigating the murder of a man we believe to have been your father, Conrad Taylor."

"I can't help you with that. I never saw my father again after we left Hampstead and went to Canada."

"Well, there's always the chance that you might be to help us with some background, and anyway we're also investigating the death of a young woman who was found in the garden of the house next door. From what your sister told us yesterday, we think you knew her. Her name was Susan Barnard."

He glanced at Elizabeth. Willis wondered how much she had told him.

"I knew her, yeah."

"Look," Willis said, "we can't really talk in here, can we? It's much too small. Why don't you let us take you over the road and buy you a nice cup of coffee?"

To their relief, he agreed at once.

"Sure," he said, picking up his jacket from the bed, "I'm always ready for a cup of Joe."

"I'll lead the way, shall I?" Willis suggested.

Desai fell in carefully behind him as he followed Willis out of the door. Elizabeth came in her turn, locking the door behind her.

"Is your room the same size as that?" Desai enquired as they went downstairs.

"That is my room. We're sharing it."

Desai said nothing, but concentrated on maintaining a space between herself and the man ahead of. She needed time within which to react should he suddenly try something. However, he seemed quite docile as they crossed the road together and went back into the coffee shop. Fortuitously, a large seating area around a corner table came free as they entered, and they headed across to it. Desai took the orders and went to the counter for the second time. If the staff found this strange, they didn't show it.

"So," Willis said when they finally had drinks in front of them, "why don't you tell us what you can remember about the day you left home with your mum and your sister?"

"My mum was a nutter," he said tersely, hunched over his cup of coffee and holding it with both hands.

He tried taking a sip but it was clearly too hot to drink. He put it down on the table and gazed into it reflectively, perhaps considering his last remark further.

"By which I mean," he went on, "that she was almost certainly mad. She was always getting angry about nothing at all, frequently stuff that it turned out she'd just imagined. My dad used to get it really bad. She couldn't be in the room with him for more than a few seconds before she'd start on at him about something or other. The last few years before we left he kept as far away from her as he could. Can't say I blame him, either."

"So you didn't get on well with your mother?"

"Hardly, no. We had regular shouting matches. But then I don't think she'd have been able to live with anybody. Our aunt in Canada sure regretted having agreed to letting us live there. But she was stuck with it, I guess."

"So what happened that day?"

"Hasn't my sister told you already? Mum just started running around saying that we had to leave, and straightaway.

I thought it was just another of her spells – you know imagining something and getting upset about it – but there was something different about it somehow. Something that made me think she was really serious. Straightaway I thought that maybe dad had died during the night. I don't know why, I just did. It was about the only thing that would make sense of mum being so upset. She was very protective of us, you know – or at least, she tried to be – and she certainly wouldn't have wanted us to see him dead in the house."

He tried his coffee again but it was still too hot.

"So I guessed that she wanted to get us all out of the house for a day or two while she arranged everything to be sorted out. It wasn't until she told us we were going off to Canada that I realised we wouldn't be going straight home again."

"And did that confuse you?"

"Sure it did. But I was sort of excited too. You know, the idea of going to Canada. Again, I thought it would just be for a short while, just a visit to my aunt. It wasn't until we got there that mum sprang the news that we wouldn't be coming back. Then we just sort of gradually got used to life there. We both got into local schools. I didn't like it very much, but then I never liked school anyway."

"Talking of school, tell us a little bit about Susan Barnard. Was she your girlfriend?"

"Sure she was. I was crazy about her. All the other boys had the hots for her, but I made sure none of them touched her. I guess I was sort of her protector."

"Did she need one?"

He scowled, and it was as if a cloud had suddenly crossed his face.

"Course she did. She was a girl, wasn't she? A pretty hot girl too, in a school full of boys."

"We heard that she didn't mind the attention of boys," Willis said innocently. "Not at all, in fact. Didn't she like being found attractive?"

"Maybe. But nobody touched her at school, that's for sure. They knew they'd have to reckon with me."

"Yes, we know. Didn't you once break somebody's nose?"

"Yeah, but he had it coming."

"Why's that, John?"

"We were behind the shops one day. We used to mess around there after school. Have a cigarette before we went home, that sort of thing. Sue started making up to one of my mates, telling him he had nice eyes, that sort of thing. I told him to leave her alone, but he wouldn't listen. So I hit him. Just once, but hard like."

"But you say that Sue was flirting with him, not the other way round. So why didn't you tell her to stop?"

"I did, but she wouldn't. Maybe she thought I wasn't serious. Well, she soon saw I was when I hit him. He went flying, and there was blood all over the place. When he got up he was crying like a baby. Gave her a nasty turn, I'll bet."

"What happened then?"

"I dunno. He went off with some of his mates. To the hospital, I reckon. I heard later he'd broken his nose. The police came to see him, but he wouldn't tell them anything. Scared of me, I guess. Sue was really pissed with me. She went off without saying anything, but I could tell she was mad as hell. Spoiled her fun, I did, see?"

"Did you know that she was reported missing the same day you left home?"

"No, I didn't."

"Did you make any effort to contact her after you went to Canada? Write to her, perhaps?"

"No, not me. Why should I? There were plenty of girls in Canada."

He tried his coffee again, and this time managed a few sips. Willis and Desai gazed at him thoughtfully, and then at each other.

CHAPTER 25

"So when did you last see Susan Barnard?" Desai asked, after taking a measured sip of coffee.

"I can't remember exactly. I saw her most days, most school days that is, so I guess maybe the day before we left."

"We may be able to help you there. We've found a record of the three of you leaving the country, and counting backwards from there according to what both you and your sister remember, we think your last day in the house would have been 26th October. That was the day before Sue was reported missing."

"OK, if you say so."

"Well, 26 October was a Saturday that year so it wasn't a school day, but the Friday would have been. Now I don't want to put words into your mouth, but maybe the last day you saw her was Friday the 25th?"

"Yeah, that would be right. Like I said, we used to see each other most days after school in that little road behind the shops."

"Did you ever walk her home at all? And, if so, can you remember whether you did that evening?"

"No, I'm pretty certain I didn't. It was starting to get dark and she said she was meeting one of her friends. I think they were going somewhere the next day, and they needed to talk about it."

"Can you remember where they were supposed to be going the next day? And can you remember the name of this friend of hers?"

"No, but it probably involved shopping. Very keen on shopping, Sue was. Always buying new clothes, new bags, new shoes, that sort of thing."

"Really? Were her parents very wealthy then?"

"I don't know. I never asked. They lived in quite a big house though, so I suppose so."

"And what about the name of the friend?"

"Well her best friend was a girl in her class called Jill. Wait a minute ... yeah, Jill East it was. She wasn't as tasty as Sue, but she wasn't bad. Great legs, she had." "

That's useful, thank you. Do you have any idea what happened to her, whether she got married, moved away, that sort of thing?"

"No, I don't."

"And that last time you saw her, Sue I mean, she didn't mention the name of anyone else she was due to meet – maybe a man? Or anything specific that she was planning to do over the weekend?"

"No, not that I can remember."

"John, I'm sorry to have to ask you this, but we have a witness who says that he saw a girl we believe to have been Sue hanging around in the street a few times and calling out to men. Do you know anything about that?"

"What you mean: 'calling out'?"

"Well, you know, he got the impression that it was sort of leading up to her offering them sex, presumably for money. Do you think that's where she might have got the money for all that shopping she did?"

"You saying she was a tart or something?"

"I'm not saying she was anything. I'm just passing on something we've been told and asking for your reaction to it. If you don't know anything about it, then fine."

The man glared at Desai.

"For your information, not that it's any of your business, Sue wouldn't even have sex with me and I was her boyfriend. So she's hardly likely to have been having it with anyone else."

"Let's move on, shall we?" Willis suggested. "Why don't you tell us what happened when you and your sister here came back to England?"

"Hasn't she told you that already?"

"She explained that you were looking to confront your father about what your mother told you," Willis replied glancing at Elizabeth, "and that's understandable. But what actually happened? You went to the house, presumably?"

"Yeah, I went to the house. There was no answer. The house looked in a really shitty condition, so I thought maybe it was empty and nobody was living there. I went round to the house next door. I didn't recognise the guy there, didn't remember him. I asked if my father still lived at Wentworth House and he said yes. So I decided to come back another day. But then I ... I got sick. I have these bad spells, you know."

"Yes, I know. I'm sorry. Just to be clear, John, did you use those exact words when you spoke to the neighbour?"

"Which words?"

"My father."

"I think I asked if Conrad Schneider still lived next door. I didn't know then that he'd changed his name to Taylor. The guy looked a bit shifty and asked me why I wanted to know. Maybe he thought I was a burglar or something. So I said I was Conrad's son."

"Are you sure about that?"

"Yeah, why wouldn't I be?"

"No reason I suppose. Look, John, I really appreciate you talking to us like this but we need to get a formal statement from you. We need to get it down on tape, then we need to get it typed up and signed by you. Will you help us do that?"

"I don't like police stations. They don't bring back good memories for me."

"I don't know what happened to you before, but you'd just be a visitor. We won't go anywhere near the cells. The interview rooms are on a different side of the building."

He shook his head stubbornly. Desai and Willis looked at each other, uncertain how best to proceed.

"John dear," Elizabeth interjected, laying her hand on his arm, "it would just be for an hour or two and then it will all be over and we can get on with our lives. Please won't you do it? For me?"

There was a silence while the three women all gazed at him.

"You won't be under arrest," Willis explained. "You'll be free to leave whatever you want. You just have to say the word."

He gazed at the table and said nothing, but then he nodded.

"Maybe tomorrow," he said.

"Tomorrow would be fine," Willis replied. Then, taking a deep breath, "look, I really hate to ask you this, but I'd like you to leave your passport with us. You too, Elizabeth. You can have them back when you come to the police station tomorrow."

John Schneider started to stand up angrily. Out of the corner of her eye Willis saw Evans slip off his stool and take a few steps towards them.

"John! Please!" Elizabeth said urgently.

He paused, uncomfortably bent over the table in the act of standing up. Then he swore under his breath and sat down again. Evans halted uncertainly, almost in mid-stride.

"Go ahead if you want," Schneider muttered.

Elizabeth fished inside her bag and handed over two Canadian passports.

"Thank you," Willis said in relief.

She glanced across at Evans and gave a small but definite shake of the head.

•

At much the same time, Simon Collison was fielding a phone call from Special Branch.

"Simon? It's Philip Newby. Listen, it's not looking good with Sophie Ho. I think we're going to have to pull her in for a formal interview. I'd like to ask her for a DNA sample as well, just in case it matches anything turned up at the murder scene."

"Have there been any developments that I don't know about, sir?"

"Yes, our friends in Singapore have been doing a little more digging and they've turned up two things which concern both them and us quite a lot. First, there's no evidence at all of her ever having had a relationship with a woman before. That raises the obvious possibility that she may just be using your officer to gain information about the enquiry."

"I've warned DS Desai about that, so I think we can be confident it won't happen."

"Nonetheless, it doesn't mean she hasn't tried. Perhaps if you have an opportunity you might try to ask your Sergeant about that, discreetly of course."

"I'll do that. But you said there were two areas of concern. What's the other one?"

"Ah, yes, distinctly worrying this one. I said there was no evidence of Sophie Ho having had a relationship with another woman before. There is however a strong suspicion that she was having an affair with one of the officers now implicated in the fake passport business."

"That's all very circumstantial though, isn't it, sir?"

Newby chuckled at the other end of the line.

"We treat evidence a little differently here at the Branch, Simon, as I hope you'll soon be learning for yourself. We have to operate on the basis of intelligence, just as the boys in the security services do. There's none of that "beyond reasonable doubt" stuff here. If something looks likely on the basis of the available intelligence, then we assume it to be the case until the opposite can be proved. So far as Sophie Ho is concerned, the pieces are falling into place. I'm sure you can see that for yourself."

"Yes, I can. You know that the bad guys in Singapore had decided to send somebody to the UK to deal with Raj. The Ho woman must be a prime suspect, partly because it looks like she may have had links to one of the people making that decision, and partly because she has at least some of the skills necessary for the mission. And I agree that it does seem very opportune that she should suddenly launch into a relationship with one of the officers on the investigation, particularly if she has no history of that sort of thing. No, if I was in your position I'm sure I would be thinking along exactly the same lines."

"Well, there you are then."

"But I'm not in your position, sir. Not yet, anyway. I'm in charge of the team here, and a damn good team they are too. I have a professional responsibility for Priya Desai's welfare, yes and for her privacy as well. It so happens that I also like a very much as a person, and I don't want her to get hurt."

"Neither do I, Simon, but in a situation like this we just do what we have to do and let the pieces fall where they may. Isn't there some sort of saying in Shakespeare about an innocent person who gets into something out of their depth and ends up having to pay the price?"

"The fell incensèd points of mighty opposites, perhaps?"

"Something like that, yes. Look, Simon, we'll handle this as gently as we can – and very discreetly too – but at the end of the day the private life of one of your offices comes a very poor second to national security. And anyway, if there's a professional killer loose on your patch then I'm sure we have a common interest in catching them, don't we?"

"Yes, of course we do. But what happens if she simply denies ever having been to the house and we can't make a DNA match? After all, if she really is a hit woman then she may well have put on a forensics suit before she went in. I remember going on a course a little while ago when they explained how the IRA worked this out in Northern Ireland during the troubles. I know that DNA technology has moved on a long way since then, but they reckoned they could get in and out of the house without leaving any trace."

"Well, let's cross that bridge when we come to it shall we? We're going to pull her in this afternoon. I'll keep you posted of course."

"Thank you, sir. And I'll try to have that word with Desai. If there's anything I think you should know then I'll pass it on at once."

"Thanks. By the way, Simon, just as one friend to another, I happen to know that the Met is not about to give up trying to transfer you over here. Don't be surprised if you get a call from the ACC very shortly. I think he's about to up the ante as it were."

"How do you mean, sir?"

"You remember that job that's about to open up over here? The Chief Super's job?"

"Yes, I do. Look, I'm fully aware that the ACC wants me to come across to the Branch as an acting Chief Super. So what? What's changed?"

"I think you'll find he's going to suggest that you get the

promotion straightaway. That you get posted to the branch as a substantive Chief Superintendent, not acting up."

"But that's absurd. I've only just been made Superintendent."

"Count the months, Simon. I think you'll find that it's coming up for 2 years. That's the minimum you need to serve in the rank."

"Oh."

"Don't sound so down about it, Simon. This would be a great opportunity for you. You'd be the youngest ever Chief Superintendent in the history of the Met; I've checked. There's something else you might like to consider as well."

"Yes?"

"I've only got about a year left in this job. After that it's onwards and upwards for yours truly. I don't mind admitting that I shall be sorry to leave this job behind. It's interesting, challenging, and it makes a difference. My next job is likely to be something much more boring and bureaucratic. But the reason I'm mentioning this is that if you take the posting when it's offered then you'll be reporting directly to me for a year or so and I'll have a chance to show you the ropes, and watch your back. This job will come vacant again about two years after that and I'm pretty sure they have it in mind for you as your next career move."

"I see."

"Yes, but if you don't take it this time then they may more or less force you to take something similar next year, and I may be gone by then, or on the way out anyway. And whoever has the job then may not see you, as I do, as a friend to be helped along his career path. They may see you as some jumped-up, over-educated teacher's pet of the top brass who's riding for a fall. Get my drift?"

"Do you know who's going to be the next Commander?"

"Unofficially and strictly between us, yes I do."

"Who is it?"

"I can't tell you that, but let's just say that he didn't go to either boarding school or university, and that he doesn't have a lot of time for anyone who did. I'd bear that in mind when the ACC calls if I were you."

CHAPTER 26

"Let's review where we are, Bob," Collison said rather tiredly the next morning. "I'm getting a bit concerned that we have hares running in all directions and we're just chasing whichever one we see next rather than having an overall plan. By the way, how are we getting on with John Schneider?"

"He'll be in very shortly for Karen and Priya to take his statement."

"Hm, I'd really like to be able to involve Peter Collins, you know. I'd like to get his take on Schneider's state of mind."

"We chatted about that last night, as it happens. His advice is that we shouldn't do anything to upset him. The slightest little thing could make him change his mind about cooperating with us. He seems to be okay dealing with Karen and Priya, so that's the way we should keep it for the time being. That's what Peter says, anyway."

"Yes, I must say it makes sense. Very well then, let's get his statement down as hardcopy, let him sign it, and then see where we go from there. There is that discrepancy by the way, isn't there? He maintains that he told Rowbotham he was Taylor's son, but last time we spoke to him Rowbotham was equally adamant that he didn't. I'm sure Rowbotham is telling the truth, but we should probably re-interview him and get that down in writing."

"Is it really significant do you think, guv?"

"Well, if you're planning to confront your father – let alone if you might already have some half formed idea about killing him in revenge having bumped off your girlfriend – you'd hardly divulge your identity to a potential witness, would you? No, it all makes perfect sense."

"Of course there something else we haven't pursued yet."

"Which is?"

"Well think about those other missing girls. If Taylor murdered Sue Barnard, then might he not have murdered them as well? That he could in fact have been a serial killer? And if so, is there any way that somebody else could have found out – a relative of one of the missing girls perhaps – and murdered Taylor by way of revenge?"

"It's a bit tenuous isn't it, Bob? If they had found out something which pointed to Taylor's guilt why wouldn't they just come to the police? Whereas we know that John Schneider hates the police and would never willingly set foot in a police station. If he suddenly found out from his mother that Taylor had been seen burying the body of a girl, then it seems much more plausible that he would put two and two together and made the connection with the Barnard girl. I just can't believe he had no idea the she'd gone missing, just like I don't believe that he made no effort at all to get in touch with her again. He was a teenager in love, and that sort of strength of feeling doesn't just disappear overnight."

"I'm no psychology expert, guv. It would be useful to get Peter's take on that."

"Yes, let's do that. Perhaps I could invite myself around for a drink this evening?"

"You'd be very welcome as always. I'll give Peter a ring later to make sure he'll be there."

"Right. You know, there's another possibility that's been nagging away at me. In fact I couldn't get to sleep last night for thinking about it. The problem is that I don't quite see how it fits all the facts."

"And what's that?"

"Well, suppose that John Schneider is a serial killer. In that case, why shouldn't Sue Barnard have been his first victim? Perhaps he was upset that she wouldn't have sex with him, and his anger got the better of him, just like it did with that boy he attacked. We're assuming that because Conrad Taylor buried Sue Barnard then he must have killed her first, aren't we? But suppose he didn't? Suppose he found her dead, having been killed by his son? He might even have found them together, the boy and the girl's corpse. In the heat of the moment perhaps he felt an overwhelming impulse to protect his son and cover-up what he'd done."

"But like you say, guv, that doesn't fit with our other theory. If Schneider murdered Sue Barnard then he wouldn't have had any reason to kill his father. You don't need to avenge something that hasn't been done."

"I've been thinking about that. You're right of course, but there could be another motive. Schneider might be wondering all these years how he got away with it. Just imagine, he must have been dreading a summons back to England to face a police enquiry whenever Susan's body was found. He must have wondered, all those years, why nothing had happened. Then suddenly he discovers the truth. Susan's body was never found because his father – literally – covered up for him. That was probably a huge relief, but at the same time a huge worry. It meant that there was somebody out there who knew he was a killer and could shop him to the police at any time. Granted, Taylor had never done anything so far by way of going to the police, but he was getting on a bit and there would always be something like a deathbed confession to worry about."

"You mean Schneider was looking to kill his father in order to silence him? To cover his tracks?"

"Yes, exactly. If we can once believe in Schneider as a serial killer – and there are those unexplained deaths in Canada to consider – then perhaps everything starts to fall into place."

"So the murders would indeed be connected because they would both have been committed by the same person?"

"Exactly, and that would also explain why he failed to tell Rowbotham that he was Conrad Taylor's son. If he was planning to kill him – or perhaps had even already done so as far as we know – he'd hardly want us to know where to come looking."

"It's an interesting hypothesis, guv, certainly."

Collison nodded and pulled a pad out of one of his desk drawers.

"Which is why thought it would be useful for you and I to review where we are. It has to be just you and I of course, because there's stuff we can't share with the rest of the team."

"OK. Where shall we start?"

"Possibility number one. The obvious suspect, Raj, killed

Conrad Taylor when Taylor discovered that he'd been stealing from him. In this scenario we have to assume that the two killings were unconnected, and that Taylor killed Sue Barnard twenty years earlier for reason or reasons unknown."

"We've been told that Sue Barnard was seen hanging around in Downshire Hill, offering men sexual favours – whether directly or indirectly – don't we? And we've been told that Taylor and his wife hadn't been sleeping together for a considerable time. So maybe Taylor took her up on her offer, but something went wrong."

"Yes, I was wondering about that as well. You see, if the Barnard girl was on the game – and that's pretty much what McKenzie's evidence amounts to – then that would also suggest a possible link to at least one of the other missing girls. It points to the possibility that Taylor was indeed a serial killer preying on sex workers. The problem is we only have one uncorroborated report about what the Barnard girl might have been up to when she wasn't at school. I've been thinking that we might ask Rowbotham about that when we re-interview him. We know that he was dropping in at the house next door in the evenings to check on the building works, so he may well have seen her too. If he had, that would be really helpful."

"OK. I'll arrange for us to see Jack Rowbotham again. And of course we're also looking for the schoolfriend, Jill East. If Sue Barnard did have any extra-curricular activities then her best friend may have known something about them."

Collison nodded to himself and drew a line across the page.

"Possibility number two. The passport mob in Singapore send someone to silence Raj. That person may or may not have been Sophie Ho. This assassin – as that's what it amounts to – gains access to Wentworth House but Raj isn't there. Either they are surprised by Taylor and kill him to prevent him raising the alarm, or they kill him deliberately either to put the frighteners on Raj or to place him under suspicion. Perhaps they even wait a little while to see if Raj returns to the house, but lose patience after a while and leave. If the killer was Sophie Ho then she subsequently takes the opportunity to befriend Priya with the intention of eavesdropping on the enquiry."

"There's a possible problem with that one, guv. We know that Sophie Ho was an expert at martial arts. Someone who was that good at karate could easily kill someone with one blow, so why bash Taylor on the head with some sort of blunt instrument?"

"Who knows? Perhaps precisely so that it wouldn't look like a professional hit."

"I guess so. So again, with this possibility, we are assuming that the two murders are not connected, and that Taylor killed Sue Barnard."

"Yes. In which case, of course, Taylor may well have killed again. That's something we'll need to investigate in due course."

"You mean we'll have to reopen all those missing persons cases? Reinvestigate them after all these years?"

"I don't see that we'd have any choice, Bob, do you? Don't get me wrong, I'm just as reluctant to do it as you are. Apart from anything else, a lot of potential witnesses may have died in the meantime. But if we do conclude – as seems likely at the moment – that Taylor killed Barnard then we would have to consider the possibility that we have an undiscovered serial killer on our hands."

"Talking of undiscovered serial killers, there's something else I should mention, guv."

"Go on."

"Well, I was talking to the gay liaison officer and he's got a bit of a bee in his bonnet about a serial killer having potentially been in operation among middle-aged gay men who frequented the Heath. Apparently there have been two others in recent years, and the M0 matches how Taylor was killed: all three were attacked at home and bashed on the head."

"I see. OK, then that's possibility number three, but let's put that on hold for a moment shall we? That would take us down the path of mounting a completely new investigation."

"Right you are, guv. So what's left?"

"Possibility number four. Susan Barnard was the first victim of serial killer John Schneider. Conrad Taylor came across her body, whether or not still in her killer's possession, and decided to cover up his son's crime rather than shop him to the police. He is spotted in the act of burying her by his wife. Horrified, she snatches both the children and leaves home, never to return. Later, as we know – much later – she tells the children what she saw. John Schneider realises for the first time why he has never been brought to justice for Barnard's murder, but knows he will always be in danger as long as his father is alive. So he resolves to come back to England and silence him once and for all. He may or may not have succeeded in doing so. If he did, then the call on Rowbotham may have preceded the crime, in which case it would have been a genuine request for information, or it may have happened afterwards and been some sort of muddled attempt to throw us off the track. If this possibility is correct then we may need to liaise with the Canadian police on a joint investigation, looking at the similar missing women cases in Ontario."

"There's always the possibility that Taylor was killed by some random intruder – a burglary gone wrong perhaps."

"Very well, Bob. Let's call that possibility number five. We know that the front door presented little problem to anybody who knew what they were doing; even I was able to open it."

Collison drew another line across the page and looked up at Metcalfe.

"Is there anything we're overlooking?"

"I don't think so. No, I'm sure not. When you think about it, this seemed a pretty open and shut case at the beginning. It looked like it was just a question of finding our prime suspect."

"Well he *is* still our prime suspect, let's not forget that. Just because things are looking more complicated as other possibilities open up, Raj is still in the frame unless and until something happens to change that. He was taking Taylor's money, and even if we can't prove he didn't have his consent during his lifetime, then that wouldn't excuse him continuing to plunder the bank account after Taylor's death. He may or may not have been Taylor's lover, so there's always the possibility that a lovers' tiff exploded into sudden violence. On his own admission he ran away from the crime scene rather than reporting it to the police. He entered the country illegally and absconded from custody. He had links with organised crime ... need I go on?"

"No, and he's still favourite for me. Don't forget all the people who said that he behaved very strangely. He certainly gave me the creeps when I met him. Did you notice that he won't look anyone in the eye? I know it's not very scientific to rely on instinct, but there's something very weird about that man."

CHAPTER 27

"I was about to make some dry martinis," Peter Collins said. "Would that be acceptable to everyone? Oh, what about you, Simon. Are you driving?"

"No, I'm taking the tube, and a dry martini would be very welcome, thank you."

Collins busied himself with pouring a London dry gin into a jug of ice, mixing in a very small quantity of Noilly Prat and then adding a couple of drops of Angostura bitters. He swirled the mixture gently for a while and then poured it into five martini glasses, each already equipped with an olive.

"Only five glasses?" Collison asked. "Where's Lisa?"

"She's upstairs," Metcalfe informed him. "She knew we wanted to discuss the case and wouldn't be able to do it in front of her, so she's gone to watch some television."

"Oh dear, now I feel guilty for having intruded. Silly of me, I should have realised."

"Nonsense," Willis said robustly. "Lisa knows the score. She's already enough of a copper's wife to realise that there's stuff she can't sit in on."

"Excellent martini, Peter," Metcalfe observed, rolling it appreciatively around with his tongue.

Collins bowed gravely. He knew full well that until a few months ago Metcalfe had not even known what a dry martini was, but he was of course too much of a gentleman ever to articulate such a thought.

"So, no surprises with friend Schneider then?" he asked.

"No, he just confirmed everything he told us yesterday. You've seen the statement which he signed."

"Yes, I have. I assume you quizzed him in particular on what he said to the neighbour – Rowbotham, is it?"

"Yes we did, and he's sticking to his story."

"But then he would, wouldn't he?" Metcalfe broke in. "If he was planning to murder his father – Taylor, that is – he wouldn't want to advertise his identity, would he?"

"That's true," Collins agreed, "and of course psychopaths tend to lie easily and instinctively; that's why they're so good at it."

"So you do think he's a psychopath, Peter?" Willis asked eagerly.

"I'm sorry if I gave that impression. The truth is I simply can't tell one way or another; I don't know nearly enough about him. I'd need to meet him, talk to him, observe him. Then perhaps over time I could come to a view. All I can say at the moment is that – assuming everything we've been told is true – he seems to have anger management issues, a disposition to violence, and a lack of empathy for others – particularly women."

"Well the lack of empathy at least would be consistent with a psychopathic state, wouldn't it?" Collison said.

"Yes, of course it would but there's much more to it than that, as you know. And even if he were a psychopath, that doesn't take us very much further. There are lots of psychopaths wandering about out there who don't become serial killers; some of them are very successful in their careers by the way. That's an aspect of this case which troubles me, actually."

"How do you mean?" Metcalfe asked.

"Well, I'm a psychologist not a lawyer, but it seems to me that unless some new piece of evidence suddenly emerges then the best we'll ever be able to do is to show that Schneider may be the sort of person to have committed murder in general terms. But what we need to do is to find some way of showing that he has actually committed at least one of these two specific murders. We've been here before, remember. Just because he may fit the profile of a murderer – even perhaps this murderer – that doesn't prove that he did it."

"Of course, of course," Collison said hastily, "I'm not suggesting for a moment that we head off down that path again."

They were all only too well aware that the events in question had resulted in Collins descending into serious mental illness, a condition from which he had been nursed back to health largely thanks to the devotion of Willis.

"No," Collison continued, "all I'm asking is whether you think – in the light of all the available information so far – this is a profitable line of enquiry to pursue."

"You mean whether I think it's possible that John Schneider may be a serial killer?"

"Yes. Do you?"

Collins took a considered sip of his martini, took out the olive and ate it.

"Yes I do," he said calmly, "but again I'd stress that it's only a possibility."

"Forgetting the psychology for a moment," Metcalfe said, "I have to say that it's a possibility I like. It's the only hypothesis that enables the same person to have committed both murders, and I just have this – I don't know, instinct I suppose – that two murders committed so close to each other, probably even at the same house, just have to be connected in some way."

"They could still be connected without having been committed by the same person," Collins pointed out. "After all, they are separated by a couple of decades."

"All true," Collison admitted. "Perhaps there's still quite a lot that we simply don't know. For example, we don't know anything about our first victim, Susan Barnard, that connects her with any suspect other than John Schneider. If she was murdered by the father – which seems the logical outcome of what the mother saw – then what was his motive?"

"Could he be a serial killer perhaps?" Collins asked. "With Barnard as his first known victim?"

"Yes, that's obviously a possibility we've been considering," Collison replied, "and if we're going to take it seriously then we'll have to reopen a lot of missing persons reports and reinvestigate them."

"There are five or six, and that's just around the same time," Metcalfe explained. "If we extend the timeframe then God knows how many we're likely to come across."

"The problem I have with that theory," Collison countered, "is that if these people were murdered then – so far as we are aware – their bodies have never been discovered. Surely if Taylor murdered Sue Barnard and buried her in a flowerbed then he would have been likely to dispose of his other victims – if there were any – in the same way. Christie buried most of his victims in and around his house, for example. So did Fred West."

"But the garden wall went up, didn't it?" Willis said. "So he wouldn't have had access to next door anymore."

"True," Collison said with a shrug, "but what the hell, a flowerbed is a flowerbed isn't it? It doesn't really matter to whom it belongs. So why shouldn't he just have used his own back garden?"

"Maybe he realised, after the wife and children left home, that he'd been spotted in the act?" Metcalfe suggested. "He could have come to the view that it was just too dangerous disposing of bodies at home anymore and that he needed to find some other way of doing it. He might even thought about digging up Barnard, but by that time the wall would have been built and Jack Rowbotham would have been living at the house full-time, so it would just have been too risky."

"But then how *would* he have disposed of the bodies?" Collison persisted. "There's no obvious possibility. He didn't have access to an allotment, or a building site, or anything like that. He didn't even go out very much."

"Would a recluse be likely to be a serial killer, Peter?" Metcalfe asked.

"Not a true recluse who never went out, no, probably not. But was he always like that? I thought the evidence suggested that he had gradually become like it over the years."

"But that would suggest that he might once have been a serial killer but then stopped killing. Wouldn't that be unusual?"

"Yes, very. Of course we'll never know for certain, but usually where a serial killer appears to have ended their activities it's either because they've died, moved away, or gone to prison for some other offence. It's unlikely they would just stop. They wouldn't be able to."

"What about this new idea, guv?" Willis asked curiously. "The one about a possible serial killer preying on gay middle-aged men who frequent the Heath?"

"We'll need to take a look at that of course, and I've asked to see the files, but I'm very much hoping that we don't need to go down that path. Can you imagine the expression on the ACC's face if I was to tell him that not only might we have had a possible serial killer at work in Downshire Hill, whom incidentally we hadn't been able to identify let alone arrest, but that I now wanted to tie up budget and manpower to investigate the possibility of another serial killer whose existence has never even been recognised?"

"I can," Metcalfe said with a smile.

"But surely that shouldn't matter, should it?" Collins asked mildly. "If there is an unsolved murder out there then it's the responsibility of the police to investigate it?"

"Oh, Peter, it's really not like that," Willis said kindly. "It's all a matter of resources these days. There's only a certain amount of money and a certain number of hours in the day. That's why even missing persons cases often don't get fully investigated, unless they involve a child or a vulnerable adult that is. Even with murders, there comes a time when an investigation has to be wound down."

"It's never formally closed, of course," Collison added hastily, "not unless we are pretty certain we know who did it but know that we'll never be able to prove it. Or perhaps where that person has died or is serving a long prison sentence for something else. But it becomes effectively a dead file being dealt with by just one officer, who usually has a lot of them in their filing cabinet, all more or less categorised as 'no further action'. And there they stay unless some fresh new evidence suddenly becomes available."

"And that's the status of these other cases right now, is it?"

"Yes, it is, Peter, and the ACC would be very unhappy to have them reopened unless there was some sort of dramatic new revelation. The same goes for the other missing girl reports, of course, but if we come to the conclusion that Conrad Taylor might have been at work in Hampstead as a serial killer, even for a limited time, then, reluctantly, the ACC would have to agree that we need to take another long look at those cases."

"I see."

Collins raised one arm and scratched his elbow distractedly.

"We have had one welcome development, though," Willis told him brightly. "We've located that school friend of Sue Barnard."

"Who is called Jill East, of course," Collins replied. "Just to prove that I really have read the file."

"Yes, exactly, Jill East. It turns out it wasn't that difficult after all. Believe it or not she was involved with the former pupils' association for a while, and her daughter goes to the school right now. The headmaster recognised straightaway who we were talking about and was able to put us in touch. She's coming in tomorrow morning to talk to us."

"Which will be an interesting opportunity to learn more about our first victim," Collison said. "If the other neighbour – McKenzie – is to be believed then she was either moonlighting as a prostitute, or something pretty close to it."

"Which is strange," Willis added, "since John Schneider claims that she wouldn't have sex with him even though, he says, she was his girlfriend. As he said, if that was the case then why should she have sex with strangers?"

"A valid question," Collins mused.

"The money might have had something to do with it," Metcalfe said dryly.

"Was the pathologist able to tell whether she was a virgin when she died?" Collins asked.

"A good question, but no," Collison responded. "There was almost no soft tissue left; just enough for a DNA sample."

"But no other DNA found on or inside the body?"

"Again no, but I don't think that's very conclusive in this case. There was almost nothing left but skeleton."

"Well, in that case," Collins said, twirling his now empty martini glass, "this lady's evidence will obviously be very interesting. I wonder what she's going to say?"

CHAPTER 28

"Superintendent Collison? Please hold for the ACC."

"Simon? How are you getting on with this Downshire Hill business?"

"We're making progress, sir. We've tracked down Susan Barnard's best friend from school and had her in for interview. She confirmed what we already suspected: John Schneider has a history of violence, anger management issues, and aggressive sexuality towards women. Dr Collins thinks his behaviour could be consistent with some sort of psychopathic condition."

"But you've nothing actually to link him to either murder, have you? No real evidence I mean?"

"No, we haven't. To tell the truth, I'm getting very frustrated with this case. I have this constant feeling that there is something we don't know, or maybe just something we're overlooking, that could unlock the door."

"Perhaps what you're overlooking is that you already have an obvious suspect in custody, for the second murder at least. I've had the preliminary report back from the CPS – I'll forward it to you by the way – and they think there's enough evidence against this Raj character to get a conviction."

"I'd be interested to read that, sir. Have they considered

the point that some of the trial may have to be conducted *in camera*?"

"Yes, they have. They're not happy of course. They burble on about public policy and so forth, but at the end of the day they don't think it would be a problem."

"If I was counsel for the defence I think I'd give them a pretty good argument on that, sir. Wouldn't we have to show that there was a risk to national security? And how would we do that? I mean, there's no evidence that any terrorists have actually taken advantage of these false passports, is there? And how could we be sure that the people on the jury wouldn't blab about it anyway?"

"I think counsel for the defence would be squared in advance, Simon. Probably the Home Office would try to make sure that the defence brief would be up for silk shortly, and would want to show that they could be responsible and take a view in the national interest. As for the jury, they'd have to be security vetted. Anyway, if there was a leak to the press we could serve a gagging order to stop them publishing anything."

"Yes, I see."

"But fortunately, Simon, counsel for the defence is not your job. You're the SIO and according to the Crown Prosecution Service you have a *prima facie* case, as you lawyers call it, against the prime suspect. So why not just call it a day and let the CPS do their job?"

"The problem with the idea that Raj murdered Taylor is that it assumes there is no connection between the two killings."

"Why should there be? They were 20 years apart from God's sake."

"Yet they happened within a few yards of each other, assuming that the girl was killed at the house. That's a pretty large coincidence, sir, you must admit."

"Coincidences happen, Simon. Get used to it. Anyway, don't we have clear evidence, albeit hearsay, that Taylor himself murdered the girl?"

"We have evidence that he buried her certainly. But that's not quite the same thing as evidence that he killed her."

"Are you suggesting that she died by accident?"

"I've considered that possibility, yes. Whatever the motive for that killing it's difficult not to conclude that it must have had some sexual aspect. We have one unconfirmed report that the victim used to hang around the neighbourhood propositioning older men. We're working on getting corroboration for that. If we can corroborate it then it might be reasonable to assume that Taylor took Sue Barnard up on her offer, but that something went wrong. Either she died accidentally – though it's difficult to imagine how that might happen – or one of them panicked and Taylor ended up killing her."

"Well there you are then. Unless Taylor bashed his own head in, the murders were in fact committed by different people."

"I didn't say they had to be committed by the same person, sir, just that I thought they were likely to be connected in some way."

"Now you're splitting hairs, Simon. Look, I'll tell you

what. I'll give you a few more days to see if you can work out one of these theories of yours – actually get some evidence to support it, I mean – but if not then I think we'll have to formally charge Raj with Taylor's murder, and issue a statement saying we believe it's likely that Taylor murdered Susan Barnard."

"What about the special branch investigation into Sophie Ho, sir? I was hoping to hear from Commander Newby."

"Dead-end, I'm afraid. She simply denies any knowledge of anything. Newby's not happy of course, but then the security boys never are. They're generally happy to proceed on the basis of a reasonable belief, but Newby's a copper and he understands that we can't take this forward without any evidence. And we have nothing to place her at the scene. In fact, the only evidence we have at all – and it's completely circumstantial – is that if she was con- cerned in Taylor's murder then it does seem mighty convenient that she should suddenly commence a relationship with one of the investigating officers, particularly as the boys in Singapore haven't been able to unearth any evidence of her being interested in other women before."

"Perhaps that's not entirely surprising, sir. Singapore is a very straitlaced society. If she was gay then she would probably have gone to great lengths to conceal the fact."

"Well, be that as it may, she's out of the picture. If the passport people did send someone to the UK to bump off Raj then maybe they're still out there, or maybe it was

Sophie Ho and she's just too smart for us. I guess we'll never know."

"Well, as you say, at least that's one hypothesis we can cross off our list. Actually, I hesitate to mention this, but there is another possibility that's being peddled by one of the officers here at the station. Apparently the Taylor murder may fit a pattern of other killings, all involving older men who had visited the Heath in search of gay sex."

"Are you suggesting that we may have a serial killer on our hands – one that is otherwise unconnected with this investigation?"

"Well, if he killed Taylor then he would be, wouldn't he? But I take your meaning."

There was a silence at the other end of the line.

"I'm sure I don't have to give you a lecture on overstrained police resources, Simon. Let this officer, or anyone else for that matter, bring us clear evidence of the activities of a serial killer and of course we'll investigate it. But let's just stay focused on this enquiry, shall we? Now, do you think – realistically speaking – you may be able to bring this investigation to a close within the next few days with a clear case against someone other than Raj?"

"To be perfectly honest, sir, I just don't know. But I'd like those few days grace to try."

"Very well, Simon. You're the SIO and I back your judgement. By the way, I wonder if you've thought any more about that job with the Branch? Not only would it be a good career move for you but I think it could be a great opportunity to bump you up to Chief Super on time served ..."

•

"So the ACC's putting us under pressure is he?" Metcalfe asked moodily. "Well, I suppose if you look at it from his point of view it's difficult to blame him. We do have an obvious suspect already banged up, after all."

"For the second murder yes, but not the first," Collison pointed out.

"But we know Taylor committed that one, don't we, guv? At the very least we have evidence that he disposed of the body."

"Yes, I know. The ACC wants us to issue a statement saying we believe Taylor killed Barnard. Again, it's easy to appreciate his point of view. That way we resolve two separate murder enquiries nice and tidily."

Collison crossed to his favourite thinking spot by the window and gazed up Rosslyn Hill.

"Well, whether we like it or not, Bob, we have to bring things to a conclusion. I hate to admit it, but unless we can prove some connection between Schneider and one or both of these murders then we're going to have to do as the ACC says."

"So we're going to concentrate on Schneider, are we?"

"Well, who else is there, apart from Raj?"

"There's that Sophie Ho woman. What's happening about that?"

"Oh, that's a non-starter I'm afraid. Special Branch haven't been able to get anything out of her at all."

"But just because they haven't been able to place at the scene, that doesn't mean she wasn't there."

"No, of course it doesn't, Bob. But unless we can come up with something ourselves then we have to forget about, and it's difficult to see how we might succeed where the Branch have failed."

Metcalfe considered this.

"We could always involve Priya ..."

"Not without breaching security we couldn't. I think we've already asked her as much as we can."

"OK then, so what's the plan?"

"We have to find a way of breaking John Schneider. Unless we can get some sort of confession from him I don't see any way forward. I think now we should openly involve Peter Collins; we don't have anything to lose. If Schneider gets upset and refuses to talk to us any more then we're no worse off than we are at the moment."

"He's already given a pretty full statement, remember."

"Yes, and we know he's lied about at least one thing. He says he told Rowbotham that he was Taylor's son. So I think what we need to do is to get formal confirmation of that from Rowbotham, and then use it to hammer away at Schneider. I still think it's a very telling contradiction, by the way. Why should he lie about it? For precisely the same reason that he didn't say it in the first place. Someone who was considering killing the man next door would hardly take the trouble to identify himself to a potential witness. So by saying that he did, he's trying to convince us of his own innocence."

"And we know from the sister that he was intending to confront his father."

"Yes, and we know from the former Jill East that he was violent, capable of bursts of sudden anger, and – in her own words – out of control. You know, it's all very well for the DPP to say that we have a reasonable case against Raj, but the way I see it it's mostly circumstantial and you could make an equally strong argument against Schneider."

"The difference I suppose is that we know Raj was living at the house where the murder took place, and that indeed he was the only other person living there. He also admitted to seeing Taylor dead but failing to report it. And don't forget he had a motive."

"Assuming that he's lying and he didn't have Taylor's authority to take that money out of the bank account."

"Assuming that, yes."

Now it was Collison's turn to pause and think.

"You know, since we have him in custody anyway, why don't you and I re-interview him and ask him all about this passport stuff? If he realises that we know stuff about him he thought was secret there's always the chance he might crack, or at least let something slip."

"Sure, again I don't see that we have anything to lose. It'll have to be just you and me though, guv."

"Of course. We're the only ones on the right side of the Chinese wall."

A tap on the door heralded the arrival of Priya Desai, looking troubled.

"Yes, Priya, what is it?" Collison asked.

She looked briefly from one to the other, but without making eye contact.

"The thing is, guv, I think there's something I should tell you. About Sophie Ho."

CHAPTER 29

"I think you'd better sit down, Priya," Collison said. "Now, tell us whatever it is you think we should know."

She perched nervously on the edge of a chair. In marked contrast to her usual self-confident air, she seemed edgy and nervous.

"I don't know how much you know about me and Sophie, guv. I mean … well, I suppose what I mean is I don't know how much you need to know."

"I certainly don't want to pry into your personal life, Priya. Why don't you just tell me anything you think may be relevant to the enquiry?"

"OK, well I just had Sophie on the phone to me, just now. She's really upset. It seems she's been interrogated by Special Branch. Did you know about this?"

"Yes I did, I'm afraid. But I can't tell you why, nor can I really explain any of the background. I'm sorry, but I'm under restraint as they say in the security services. Bob and I have been made subject to the Official Secrets Act."

"Oh, I see."

She clasped her hands together and darted a quick glance around the room.

"Or rather, I don't see," she went on. "But if you can't tell me then that's that."

"What is it you want to tell me, Priya?" Collison asked her gently. "I promise that Bob and I will treat it in the strictest confidence in so far as we are able to."

"Well, she says Special Branch have been asking her about the case; our case, that is, the Downshire Hill enquiry. She seems really confused because the first she heard of it was when she came here to the nick to meet me."

"So she says," Metcalfe interjected.

Collison shot him a quick glance and subtly but firmly shook his head.

"Go on, Priya," he said.

"They've been asking her if she's ever been to the house, almost as if they're treating her as a suspect. But she isn't, is she? That would be ridiculous. She doesn't have any connection with Conrad Taylor."

Collison thought deeply for a moment.

"I can't comment on the last bit, but I can confirm that she has been treated as a suspect. We weren't allowed to investigate her ourselves because there were security aspects which only Bob and I were allowed to know about. But if it makes you feel any better, my current understanding from the Branch is that we are no longer to treat her as a suspect. Certainly we are no longer pursuing that possible angle."

"Oh, that's a relief. But then, I wonder..."

"You wonder what, Priya? What was it you wanted to tell us about?"

"Well, I remember you asking me if Sophie had tried to get any information out of me about the investigation, and I said no. It's just that the last few times I've seen her, or we've spoken on the phone, she has actually asked about the case, even though I told her not to. We had a bit of a row about it actually. She said she was just trying to take an interest in my job."

"She really should know better, shouldn't she? After all she was with the police in Singapore for some time."

"Yes, but she's not a copper, not like us. She was just a translator. A sort of adviser really, I suppose, maybe a bit like Dr Collins."

"Dr Collins may not be a police officer," Collison said quickly before Metcalfe could intervene, "but he certainly understands the need for confidentiality. He's a professional, and I would expect the same from Sophie Ho. What sort of things has she been asking about, by the way?"

"Oh, it's just general stuff. Whether we are going to charge Raj, that sort of thing."

"If she interested specifically in Raj?" Collison asked carefully.

"Is that important, guv?"

"It might be, yes."

"Well then I suppose yes, she is. And I got to wondering …"

"Wondering about what exactly?"

"It's just that I know that Raj's background is in Singapore. That's where Sophie is from, as you know. So I just got to wondering whether there might be some connection between them. Maybe they knew each other out there or something. Oh, I'm probably just being stupid but I can't get the idea out of my head. I can't even sleep properly for worrying about it."

"You're not being stupid at all, Priya," Collison replied with a smile. "On the contrary, you're just proving what a very fine police officer you are. You've made a connection which neither Bob nor I can comment upon, and to be honest we don't really know whether you're right or not. But we share the same sort of concern."

Desai gazed at him intently and gnawed at her lip. She seemed close to tears.

"It's just ..."

"It's just that you're wondering whether she really wanted to see you for yourself or just to pump you for information about the investigation," Collison prompted her softly.

"Yes, exactly that. How did you know?"

"I'd have to be pretty insensitive not to know."

"And you're not that are you? Oh, why do you have to be so nice all the time?"

She broke off at this point, buried her face in her hands, and started sobbing silently. She took her hands away and looked helplessly around the room, a frown of utter self-disgust on her face. Collison watched her equally helplessly; he could guess what it was costing her to be seen crying like this. Metcalfe slipped out of the room and returned shortly with a box of tissues. Their delicate lilac colour marked them as the property of Karen Willis; lilac was one of her favourite colours.

"Oh, thank you, guv," she gulped through her tears and, seizing a handful, blew her nose violently.

"I'm so sorry," she said, dabbing at her eyes, "this is stupid. I'll be all right in a minute."

"Take as long as you need," Collison advised. "We know this must be very upsetting for you."

She crumpled the tissues in her fist and gazed at him fixedly.

"You know, don't you? About Sophie and me. I don't know how, but you know."

"Yes, we do, but it's really none of our business and there's certainly no need for anyone else ever to know."

"Are you ... you know, shocked?"

"Why on earth would I be shocked? People meet, they are attracted to each other, they have a relationship. It happens every minute of every day. What's there to be shocked about?"

"Oh, you know..."

"We know nothing, Bob and I. And that's the way it's going to stay, Priya. Your personal life is your personal life. It's none of our business."

"But can I ask you ..."

"Can you ask me if I think she's been using you?"

"Yes. Please be truthful. I'm really so confused ..."

"The only truthful answer I can give you is that I don't know. Can we ever really be sure of anyone? That's the essence of a relationship, I think. That you have to be prepared to take somebody on trust even though in so doing you open yourself up for them to hurt you. You have to trust them not to. It's a bit like the Boy Scout handshake – do you know that story?"

"No, I don't."

"Well, I used to be a Scout and when you met another Scout you had to shake hands with your left hand."

"Why the left-hand?"

"That's the whole point I'm trying to make. Baden Powell spent time in Africa and he saw the tribesmen there would put down their shield, which they held in their left-hand, leaving the person they were greeting still holding their spear. It was a sign of trust, you see. I've always thought that relationships are a bit like that."

"You come out with some really weird stuff, guv. Do you know that?"

"I'm sorry. Maybe my mind just works a bit differently to other people's."

He reached out for her damp and crumpled tissues and tossed them in the bin.

"At least your mascara hasn't run," he observed. "How do you manage that?"

"I don't wear mascara," she said in surprise. "I hardly ever wear any make-up at all. Haven't you noticed?"

"No I must confess I hadn't," he said awkwardly. "It must be because you-"

He broke off and cleared his throat.

"Well anyway," he went on, "speaking purely as police officers, unless you think that Sophie's level of interest in the case is truly remarkable, then I don't particularly feel like reopening the possibility of her being a suspect. To tell you the truth, I don't think we have the time. We've been put under pressure to bring this enquiry to a conclusion as quickly as possible one way or the other. I'd just been chatting to Bob about it before you came in. I'm desperate to find some way of placing John Schneider with either victim, or preferably both. If we can't do that then we're going to have to hand the file over to the CPS, and they will proceed against Raj."

"Well, he is the obvious suspect," she murmured.

"Yes, and the CPS think there's a pretty clear case for him to answer."

"Well there is, isn't there?" she pointed out.

Metcalfe smiled. Collison saw it, and smiled sheepishly himself.

"Yes, you're right of course. And please don't say that it's just because of my natural reluctance to believe that the most obvious suspect must have committed the crime. It's not that at all. It's more that I find it very difficult to believe that these two murders are not connected in some way."

"And there's no way that Raj could be involved with the first one, is there?" Desai said.

"Hardly. He would only have been a few years old. And so far as we know he had no family connection with the UK."

"So far as we know," Metcalfe pointed out.

"You're right, Bob, we should have checked that. Let's run some searches before we interview Raj again."

"I suppose they couldn't be some other sort of connection?" Desai proffered hesitantly.

"Like what?"

"I don't know. I'm just thinking aloud really."

"Nothing wrong with that. Carry on."

"Well, we know that Taylor killed Sue Barnard, don't we?"

"We know that he buried her, which isn't quite the same thing. Probably more accurate to say we assume that he killed her in the absence of evidence to the contrary."

"Yes, OK, whatever. Let's just say that he had something to hide. Well, suppose that Raj found out about it in some way. He might have been blackmailing Taylor. Perhaps that's what the payments from the bank accounts were."

"It's a nice idea," Collison replied, "but victims tend to murder their blackmailer, not the other way round. It wouldn't give Raj a motive for killing Taylor. No, the CPS are quite right. If Raj is our killer – and he's the only person we can place at the scene apart from possibly a fleeting visit by Schneider – then the most likely explanation is that Taylor found out he was stealing from him and Raj panicked and killed him."

"I've been thinking about that fleeting visit, as you call it," Metcalfe observed. "We only have his word for it that he wasn't able to gain access to the house. Suppose that he did get in, and killed Taylor. Wouldn't it be a really cute stratagem to go next door and tell the neighbour that you haven't been able to get any answer?"

"A bit too cute, surely. Wouldn't his natural instinct be just to slip quietly away and hope nobody would notice him?"

"Yes, I guess so," Metcalfe conceded reluctantly.

"I suppose it's always possible that he might have seen Rowbotham looking out of the window, or somehow just thought that he'd been spotted," Desai suggested.

"You mean he just made the best of a bad job – decided to brazen it out?" Collison asked.

"Yes. And that would explain why he didn't identify himself to Rowbotham. We know that he and his sister were planning to go back to Canada. The only reason they haven't gone already is that they couldn't get jobs and ran out of money. So all Schneider would have left behind him was the memory of Rowbotham having met a complete stranger, and us with no way of being able to identify him."

"It's a puzzle isn't it?" Collison asked ruefully. "Well, it just goes to show that our only chance now is being able to break John Schneider when next we see him. It seems that once again we shall have to rely on Peter Collins."

CHAPTER 30

"OK, people, listen up please," Collison said that afternoon in the incident room. "I'm afraid we're running out of time. The CPS think we have an adequate case against Raj for the Taylor murder, and the powers that be are pressing us simply to hand the file over and close down the enquiry."

There was a silence.

"To be perfectly frank, I don't want to do that," he went on. "For one thing, it seems to me that we still have at least one other viable suspect for that killing. For another, it would mean abandoning any thought of the two murders being related to each other, and I'm not ready to do that yet."

He walked over to the whiteboard and gazed at it thoughtfully.

"There's so much about John Schneider to find disturbing. We know that he had anger management issues, and a tendency to violence. We know that he's demonstrated aggressively sexual behaviour towards women. We know that he's lied about what he said to Jack Rowbotham. So what else might he have lied about?"

"There's also the question of these dead women in Canada, guv," Metcalfe proffered. "The Canadian police have already said that if we have reasonable cause to think Schneider may be a serial killer then they'll be wanting to take a serious look at him themselves."

"Agreed. However – and it's a big 'however'– we don't have a single piece of solid evidence against him. Everything is either supposition or highly circumstantial. As Dr Collins reminded me the other day, it's not enough for us to show that he could have committed the crime, or even that he's the sort of person who is more likely to commit this sort of crime than other people. We have to get something firm on him, something that strongly suggests he actually committed this specific murder."

"And how do you propose to do that, sir?" Evans asked.

"We have to break him," Collison replied grimly. "We're going to get him back in for another interview tomorrow, and this time I'm going to let Dr Collins loose on him. I realise it's a gamble; he may simply clam up, particularly as we're going to have to let him have a lawyer this time. But I don't see that we have any choice. Like I say, we're running out of time."

"So you still fancy him for the Taylor killing, guv?" Desai enquired.

"Yes, I still like the hypothesis that when he found out about Taylor killing Barnard he resolved to come back to England and take revenge. We're pretty sure that he returned just before Taylor was in fact killed. He doesn't have any proper alibi – only his sister – and I don't necessarily buy the story of him not being able to gain access to the house. For all we know it might just have been a clumsy attempt to throw us off the track, or muddle the timing. I'm going to re-interview

Jack Rowbotham, by the way, so that we can nail Schneider's lie once and for all."

"What about Raj, sir?" Goodwin asked. "He is still the prime suspect after all. If we get left with him and nobody else, we still need to be able to build the strongest possible case against him."

"Quite correct," Collison agreed. "At the same time as DS Willis and Dr Collins are interviewing Schneider, DI Metcalfe and myself will be talking to Raj and *his* lawyer. It has to be the two of us, I'm afraid, as there may be some security implications which we're not allowed to share with the rest of you."

Though this was hardly fresh news, it still prompted some sidelong glances among the team. Evans put his hand up.

"Yes, Timothy?"

"Have we found anyone to corroborate the story about Barnard offering herself to men in Downshire Hill, sir? I know her school friend confirmed that she may have been on the game – well, sort of, anyway – but can we actually place her at the scene?"

"Well, we know she was buried there," Collison replied with a grim smile, "but I take your point, Timothy. It's always possible that she was killed elsewhere. We know that Rowbotham's back garden was not secure at the time. That's something else I want to ask him about. If he was coming and going frequently in the evening as he says, then he may well have seen her hanging about himself."

He looked around the room.

"Anything else? No? Well, in that case I'd like everybody

to get away early this afternoon – no later than five say – because it's going to be a long day tomorrow."

•

Shortly after five Collison found himself once again in the large living room of the house in Frognal.

"I really can't make up my mind," Collins said, "whether it's too early for cocktails or too late for tea. What do you think, Simon?"

"I'd be very happy with tea, thanks. I have a feeling I'm going to be very late tomorrow evening, so I'd rather like to get back to Caroline as soon as I can."

"I'll make it," Lisa volunteered, "and then I'll go upstairs so you four can chat properly."

They all murmured their thanks as she slipped from the room.

"Well, there you are, Peter," Collison said. "You've probably already heard from the others that we have one chance left at Schneider, and one only. If we can't get some sort of confession out of him tomorrow then we're going to have to let the CPS go ahead against Raj."

"And you don't like that idea?"

"You know I don't. Oh, I know he's the obvious suspect and I know it's likely a jury would convict on the basis of what we know, but I just feel there's something wrong. Something we've missed, perhaps."

"I see."

"So how do you propose we handle Schneider? When I say 'we', by the way, I mean you and Karen. Bob and I are going to be busy with Raj."

"Well, it's very difficult preparing a profile on Schneider when I've never even met him. But I've read everything on the file, and of course I've had long chats with Karen about her impressions each time she met him. I've got some notes here, but the short answer is I think we have to appeal to his vanity."

"Vanity?"

"Yes, he clearly has a strongly egotistical view of himself and his environment. We all do, of course. We all view the world looking outwards from ourselves and so it's perfectly natural that our perspective should be egocentric. But with people like Schneider, that becomes exaggerated, partly because they have such low levels of empathy. The less you care about or feel for other people, the more emphasis you're likely to place on yourself and your own needs."

"You're describing a psychopathic state of mind, aren't you, Peter?" Metcalfe asked.

"Yes, though of course not all psychopaths are killers, or even violent. But this lack of empathy, and corresponding high regard for the self, is typical of such a state. Some of this is a bit controversial, but personally I'm a strong supporter of the view that environmental conditioning plays a very large role here. Psychopaths who develop into serial killers tend to have a very distorted parental relationships. Either one parent is missing entirely, – usually the father – or the emotional relationship with one parent is either very distant or over-close."

"And you think that ego plays a part in what they do – the killing?"

"Not directly, no. The urge to kill goes to something else, some emotional or perhaps sexual need that at a certain point can only be fulfilled by killing. You see, along with this heightened egotistical sense often goes an actual inadequacy, whether sexual, social, emotional, or a combination of the three. Serial killers tend not to be people who are hugely successful in their careers, for example. This combination of factors can lead to a craving for control, and killing is of course the ultimate form of control. It's significant in my view that in many cases the killing itself is preceded by lesser but nonetheless effective means of control. Gacy used handcuffs, for example, and Christie sometimes used gas to render his victims unconscious, as Sutcliffe did with a hammer."

"So where does the ego come in, then?" Collison prompted him.

"Once they are discovered. Once they realise the game is up then ego kicks in and makes them want the world to know just how effective they have been as a serial killer. In a perverted sort of way I suppose it's them trying to convince the world – and themselves – that they really have been a success after all. Gacy, for example, was anxious that he should get full credit for all his killings, not just the few the police were already investigating. But equally, they tend to hold a few back, just so they can think that they still somehow hold the upper hand, that there's something they know which the police haven't found out. I think that's why Brady would never reveal the location of all his victims; it gave him a warped sense of superiority."

"And of course his lack of empathy meant that he had no

feeling at all for the families of his victims and their need for closure," Willis put in.

"Yes, exactly, Karen. I must say that had I been advising on that case I wouldn't have tried that approach at all. I think it was doomed to failure."

"So how would you have played it then?"

"Well, it's easy to be wise after the event, but I would have been tempted to cast doubt on the number of people he had actually killed and challenge him to prove it."

There was a silence while Collison digested this.

"I can see a possible flaw in such an approach, Peter," he said at length.

"What's that, my old Parker bird?" he asked in his best Lord Peter Wimsey manner.

"You said that ego kicks in when they realise the game is up, when they've been caught. But we haven't caught Schneider, have we? On the contrary, we are trying to get him to convict himself out of his own mouth."

"Yes, you're quite right. I was just coming to that, actually. And even if he did commit the Taylor murder, that doesn't necessarily show that he's a serial killer, does it? He might just have been driven by his historical feelings for the Barnard girl. But you're right, of course; if that's the case, then my approach won't work. So we have to assume that it *is* the case. It's a bit like one of those situations in bridge when you have to put the cards where you want them to be, because if they're not then you can't make the contract anyway."

"I see," Collison said unhappily. "I was rather hoping that

you might come up with some brilliant scheme to persuade him to admit to the Taylor murder."

"Nothing specific that I can put my finger on," Collins replied uncomfortably. "I'm afraid this is just one of those situations where we have to do our best and see what happens."

"What's your instinct, Peter?" Metcalfe asked curiously. "Forget what we can prove and just look at what we know, or think we know. Do you think he would have been capable of killing all those women in Canada?"

"It's a difficult question to answer without knowing how he's developed as a person in the last twenty years: what he's done, what sort of relationships he's had, whether he's been in trouble with the police, that sort of thing."

"Well, we know he hasn't been able to hold down a job," Willis reminded him.

"And that he dropped out of college, and that he doesn't seem to be in a long-term relationship," Metcalfe went on.

"Yes, yes," Collins acknowledged. "Oh, I do so hate speculating like this on the basis of incomplete information, but yes, I do. Based on what we know of his teenage years here in Hampstead and what little we know of his time in Canada, then I think he does have the sort of psychopathic personality which would be consistent with him being a serial killer. But, as I've pointed out several times already, that doesn't prove that he did actually kill Conrad Taylor. That's a job for you chaps."

"And for you, Peter," Collison said with a grin as he got up to leave. "It's you who's going to be interviewing him, don't forget. I have every confidence in you, by the way. If you can't break him down then nobody can."

"Oh dear, yes, I was forgetting that," Collins said worriedly.

Taking off his glasses, he began to polish them in a distracted sort of way with his handkerchief.

CHAPTER 31

Raj sat impassively while Metcalfe turned on the tape recorder and recited the formal caution. Collison tried to gain some impression of the duty solicitor sitting alongside the suspect. He was an earnest-looking young man in glasses who already had his pen poised over his blue legal notebook with its perforated pages. Collison guessed that he was likely to be a stickler for the rules, but time would tell.

"Mr Rajarshi," he began once Metcalfe had finished, "is it OK if I call you Raj? I understand everybody does."

There was an almost imperceptible nod by way of response.

"As you know, you are being interviewed as a suspect in the murder of Conrad Taylor. You have been cautioned, and you have exercised your right to have a legal adviser present."

"Speaking of which, Superintendent," the young man cut in, "perhaps we could explore the status of this interview. My client has already been charged with Mr Taylor's murder, and presumably you have also already taken the decision to proceed with his prosecution. In those circumstances I really must question whether it's proper for you to be interviewing my client again."

"Let me choose my words very carefully," Collison replied. "It is of course true that your client has been charged with Mr Taylor's murder. However it is not true – at least not from my viewpoint as the Senior Investigating Officer – that a final decision has been taken to launch a prosecution. If your client would rather not proceed with this interview, that is of course his prerogative. But I do assure you that I am still genuinely trying to eliminate him from our enquiries."

He gazed steadily at the solicitor, who was the first to break eye contact.

"Very well," he said unhappily. "I will allow the interview to proceed but I may at some stage advise my client not to answer particular questions."

"That is of course what you are here for," Collison observed, hoping that he was not coming across as sarcastic. "But, before we begin, there is a formal matter which I must raise with you."

"What's that?"

"Both DI Metcalfe and I have been made subject to the Official Secrets Act in respect of various issues which may form part of your client's defence should this matter go to trial. I know that you are bound anyway by the usual duty of confidentiality to your client, but I must stress that you should not discuss anything you are going to hear during this interview with anyone other than your client, and his counsel should that become necessary. Is that understood, please?"

"Yes, of course," from the lawyer, but with a clearly surprised sideways glance at his client.

"So, Raj," Collison said, "it may interest you to know that we have been in contact with the police in Singapore. Is there anything you'd like to volunteer about that?"

A slight shake of the head was the only response.

"For the tape, the suspect has shaken his head. Very well. We understand from the Singapore police that you were sent to England in the guise of a refugee from Sri Lanka, but in fact as an undercover informant with a mission to penetrate and expose the British end of a fake passport racket."

Raj again sat impassively while his lawyer, after an initial look of disbelief, hurriedly scribbled in his notebook.

"However, you didn't stick to that mission, did you? On the contrary, having been allowed into the UK with temporary leave to remain pending further interviews, you simply disappeared. Why was that?"

Raj shrugged.

"Please do try to give verbal responses for the tape, Raj. You've just shrugged. What you mean by that? Are you denying what I've just said?"

"Please don't put words into my client's mouth, Superintendent," the solicitor said. "Raj, perhaps it might be better if you simply said 'no comment' if you don't want to answer a question."

"Then no comment," Raj said flatly.

"Very well. I should say however that we are quite confident we can prove in court everything I have just told you. It may interest you to know that our own police force – Special Branch to be precise – was informed of your mission by the authorities in Singapore and gave their permission for it to proceed as they were concerned that these forged passports might be used by terrorists to gain entry to the UK."

The solicitor glanced at his client and then back at Collison.

"I think it's clear my client doesn't want to comment on that, Superintendent. Why don't we proceed?"

"Very well, then let's go directly to the circumstances surrounding the murder of Mr Taylor. How long had you been living with him, Raj?"

"About two years I guess."

"Yes, and you've previously described to us how you came to meet him. But let me press you on one point. What was the nature of your relationship?"

"I lived with him and I worked for him. First just as a researcher, but then I took on all the rest of his stuff. I did the shopping because he didn't like to go out. And he asked me to handle his financial stuff as well."

"Let me just stop you there. I'm sure you can understand that is very important we get all of this absolutely right. When you say that he asked you to handle his financial affairs, how did he do that?"

"What do you mean?"

"Well, did he give you some sort of letter of authority to act on his behalf?"

"No, nothing like that. He just asked me."

"Do you remember when this was?"

"Maybe a year ago. Something like that."

"Well, it may interest you to hear that we've asked the bank to send over everything they have on record concerning Conrad Taylor. We've also taken a statement from the bank manager, and the one before her. And there's no record – nothing at all – to indicate that Mr Taylor ever gave anyone other than himself authority to operate his bank account."

"He didn't need to. We did everything online. All I needed was the password, and he gave it to me. The PIN on his cash card as well."

"Well there again, perhaps we could explore that a little more deeply. You see, the bank told us that Conrad Taylor had never used online banking until a few months before his death. He seems to have been an old-fashioned sort of bloke who used cheques but nothing else. He even used cheques to draw out cash over the counter at his bank branch. Then suddenly the bank received a request for online banking, and at the same time the cash card which had been issued to Mr Taylor, but never previously used by him, became active. Somebody was using it to draw out cash on a regular basis, and that somebody was you, wasn't it?"

"You know it was. There's no secret about it. I told you all of this. Conrad asked me to use the card when he needed cash. He didn't like going out of the house, so I did it for him."

"And the online banking? How did that come about?"

"I told him that if he wanted me to look after his money it was much easier to do it online. I got the form from the bank and he filled it in and signed it."

"I should tell you that we are having that signature examined by an expert and that his initial view is that although it is superficially similar to Mr Taylor's, it is probably a forgery. If you magnify it, it appears to be made up of a number of individual strokes, exactly as you would expect from a rather amateur forger."

"My client has not been charged with forgery,

Superintendent, so I fail to see the relevance of this line of questioning."

"It goes to the murder charge."

"I'm sorry, but I don't think it does. It is at best background context, and largely irrelevant. My client is quite clear that the deceased gave him permission to operate his bank accounts. If you want to try to disprove that, so be it. But I'm going to advise my client not to comment further on these matters."

"Very well, but in passing you will of course be aware as a lawyer that even if such authority was given by Mr Taylor it would have lapsed on his death, and your client has already admitted that he continued to withdraw cash from the account during the following weeks."

"What my client has told you is a matter of record, Superintendent. Again, I would advise my client not to comment on these matters unless and until he is charged with some relevant offence."

"Then let us come back to the moment when your client claims he discovered the dead body of Conrad Taylor. If, as you say, Raj, Mr Taylor was already dead why didn't you simply come to the police straightaway? It must have been clear that he'd been murdered. Part of his head was bashed in, wasn't it?"

"My client has already dealt with these matters," the solicitor said, rummaging through the file and flourishing the earlier statement. "I really don't see what purpose can be served by rehearsing all of it again. My client's account is quite clear. He found Mr Taylor is dead, panicked, and ran away."

"Yes, but why? Surely an innocent person would have been

eager to report the crime as soon as possible? If he cared for Mr Taylor when he was alive, then surely he would be anxious to see his murderer caught?"

The solicitor sighed.

"Really, Superintendent! Your own case, as you've just outlined it, is that my client entered the country under false pretences and then absconded. That he became effectively an illegal immigrant who would surely be in danger of deportation were he to be apprehended by the police. Assuming that were in fact the case – and note that I say 'assuming', because we're making no admissions on that score – then wouldn't it be entirely logical and understandable for my client not to want to come into contact with the police? In which case, he wouldn't have felt able to report the murder. That's not the same thing as not wanting to report it. On the contrary, my client is very anxious for Mr Taylor's killer to be identified and prosecuted."

Collison sat silently for a moment and then, ignoring the solicitor, spoke directly to the suspect.

"But something you may not be aware of, Raj, is that things didn't proceed according to plan. You see, it seems that there were some rogue police officers involved in the passport scam, and all the details of the enquiry were passed back to the criminals behind the scheme. One informant has already been murdered in Singapore, although they were supposed to be under police protection at the time. And it is possible – and I must stress that we don't know for certain – that a hired killer has been dispatched to the UK to take care of you."

Raj looked visibly shocked, as did his solicitor.

"Are sure about this?" the latter asked.

"No, as I said, we can't be absolutely certain. But I can tell you quite truthfully that information to that effect has been received by Special Branch and that they are taking it very seriously. So, in the circumstances, if there is anything that your client would like to tell us about the people behind these forgeries then he would be doing himself a huge favour. Not only might it make a jury more inclined to believe his story about the murder, but it might help Special Branch locate and arrest whoever it is has been sent over here to find him and – we believe – kill him."

Raj swallowed hard while the other three occupants of the room stared at him.

"No comment," he croaked at last.

An idea suddenly occurred to the solicitor.

"Has it occurred to you," he asked, glancing first at Collison and then at Metcalfe, "that whoever this hired killer might be could have called at the house, found my client out, and killed Mr Taylor? To send a message to my client, perhaps?"

"Yes, it has occurred to us," Collison said evenly. "But the fact remains that your client is the obvious suspect in this case. Just think about how it will look to a jury. He entered the country illegally and then absconded from the immigration authorities. It is common ground that he's been operating the deceased's bank account, both before and after his death. He lived with the deceased, on a basis which has yet to be fully explained, for some time. He was the only person other than the deceased who had access to the murder scene. He admits to having discovered the body of the deceased. He claims to want to see the murder apprehended, yet took no steps to make the police aware that the death had even occurred. He ran away from the murder scene and was later arrested by some of my officers while withdrawing money using the cash card of a man he knew to be dead."

He paused, giving time to his words to be considered by the two men on the other side of the table. The solicitor pretended to be absorbed in jotting down a few further notes, but then glanced quickly at his client, who shook his head once again. Collison felt frustration building within him; it was obvious that Raj was not telling the whole story, and becoming equally obvious that they weren't going to get it out of him.

"Interview terminated at 1158," he said, trying to keep the irritation out of his voice.

CHAPTER 32

John Schneider was also accompanied by a solicitor, though this one was less of an unknown quantity as he appeared regularly at Hampstead police station, as well as at local magistrates courts. He was a middle-aged man in a shabby suit and as they sat together in the second interview room Willis was acutely reminded that he habitually smelt in equal parts of stale cigarette smoke and body odour. As she finished the business with the tape machine she was wishing that she had applied just an extra few dabs of perfume before entering the room.

"Now then, John," she said after they had all identified themselves for the tape, "you do realise that this interview is proceeding under caution, don't you? You were cautioned by the duty Sergeant when you arrived at the police station and I'm sure your solicitor has advised you what that means."

"So, just for the record," the solicitor commented, "my client is being interviewed as a suspect is he?"

"He is one of a number of suspects whom we are trying to eliminate from our enquiries, yes."

"And I'm sorry, but I didn't quite catch this gentleman's rank...?"

"Oh, I'm not a police officer," Collins explained, taking off his glasses and rubbing them gently on his handkerchief. "I'm a psychologist."

"Dr Collins is a registered adviser to the Metropolitan Police," Willis said hastily, "and has assisted us with a number of investigations. He has some questions which he'd like to put to your client."

"This all sounds very irregular," the solicitor said sourly, "but go ahead and ask your questions. I can't guarantee that I will advise my client to answer them though."

"I wanted to ask you about Susan, John," Collins began. "Do you remember her well?"

"Sue? Sure I do. Why shouldn't I?"

"No reason at all. On the contrary, we all tend to have very strong memories of our first love."

"Yeah, I suppose so."

"And she was that, wasn't she, as I understand it? Your first love I mean."

"Sure, I was in love with her."

"And she with you?"

"Of course she was. What are you getting at?"

"Well, if she was in love with you as you say, how do you explain the fact that she might have been offering herself to other men, presumably for money?"

"That's rubbish, that is. I told you lot that when you tried it on before."

"We do have evidence from two different witnesses, including someone who was one of her best friends at school."

"What do they know about it? She was my girlfriend, so I should know."

"When Karen here – sorry, my colleague that is – put this to you before you said that you and Susan weren't having sex together. Is that right?"

"Yeah, what of it? She said she wanted to wait. Well, for full sex anyway. She was only 15 you know. And that's why this is such crap, what you're talking about. If she wasn't having sex with her own boyfriend, why would she be offering it around to other men?"

"For money, we understand, but just for the record, so far as you're aware she wasn't indulging in any sexual activity – on whatever basis – with anybody other than you?"

"Of course she wasn't. Why, if I'd thought for a moment she was up to anything like that I'd-"

He stopped suddenly.

"You'd what, John?" Collins asked softly.

"Well, I'd have done something about it, wouldn't I?"

"Yes, I rather think you would. Like that other boy when Susan wanted to get fresh with him, do you remember? You punched him in the face and broke his nose."

"So? I got angry. It could have happened to anybody. And anyway, it wasn't her getting fresh with him, it was the other way round. I told him to stop and he wouldn't, so I hit him. Simple as that."

"It's interesting that you think that, John."

"Think what?"

"That responding with violence is a natural reaction when somebody annoys you."

"Anybody would have done the same. She was my girl, wasn't she?"

"Well no, I'm not sure they would have done, actually. You see, most people don't get violent, because they're able to control their feelings of anger. I think you have problems with that, John, don't you?"

"I don't think you should answer that," the solicitor said, addressing Schneider but staring at Collins.

"All right, then let me change the subject," Collins went on. "Do you remember something else that happened when you were at school, John? The thing you got into trouble with the police about?"

"Why do I need to tell you? You must have it all on file. All those lies those women told and everything."

"What lies, John?"

"About what I'd done to them."

"But it was all true, wasn't it? Your schoolmates admitted it quite readily, and they all named you as the ringleader. More than that, actually. They said you made them do it."

"It was only a bit of fun. Nothing would have happened if those women hadn't come to the school and made trouble."

"It was the police who came to the school, John. Don't you remember that? They brought some of the women with them, yes, but only to identify you."

"But I hadn't done anything. I keep telling you, it was just a bit of fun. They blew it out of all proportion, made it sound worse than it was."

"I actually read the file just yesterday, John, so it's pretty fresh in my mind. What you did to them may have been a bit of a joke to you, but some of them required counselling. One of them was so badly affected that she became scared to go out of the house; she had to give up her job. Don't you understand? It wasn't just the shock and embarrassment of having your hands all over them; they were scared out of their wits. You made them frightened to walk down the road – any road."

"Where you going with this, Dr Collins?" the solicitor cut in. "Whatever you're referring to is obviously a very old police matter and you've had plenty of time to bring charges against my client if that was your intention. Why are you dragging it all up again now?"

"I'm trying to understand your client's perspective, his attitudes. His attitudes towards women in particular."

"His attitudes towards women are his own affair. This is an interview, not a psychiatric examination."

"Well then, perhaps I could pose a hypothetical question, or rather two hypothetical questions. John, I know you told us that Susan wasn't offering herself to other men, but just suppose for a moment that you had seen her – perhaps in Downshire Hill itself outside your own house – propositioning passers-by. Offering them what she wasn't prepared to give you. How would you have felt about that? You'd have been pretty angry, wouldn't you?"

"Don't answer that," the solicitor said quickly.

"All right, then let me move onto my second question. John, suppose it had been you rather than your mother who saw your father burying Sue's body in the next door garden. What would you have done?"

"I'm not going let my client answer that question either. This is all just some sort of fishing expedition. If you have facts you want to ask my client about then go ahead and we'll try to help you, but I'm not going to let you try to get inside my client's head. That's not what this is about."

"All right," Willis said in conciliatory fashion, "let's stick to the facts as you ask. John, when you spoke to us before you told us about the time you tried to see your father. But I'm going to ask you about that again, because you weren't under caution at the time. Can you tell us what happened, please?"

"I went to the house and knocked on the door, but there wasn't any answer. I tried looking through the windows but I couldn't see anything. I was just walking away up the road when I had the idea of asking the bloke next door if my dad still lived there."

"You say you looked through the window but couldn't see anything. Do you mean anything or anyone?"

"Anyone, I suppose. I think there were chairs and tables and things, like you'd expect."

"But nothing out of the ordinary?"

"What you mean?"

"Oh, nothing. Let's move on. Do you remember what you said to the man next door?"

"Yeah, I asked him if my dad still lived there."

"Did you actually say 'my dad' or did you just say 'Conrad Taylor'. Can you remember?"

"I'm sure I said 'my dad'. At any rate I told him he was my father. And I wouldn't have said 'Conrad Taylor' anyway. I still think of him as Schneider. It's only since I've been talking to you guys that everyone keeps calling him Taylor."

"Did you recognise him – the man next door I mean?"

"No, but then I wouldn't, would I? Not after 20 years or so. Anyway, I think our neighbours on that side changed at about the same time we went away."

"Yes, but Mr Rowbotham – that's the neighbour – says he was coming and going from the house because he was checking on the progress of some building works he was having done."

"I don't remember anything about that."

"What, you don't remember the works? Surely there must have been a lot of noise mustn't there? And what about when they took the fence down between the two gardens?"

"Oh yeah, I remember something about the works, but I don't remember ever seeing that guy before."

"When did you last see Sue Barnard, John?"

"On the Friday, like I said before. It was a school day so we would have met up after classes."

"And gone to that service road behind the shops?"

"I expect so, yeah. We did most days."

"And that was when you last saw her? When she left the service road to go home?"

"Yeah. I think I walked to the bus stop with her and then I carried on up the hill. I used to most days. I usually couldn't be bothered to wait for the bus, and it's not that far."

"Was anyone else with her when last you saw her at the bus stop?"

"Some of her mates, I think."

"Do you remember a friend called Jill East?"

"You asked me that before. Yeah, of course I do. She was

pretty hot. If I hadn't already been going with Sue then I'd have given her a go."

"So just to be clear, John, you went to the house once and once only, you couldn't get any reply when you knocked, and you never got to see your father, either dead or alive?"

"Yeah, that's right."

"I wonder if we could ask you about your time in Canada, John?" Collins asked suddenly.

"What about it?"

"Were you happy there?"

"Yeah, I suppose so."

"Really? That's not the impression I gained from reading what your sister said."

Schneider glared at him suspiciously.

"Why? What's she been saying about me?"

"Well, isn't it true that you dropped out of college almost immediately? And that you've had problems holding down a job ever since?"

"Yeah, but it's not how you're making it sound. You know what women are like. They make things up. They make things sound worse than they are. They make trouble for you. They're women, you know?"

"It sounds like you don't like women much, John."

"Of course I like them. I'm a normal guy, aren't I?"

"I don't mean physically, John. I'm sure you like having sex with them well enough. But you don't really like being around them, do you?"

"I'd rather just have them around for sex, sure. Who

wouldn't? But it doesn't work like that, does it? They want the whole relationship bit."

"And relationships don't seem to work for you, do they?"

"I do all right."

"Maybe they're frightened of you, John. Do you ever stop to think about that? We understand that everyone was scared of you at school. How did that make you feel? Did it make you feel good, strong, important?"

" Who says so?"

"Never mind who says so. We've got it all on the file. Come on, John, admit it; it makes you feel good when people are scared of you, doesn't it? Course it does, why shouldn't it? Did you feel good when you broke that boy's nose? Did it make you feel good when you assaulted those women? I bet you could see they were scared, couldn't you? You liked that, didn't you? Come on, you can tell us."

"All those other women too," Willis interjected. "The ones in Canada. Were they scared of you, John? You must have been sorry you had to kill them in that case. But maybe you kept them alive for a while first, eh? Kept them prisoner somewhere maybe?"

"Look, what is this?" the solicitor exploded. "You say my client's a suspect in the Conrad Taylor killing, then you start dragging up all sorts of totally unconnected stuff from the past, and now you're talking about Canada for God's sake. I'm sorry but unless you have some direct factual matters to put my client then this ends right here."

They all looked at each other, apart from Schneider who gazed blankly at the wall. Willis found she had been holding her breath, and exhaled gently but deliberately. As she inhaled again, she glanced at her watch.

"Interview terminated at the request of Mr Schneider's legal representative at 1204," she announced, reaching out to turn off the tape recorder.

CHAPTER 33

It was a gloomy foursome who gathered to compare notes in the King William IV that lunchtime.

"Was there really nothing?" Collison asked in despair.

"Nothing specific that can tie John Schneider to either murder, no," Willis confirmed, gazing moodily into her mineral water.

"The really frustrating thing," Collins observed, "is that now I've had a chance to observe Schneider in person I'm more convinced than ever that he's dangerous. He has very low empathy levels, apparently low anxiety levels, and an obvious anger management issue. He is also quite self-delusional, which is a quality I've seen before in psychopaths. People think that they lie automatically to cover their tracks, but I'm not convinced that's the case. I think a lot of the time they have this ability to weave an instant alternative reality, one in which perhaps they believe themselves as they present it. But Karen is quite right I'm afraid. There was nothing he said that could link him to either murder, evidentially that is."

"We know he was at the scene of the first murder," Collison said doggedly.

"Actually, Simon, I'm not sure that we do, do we? That only holds good if Sue Barnard was killed at or very near Wentworth House. Whereas we know it's possible that she could have been killed elsewhere and brought round the side of the house next door quite easily."

"True, but that doesn't sound very likely, does it? And it would still have needed the killer to be somebody who knew that the site was insecure."

"I agree. I suppose I'm just raising the sort of points that Schneider's defence counsel might make. Actually, I have come up with a new hypothesis which allows for John Schneider having committed both murders. If you remember, we've been told that at the time of the first killing he was big for his age, both tall and strong. Well, what if it wasn't Conrad Taylor – or Schneider as he then was – who was seen by his wife burying Barnard's body? After all, there was no artificial light in the garden and I've checked the moon for that date. It was only about a half-moon, so it would have illuminated the scene to some extent, but not totally."

"You mean John Schneider might have been seen by his mother as he buried Sue Barnard's body, but been mistaken by her for his father?"

"Exactly. So when he was whisked away by his mother the next morning – who, so far as we know had not attempted to address a word to her husband in the meantime – he must have wondered what the hell was going on. And he must have spent the next 20 years assuming that he'd got away with it. That nobody had seen him, and that nobody had discovered the body since."

"In which case it must have come as a very nasty shock when his mother made her deathbed confession."

"A very nasty shock indeed. But at the same time an

insurance policy, don't you see? After all, she had also told the same story to his sister. So all he had to do was to get rid of his father and then nobody would have been able to contradict his mother's version of events."

"So he didn't come to England seeking revenge after all?," Metcalfe asked. "But rather to silence the only person in the world whose version of events could finger him for Barnard's murder. After all, if it wasn't the father burying the body, then who was it? We know Rowbotham wasn't at the house at the time, so John Schneider would have been the only other available male."

"Yes, so if I'm right John had a very powerful motive indeed for killing his father. Under my hypothesis I'm assuming that he did actually gain access to the house, where he found his father alone and killed him with a hammer. However, there was a problem. He'd told his sister that he was going to pay the house a visit, so when she heard about their father being found dead she'd put two and two together and assume – correctly as it happens – that he'd carried out his threat, although she would have thought it an act of revenge for Barnard's killing."

"So he goes next door," Collison said, taking up the thread, "and – naturally without revealing his identity – says that he's been unable to rouse anyone at the house next door and asking if Mr Taylor still lived there."

"Mr Schneider, not Mr Taylor," Willis said quickly. "He told us that he always referred to his father as Schneider because that's what he thought of him as. According to him it's only in the last few days that he's picked up the habit of calling him Taylor from us."

"My word, yes," Collison agreed excitedly. "So if Rowbotham should remember that he called his father – or rather the man next door, since we are assuming he didn't refer to him as his father – Taylor rather than Schneider then that's two lies that we can catch him out on. Not a lot by itself may be, but powerful nonetheless."

"You mean because if he deliberately referred to his father as Taylor then it can only have been because he was trying to conceal his own identity?" Willis asked.

"Yes. After all, if he was a tax inspector, or from the council, or even from the police, he would have called him Taylor because that's how he'd been known for the last 20 years. Whereas we have the son on tape and under caution saying that he would never have done that because he thought of him as Schneider."

"It's all a bit circumstantial isn't it, guv?" Metcalfe observed dubiously.

"Yes, of course it is, but then so is the Crown Prosecution Service's case against Raj and they seem comfortable enough with that. Suppose that we might be able to put together an alternative scenario supported by equally strong circumstantial evidence?"

"That might not go down very well with the ACC, guv. After all, the CPS are champing at the bit to launch a prosecution against Raj. If we come up with some other hypothesis that is even half credible, then doesn't that undermine their efforts? Don't forget, we'd have to disclose to the defence the presence of any alternative suspects. Right now we don't have any, or none supported by firm evidence anyway. The Branch couldn't break Sophie Ho and there's nothing against Schneider other than his presumed presence at each murder scene at or about the time of the killing."

Collison gave him a hard stare.

"Are you suggesting, Bob, that we should pull back from investigating Schneider just because it might inconvenience the CPS?"

"I'm not suggesting that we should pull back, guv. I'm just suggesting that we take an informed decision. There could be a trade-off here. By finding out more about Schneider we might succeed only in weakening the case against Raj. Have you thought of that?"

"No damn you, I haven't. Oh, why do bloody politics have to get in the way of everything?"

The others gazed at each other awkwardly. Characteristically, it was Collins who broke the silence.

"Surely it's not so much politics as practicality?" he asked gently. "There are trade-offs inherent in just about every decision we make; it's just that most of the time we don't consciously articulate them. I'm not a copper like you chaps, but I can see the force in what Bob is saying. If we can't make out a watertight case against Schneider, then why not let the CPS proceed against Raj? It's their decision after all, their responsibility."

"I don't want it to come to that. For God's sake, Peter, you said yourself the man's dangerous."

"And I stand by that opinion. But you know how the

courts will look at it, Simon. They don't want to hear some expert like me pontificating in the witness box about how Schneider is the sort of person that could have committed these crimes – yes and perhaps other crimes too. They want firm evidence that he did actually commit at least one of the specific murders. And anyway, you know how things go when a case comes down to expert evidence. The other side will simply get another expert to say that I'm completely mistaken, that Schneider is good with animals and children, and that he regularly escorts little old ladies across busy roads."

There was another silence.

"Okay, I'll tell you what we'll do," Collison said determinedly, glancing at his watch. "We've got until close of play today to come up with something that may persuade the ACC to put the brakes on the CPS. Well, it's only just after 2 o'clock. Why don't we at least have one last go with Jack Rowbotham? If we have him on tape saying that John Schneider didn't refer to Taylor as his father, and nor did he actually use the name Schneider, then at least that's something. We can argue that he deliberately tried to mislead Rowbotham into believing that he knew nothing about the man next door, and why would an innocent man do that?"

"I still don't think it's enough, guv," Metcalfe replied uncomfortably.

"No, it may not be," Collison sighed, "but at least we'll be doing something."

"There is just one thing that might make a difference," Collins said slowly.

The other three chorused "what?", "go on", and "yes?",

creating in the process much the same sound as many contemporary operas.

"Well, it's only just occurred to me, and it's a very long shot, but what about this? Rowbotham told us that he used to come and go in the evenings to check on the progress of the building work. Well, surely Saturday evening would be a very logical time to visit since even if the builders had been working on a Saturday, they would presumably by then have knocked off for the weekend. Also, he'd have been able to run all his errands during the day, which he wouldn't have been able to do during the week. I'm just thinking about it, and if I had the choice between heading across London after a hard day's work and doing so over the weekend, I'd choose the weekend any day of the week – oh dear, no pun intended."

The others looked at him uncomprehendingly.

"Sorry, I'm waffling again, aren't I? Well, all I mean is this. We have Schneider saying on tape and under caution that the last time he saw Sue Barnard was when they parted at the bus stop after school on Friday. So we can't place him with Barnard any time later than that; at the time she was murdered, for example. But suppose that Rowbotham was there that Saturday evening and suppose that he saw Barnard hanging around in Downshire Hill, as another witness did although not necessarily on that particular day. But just suppose that she was there and that Rowbotham saw her ..."

"How does that help us? She must've been on Downshire Hill sometime late on the Saturday if she was murdered there later that night."

"Yes, I know. But just suppose that Rowbotham might

have seen Barnard and John Schneider together? You see, my alternative hypothesis depends upon John Schneider having had a motive for killing Sue Barnard, and what might that have been?"

"Perhaps that he wanted sex with her – full sex I mean – and she wouldn't give him what she wanted?" Collison suggested.

"Yes, that would work, but if that were the case then why should he suddenly have snapped now? I got the impression that he'd asked her quite a few times and always got the same response. No, I have another idea in mind."

Being the only one not on duty, he was able at this time to sip gravely at his gin and tonic.

"Suppose that Schneider saw Barnard soliciting in Downshire Hill. Can you imagine how angry that would have made him? Firstly just the fact that she was on the game, and parading the fact right outside his own house. Surely his over-active male ego would have felt humiliated by that. And then there was the fact that she was apparently offering to other men what she was withholding from him. From what I've been able to learn of his personality, Schneider would almost certainly have exploded. And if she was with him at the time then it's entirely possible that he killed her there and then."

"Peter, I think you're onto something," Willis said excitedly. "After all, he said during our interview with him that if he'd had any inkling that she was up to that sort of thing then he'd–"

"That he'd do something, yes, although he wasn't specific

302

about what the 'something' was. But I think we can guess, can't we?"

"Well, it's something anyway," Collison said brightly. "Bob, why don't you give Jack Rowbotham a ring and ask if he can come round to the station this afternoon to give us another statement?"

He finished his orange juice with every appearance of distaste, and then put the glass back down on the table with a sharp tap.

CHAPTER 34

"I'm very sorry to have to drag you here again, Mr Rowbotham," Collison began. "To be honest, we've come to something of a dead end and we are desperately trying to find something that will help us kickstart the investigation."

"But you've got Raj in custody, haven't you? I thought I read in the press that you'd charged him with Conrad's murder."

"Yes, that's quite true but no formal decision has yet been taken actually to prosecute him. That's down to the Crown Prosecution Service you know. But even allowing for that, we have a couple of problems."

"Oh yes?"

"Yes. The first is that – and I probably shouldn't be telling you this but I just want to make sure that you understand the context of this conversation – we actually have another potential suspect for Conrad's killing. The second point – and its related because the same suspect is involved – is that I have to believe the two murders were in some way connected even though they were separated by a period of 20 years or so. Raj was a child at the time of Sue Barnard's murder, and living thousands of miles away. So if he did kill Conrad Taylor then that's inconsistent with any theory about the two crimes being connected."

"But if a hypothesis is inconsistent with the known facts then surely one abandons the hypothesis and forms a new one? That's what I was taught at university anyway."

Collison smiled.

"Yes, you're quite right of course. Actually I do recognise it as a weakness in myself that I'm sometimes too slow to abandon a hypothesis. But anyway, we'd like to ask you about a couple of matters in particular."

"Fire away, Superintendent."

"Now I know you've answered this question before, but it's become a point of some importance. Can you remember exactly what John Schneider said to you – he was your mystery visitor – when he came calling at your house?"

"Oh, so that's who it was? Yes, he asked me if Conrad still lived next door."

"Now, I have to be very careful not to put words into your mouth, Mr Rowbotham, but I'd like you to try to remember exactly what was said. See if you can remember the actual conversation."

"I think he said 'can you tell me if Mr Taylor still lives next door' or something like that."

"Okay, this could be really significant. That's why we are recording this interview and that's why we need you to be as precise as possible. Are you sure that he said Taylor rather than Schneider?"

Rowbotham gazed at the wall and frowned as he thought.

"Take your time," Collison urged him.

"You know, I think I *am* sure," he said slowly. "After all, I've always thought of Conrad as Conrad Taylor, so it would have seemed very odd suddenly to have heard him called something else. I'm sure I would remember that. So yes, he said Taylor."

"OK, I'm now going to ask you what barristers would call a leading question, but I don't see there's any other way of doing this. Did he make any mention of Conrad Taylor being his father? Did he say 'I'm looking for my father, can you tell me if he still lives next door?' or anything like that."

"No, absolutely not. I would definitely have remembered if he'd said something like that. I had no idea he was Conrad's son."

Collison and Metcalfe looked at each other. It was something at least.

"Now, I'd like to turn your attention to the first murder, the killing of Susan Barnard. We know that she went missing on a Saturday evening and we were just wondering whether you might have visited the house at all that weekend. If it helps jog your memory, we believe it was 26th October."

"No, I can tell you straightaway that I wouldn't have been there that weekend."

"How can you be so sure? It was 20 years ago after all."

"Oh, I can be very sure. You see, my birthday is on the 25th and I would have had my mother staying with me at my flat from the Friday evening right through the weekend. I would probably have gone to pick her up after I finished work."

"Oh, that is disappointing. By the way, just for the record, would your mother be able to confirm that?"

"I'm afraid not. She died a few years ago. But I can be absolutely certain. You see it was a fixed routine with us; we always used to spend my birthday together, and when it fell over a weekend then she used to stay for a few days."

"Can you remember when you would last have visited the house – prior to the 26th, I mean?"

"No, I can't, but it would probably have been one evening earlier that week. I tried to drop in every few days just to keep an eye on things. The builders turned out to be a bit of a disappointment, I'm afraid. They ran way over time and left the place in a dreadful mess. I had to get some industrial cleaners in before I could move in myself."

"Well, there is one other thing you may be to help us with. You see, we've heard from a couple of different people that Sue Barnard may have been offering to have sex with men for money. That she used to call out to men in the street as they went past, presumably in the hope that she could engage them in conversation and then proposition them. I know it seems hard to believe, a nice girl from a respectable family, but as I say we've heard the same story from two different people so we have to take it seriously."

"Go on. What do you want to know?"

"We've heard that Downshire Hill might have been one of her patches as it were. That she might actually have been parading herself up and down the road, perhaps even outside your house. Now please cast your mind back. When you used to visit the house in the evenings to check on the building works do you remember ever having seen a young girl hanging around in Downshire Hill? Perhaps she might even have called out to you?"

"A young girl, you say?"

"She was only 15 actually, but could look a lot older. You know, with heels and make up, and things. If it helps, here's her photo."

Rowbotham slid it across the table towards himself and studied it intently.

"You know, now you come to mention it, I think I did see her, maybe a week or two before that. I was walking down the hill from Hampstead tube station and as I turned into Downshire Hill a girl did call out to me. I'm not sure I could swear to it being this particular girl though. It was a long time ago."

"Can you remember what she said?"

"I think she asked if I'd like to buy her a drink. Something like that anyway."

"I do appreciate that it's a very long time ago, but can you remember anything about her at all? Anything that might help us to identify her?"

Again, Rowbotham thought hard.

"Yes, I think I can. You see she was wearing a pink raincoat, and the light coming from the shop window on the corner made it seem really bright. Almost like a Hopper painting or something like that."

"You're a fan of Hopper, are you?"

"Yes, I am. I must admit I'm not a great one for abstract art, but I do like something that paints a scene, something you can identify with."

"Yes, I'm with you there. Now just to be clear, Mr Rowbotham, when you saw this girl was she on her own or with anybody else?"

"On her own definitely."

"I see. Oh well, it was worth a try I suppose."

"I'm sorry. Have I been a disappointment?"

"Not at all. All you can do is tell us what you saw and heard, and you've done that very well, so thank you very much. Oh, I almost forgot. We owe you a debt of gratitude for your assistance in apprehending Raj as well, don't we?"

"Well, all I did was pass on the sighting I had of him to that nice lady Constable. Oh, I should say Sergeant now, shouldn't I?"

"Yes you should," Metcalfe agreed with a grin as he closed his notebook and put his pen away.

"Interview terminated at 1620," Collison said as he looked at the clock and Metcalfe reached out to turn off the tape recorder.

"Well, I can't tell you how much we appreciate you making yourself available like this, Mr Rowbotham. Hopefully we won't have to trouble you again but depending on how we decide to proceed you may be called upon to give evidence in court in due course."

"No problem at all. Always happy to help."

•

The ticking of the clock in the incident room seemed unnaturally loud and reminded Collison all too clearly that the enquiry was literally running out of time.

"Well, there you are. We've had one last throw of the dice, and it's moved us forward a little, but whether it's enough I really can't say. You've all had a chance to see the transcript of our meeting with Jack Rowbotham this afternoon which is hot off the press. You'll see that according to his evidence, and contrary to what Schneider told us under caution, there was no mention of Conrad Taylor being his father when he called on Rowbotham, and nor did he use the name Schneider. I would argue that the only logical explanation of this was that he was deliberately trying to conceal his identity. And that this would be consistent with him having just visited Wentworth House and murdered his father."

"By way of revenge for the murder of Sue Barnard, sir?" Evans asked.

"That's what his sister would have believed, yes, and that's why it was important for him to conceal the fact that he'd been able to gain access to the house. But in reality, it's possible that he was killing his father in order to silence him. In order that he would never be able to cast doubt on the mother's story. To conceal the fact that it was not her husband whom Mrs Schneider had seen burying Sue Barnard but her son. Because it was the son who killed her."

There was a long pause. Finally, it was broken by Godwin.

"I get the fact that he lied, sir, but ... excuse me if I'm missing something here ... but, well, the rest is just supposition isn't it? I mean, I get it like I say, but how are we going to prove it?"

"That is the question," Collison replied heavily. "Like you say, Susan, there's a lot of supposition but not enough proof. Why, apart from the fact that we are assuming she was killed there, we can't even place our first victim at the scene or with any of our suspects. There is ample evidence that she was turning tricks in the immediate vicinity, but no sighting of her on the evening in question."

The minute hand of the clock, which seemed to have been poised for an eternity at one minute to six finally jerked upright. As if on cue there was a knock at the door and a uniformed constable stepped into the room.

"Personal call for you, Superintendent. It's the ACC's office."

"Thank you, Constable. I'll take it in my office."

He felt a rising sense of panic as he moved towards the door. He really had no idea what he was going to do but he knew he only had for as long as it took him to walk upstairs to make up his mind.

Suddenly, from behind him, Desai, who had been staring at something in the file with a growing frown, called out "sir, wait ..."

CHAPTER 35

Mr Justice Ingram scratched his nose with the end of a pencil reflectively as he gazed at the two notes which his clerk had just placed before him. The good news was that there was steak and kidney pie for lunch in the judges' dining room; he ticked the box and handed the slip back to the hovering clerk. The bad news was that England were 28 for 3 against Australia.

His gaze swept the waiting courtroom. Seated away by the jury was the leading defence counsel, Andrew Fuller QC. His presence had added a certain frisson to the proceedings as the seat on the High Court bench to which the honourable Mr Justice Ingram had but recently been appointed – together with its accompanying knighthood – had been widely rumoured to be reserved for Fuller until he had been unfortunate enough to fall under suspicion for the murder of his wife. The fact that he was appearing for the defence also spoke volumes as to the sharpness with which his stock had fallen in official circles; he could normally have expected to have been offered the prosecution brief in such an important case. Important enough that Mr Justice Ingram had been dragged from the rarefied atmosphere of the Royal Courts of Justice discussing the small print of commercial contracts to sit as a red judge at the Old Bailey.

He consulted his notes and then began his summing up.

"Members of the jury, may I first thank you all for your long and untiring attention to what has been a very difficult case. Very shortly I will ask you to retire and consider your verdict but first there are certain points which I would draw to your attention."

"In this case the same person stands accused of having committed two murders, each separated from the other by some 20 years or so. Yet, as you have heard, the prosecution believe that the cases were in fact connected. Mr Barratt has presented a hypothesis under which the accused murdered Sue Barnard – for reasons which remain unclear but may well have had something to do with an argument over the provision sexual services – and, in a fit of panic at what he had done, hid the body on a temporary basis in the back garden until he could decide what to do with it. You should note, as you have been shown on the plan of the properties concerned, that at the time the two back gardens were effectively one, since the fence previously dividing them had been removed for building works."

"Imagine the accused's surprise, as Mr Barratt invited you to do, when that night Conrad Taylor – or Schneider as he was then known – found the body and buried it, presumably with the intention of covering up for his son, John Schneider, whom he believed to be the girl's killer. In reality, Mr Barratt says, this belief was erroneous. Susan Barnard had in fact been killed by the accused, Rowbotham, who lived in the house next door."

Andrew Fuller QC gave the merest hint of rising to his

feet. It was such a well-practised manoeuvre from such a consummate courtroom performer that the merest hint was sufficient.

"Let me amplify that last statement," the judge said smoothly. "The accused had recently become the owner of the house next door but was not actually living there at the time in question. He does admit however that he was in the habit of making regular visits to check on the progress of the building works which he had commissioned, and it is the prosecution's case that he was in fact there that night."

"We have heard from two separate witnesses that the burial of Susan Barnard was witnessed by Judith Schneider, Conrad's wife, who happened to glance out of an upstairs window and see what was happening. Deeply shocked, and quite naturally believing that it was Conrad himself who had killed the girl, she hustled both her children out of the house first thing next morning never to return. We have heard that she took the children to live with a relative in Canada and only told them what she had seen shortly before she died a year or so ago."

"It is worth noting that the murdered girl, Barnard, had attended the same school as both the Schneider children and seems to have been the girlfriend of the son, Johann or John. When they heard their mother's story, both children determined to come back to England as soon as they could and confront their father with what they had learned."

"So, as Mr Barratt would seek to persuade you, Conrad Taylor lived out the last 20 years of his life believing that his son was a murderer, and with the knowledge that he had himself quite unlawfully buried the body of Susan Barnard in order to protect his son from prosecution. And all this time, of course, the accused, Rowbotham, lived next door only too well aware of what had happened and doubtless believing that his secret was safe. But something was about to go wrong. One day there was a knock at the door and John Schneider presented himself. You have heard from Mr Schneider how he told Rowbotham that he was looking for his father, and asked if he still lived next door. In fairness to the defence, you should remember that this account of the conversation is disputed by the accused, who denies that Schneider made any mention of the man living next door being his father."

"Now, Mr Barratt says, Rowbotham panicked for a second time. He must have known that as soon as John Schneider was able to speak to his father and tell him what his mother had seen and assumed, Conrad Taylor would know that he had been tragically mistaken. He would also be able to put two and two together: if neither he nor his son had murdered Susan Barnard, then who was the only other possible suspect for the girl's murder? Rowbotham."

"And so the prosecution case is that Rowbotham went to the house next door, managed to persuade Conrad Taylor to let him in, and murdered him there and then by striking him over the head with a hammer. There are two points you may remember from the evidence here: first, the murder weapon has never been found; second, traces of the accused's DNA were found in the room where Conrad Taylor's body was subsequently discovered by the police."

"For the defence, Mr Fuller argues that the accused

has freely admitted having been in Wentworth House on a number of occasions and so it is hardly surprising that his DNA would be found there. He also argues that the prosecution's case rests largely on supposition. He says that there is no evidence linking the accused directly with either victim at the time of their murder. Strictly speaking, this may be true, and yet..."

"And yet the prosecution alleges that the accused made not one but two fatal blunders, one in respect of each killing. This may be a convenient moment to introduce the point, which Mr Fuller has quite understandably emphasised repeatedly, that until very late on in the enquiry the accused was not an obvious suspect in respect of either killing; in fact he was not a suspect at all. The police actually had in custody a man – a man arrested incidentally with the active cooperation of the accused – whom they had charged with Conrad Taylor's murder. You have heard Superintendent Collison explain very frankly and honestly that at the time the case against this man – a Mr Rajarshi – seemed very compelling. He had been living with the deceased, he had been removing money from the deceased's bank account, he admitted finding the deceased's murdered body but took no steps to alert the police, he effectively went on the run to conceal his whereabouts, and it was known that he was an illegal immigrant who had previously lied about his circumstances and then absconded from the authorities."

The judge paused and took a measured sip of water.

"You then heard how a seemingly random statement by the accused turned the police investigation in a very different direction. While being interviewed by the Superintendent and one of his colleagues, the accused claimed to have seen the deceased, Barnard, about a week before her death wearing a very distinctive pink raincoat. It suddenly struck the police that they had previously taken a statement from a school friend of Susan Barnard with whom she had gone shopping in the West End on the day before her murder, the day on which she had bought the pink raincoat in question. In other words, for the accused to have known about the raincoat he can only have seen it at some time during the few hours leading up to Barnard's murder, a time when he said he was nowhere near Hampstead but was in fact spending the weekend with his mother elsewhere in London."

"It is only fair to point out, as the defence have done very ably, that this interview was conducted on the basis of the accused being a witness rather than a suspect. The defence have sought to have this evidence excluded on that basis, but I have ruled that the police acted properly. At the time of the interview they had no reason to believe that Rowbotham was a suspect, and were therefore under no obligation to treat him as one."

He looked down at his notes again.

"You should also remember that when Rowbotham gave evidence in his own defence he said he had seen the pink raincoat as he was looking out of the widow when the remains of Susan Barnard were removed from his back garden. However, this is flatly contradicted by the Scene Of Crime Officers, who say that the excavation was concealed by a tent, and that it is common practice to cover a body with a tarpaulin before removing it from the ground. The photographs of the scene taken at the time which you have seen – and I'm sorry if they were distressing – bear this out."

"Turning now to the second murder, we come to what the prosecution say is another damning slip by the accused. As the police started investigating the crime afresh, this time with Rowbotham as the prime suspect, one of the police officers, Detective Sergeant Desai, remembered a conversation with Rowbotham before the apprehension of Rajarshi in which he referred to the deceased, Taylor, having been struck on the head. It suddenly occurred to the Sergeant that the accused could not possibly have known this, as no details of the cause of death had been released to the media. Could not possibly have known it, that is, unless the accused were himself the murderer."

"Unsurprisingly, this evidence has been hotly disputed by the defence. You have heard Mr Fuller, when cross-examining Sergeant Desai, suggest that she simply made it up in order to incriminate the accused, a suggestion which she steadfastly denied. You have similarly heard Mr Barratt cross-examining the accused, whose case is that he never said such a thing, although he did at one stage suggest that the Sergeant might herself have imparted this information, a suggestion which she in turn denied."

"Members of the jury, this is clearly a point of great importance since it is the only direct, as opposed to circumstantial evidence linking the accused to the murder of Conrad Taylor. In the case of such a direct conflict of evidence I can only say this: you have heard both witnesses give evidence, and it is for you to decide whose version of events you prefer."

The judge now began to give the standard direction on reasonable doubt. As he did so his pace quickened perceptibly since he had one eye on the clock, and half his thoughts on steak and kidney pie. With a facility which argued for a long and successful future career on the bench, he brought his summing up to a masterly conclusion at precisely one minute before the luncheon adjournment, and then stood with the rest of the court as the jury filed off self-consciously to their room.

Afterwards the detectives stood around in a rather tense group with the prosecuting counsel. Adrian Partington, Patrick Barratt's habitual junior, contrived to stand next to Karen Willis.

"What do you reckon?" Collison asked nervously.

Barrett shook his head.

"On the second one, impossible to say. It all comes down to whether the jury will believe the police evidence or not. On the first one, I'm pretty confident."

"But saying you've been verballed is the oldest trick in the book, isn't it?" asked Desai, clearly not overawed by the august presence of a Queen's Counsel complete with wig and silk gown. "Surely they won't fall for that?"

"It's an old trick for us, but not for them," Barratt pointed out gently. "They won't have heard it before, but they may well have seen lots of television programmes where the police stitch people up in the cells."

He glanced longingly at the swinging door to the outside.

He was anxious for a smoke, but it was clear that it was pelting down with rain in the road beyond.

"Would you like to borrow my umbrella, Mr Barratt?" Willis asked mischievously, having divined his purpose.

He looked with dismay at the colourful object proffered to him. Craving competed briefly with potential embarrassment, but lost the unequal struggle.

"Thank you, no," he said reluctantly. "I must say, it's very … what colour is that exactly?"

"It's magenta, and it matches her stockings," Desai said enthusiastically. "It's nice isn't it?"

Collison had been momentarily distracted as Andrew Fuller walked past him with a tight little smile of acknowledgement, but now came to the rescue.

"Why don't you borrow mine, Patrick? It's black and it matches my socks."

Later, a little while later, they watched Jack Rowbotham stand unsteadily in the dock while the jury delivered their verdicts: guilty of murder on both counts.

GLOSSARY

RANKS IN THE METROPOLITAN POLICE FORCE

Constable

Sergeant

Inspector

Chief Inspector

Superintendent

Chief Superintendent

Commander

Deputy Assistant Commissioner

Assistant Commissioner

Deputy Commissioner

Commissioner

Note (1): All officers with a rank of Commander and above are described generically as "Chief Police Officers"

Note (2): All ranks up to and including Chief Superintendent may be prefixed with "Detective" if the officer is serving with CID.

METROPOLITAN POLICE ACRONYMS OR ABBREVIATIONS

AC	Assistant Commissioner
ACC	Assistant Commissioner (Crime)
CID	Criminal Investigation Department (the Detective branch of the Met)
CPO	Chief Police Officer (see above)
Con(n)	(1) A conference with a barrister (courtroom lawyer) at his chambers (offices)
	(2) A convict
Con(v)	To deceive
Con Man	A fraudster, one who steals by deception
CPS	Crown Prosecution Service
DC	Detective Constable
DCI	Detective Chief Inspector
DCS	Detective Chief Superintendent
DI	Detective Inspector
DS	Detective Sergeant, but also Detective Superintendent
Guv	Guvnor, an acceptable informal substitute for "sir"
Met	The (London) Metropolitan Police Force
SIO	Senior Investigating Officer
SOCO	Scene of Crime Officer(s)
Super	Superintendent
Yard	Scotland Yard, the headquarters of the Met

SLANG USED BT THE METROPOLITAN POLICE

Bang to rights	The situation of a suspect against whom there seems to be an unanswerable case
Blues and Twos	The sirens and flashing blue lights used by emergency vehicles in the UK
Brief	Applied generically to any lawyer representing or advising a suspect
Chummy	Often used as a name for an as yet unidentified criminal (US 'perp')
Force	"the force" = the Met
Job	"in the job" = to be a police office
Nick(n)	A police station, as in "down the nick"
Nick(v)	To arrest or apprehend, as in "you're nicked"

GUY FRASER-SAMPSON is an established writer, having published not only fiction but also books on a diverse range of subjects including finance, investment, economics and cricket. His darkly disturbing economic history *The Mess We're In* was nominated for the Orwell Prize.

His *Mapp & Lucia* novels have all been optioned by BBC TV, and have won high praise from other authors including Alexander McCall Smith, Gyles Brandreth and Tom Holt. The second was featured in an exclusive interview with Mariella Forstrup on Radio 4, and Guy's entertaining talks on the series have been heard at a number of literary events including the *Sunday Times* Festival in Oxford and the *Daily Telegraph* Festival in Dartington.

THE FIRST THRILLING TITLE IN THE HAMPSTEAD MURDERS SERIES

£7.99, ISBN 978-1-910692-93-6

The genteel façade of London's Hampstead is shattered by a series of terrifying murders, and the ensuing police hunt is threatened by internal politics, and a burgeoning love triangle within the investigative team. Pressurised by senior officers desperate for a result a new initiative is clearly needed, but what?

Intellectual analysis and police procedure vie with the gut instinct of 'copper's nose', and help appears to offer itself from a very unlikely source a famous fictional detective. A psychological profile of the murderer allows the police to narrow down their search, but will Scotland Yard lose patience with the team before they can crack the case?

Praised by fellow authors and readers alike, this is a truly original crime story, speaking to a contemporary audience yet harking back to the Golden Age of detective fiction. Intelligent, quirky and mannered, it has been described as 'a love letter to the detective novel'. Above it all hovers Hampstead, a magical village evoking the elegance of an earlier time, and the spirit of mystery-solving detectives.

THE SECOND GRIPPING TITLE IN THE HAMPSTEAD MURDERS SERIES

£7.99, ISBN 978-1-911331-80-3

The second in the Hampstead Murders series opens with a sudden death at an iconic local venue, which some of the team believe may be connected with an unsolved murder featuring Cold War betrayals worthy of George Smiley.

It soon emerges that none other than Agatha Christie herself may be the key witness who is able to provide the missing link.

As with its bestselling predecessor, *Death in Profile*, the book develops the lives and loves of the team at 'Hampstead Nick'. While the next phase of a complicated love triangle plays itself out, the protagonists, struggling to crack not one but two apparently insoluble murders, face issues of national security in working alongside Special Branch.

On one level a classic whodunit, this quirky and intelligent read harks back not only to the world of Agatha Christie, but also to the Cold War thrillers of John Le Carré, making it a worthy successor to *Death in Profile* which was dubbed 'a love letter to the detective novel'.

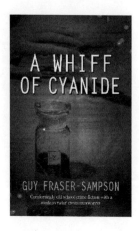

THE THIRD GRIPPING TITLE IN THE HAMPSTEAD MURDERS SERIES

£7.99, ISBN 978-1-911129-76-9

The third volume of the bestselling Hampstead Murders sees the team become involved with a suspicious death at a crime writers' convention. Is this the result of a bitterly contested election for the Chair of the Crime Writers' Association or are even darker forces at work?

Peter Collins, who is attending the convention as the author of a new book on poisoning in Golden Age fiction, worries that the key clue to unlock this puzzle may be buried within his own memories. A character called Miss Marple offers her advice, but how should the police receive this?

Meanwhile an act of sudden, shocking violence and a dramatic revelation threaten tragic consequences...

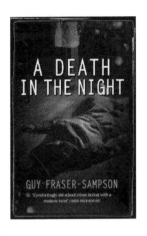

THE FOURTH GRIPPING TITLE IN THE HAMPSTEAD MURDERS SERIES

£7.99, ISBN 978-1-911583-46-2

When a woman identified as the wife of a prominent lawyer dies at an exclusive women's club, the team from Hampstead police station find themselves thrown into a baffling investigation with very little evidence to offer any guidance.

By coincidence, Metcalfe, Collins and Willis were all attending a vintage dinner dance at the club at the estimated time of death. Can they remember anything between them which might indicate a solution?

Set against a background of professors, barristers, and serial adultery, the fourth in the Hampstead Murders series continues the pattern set by its predecessors: strong, character-driven contemporary narrative written in the spirit of the Golden Age of detective writing. Praised by leading crime-writers, and garnering rave reviews from book bloggers, the books have been described as elegant, intelligent, quirky and 'a love letter to the detective novel'. All agree they are very 'different' from the standard fare of modern crime fiction.